CH01507070

James Darcy was born in England, one of man compromise. Asked rec them as 'interesting', adding 'Most struggles have more than one dimension'. Refusing to let the past shape his future he has lived his life with a simple message which can be found in his wallet today, the poem by Calvin Coolidge, *Persistency*. Having completed his education the last three decades have been spent immersed in the world of finance providing funding for business acquisitions. Describing his career choice as a 'contradiction', he concedes it has been 'good to him' providing opportunities far beyond his early expectations and a platform to explore his artistic side while working within a profession he defines as soulless, 'It's all about balancing it out, it's not something I'm particularly good at but then who is? I'm disciplined, my brother would say, 'Jimmy, how many lists do you have on the go today?' He knew me as well as anyone, I still think of him constantly when I'm writing, he was a great brother and friend…'

Preferring to write early evenings, his desk, an old Victorian flip lid complete with clay inkwell, can be found covered in poems, short stories and manuscripts fighting for space with a small light and a laptop that has seen better days. His writing style is driven by human observation and an emotional journey often tinged with sadness recognised and embraced by those that claim to have 'lived a life', be it now or in the past.

Having lost both parents, the first, his father, when he was just 18 years old, he is under no illusion that life owes you anything, 'It's there to be lived, no one said it was going to be easy, we all have opportunities, it's up to us to take them'.

James Darcy lives alone writing and working and not always in that order.

Last Known Address

James Darcy

October Road Limited
www.octoberroad.co.uk

Published by October Road Ltd
Lower Ground Floor, South Western House,
Canute Road, Southampton,
Hampshire SO14 3AL,
United Kingdom
www.octoberroad.co.uk

Typeset by October Road Ltd
Printed in the United Kingdom by Hobbs the Printers Ltd
Totton, Hampshire
www.hobbs.uk.com

Cover photograph © Chris Knox Photography
www.ckpimaging.com
With special thanks to Buckler's Hard, Beaulieu, Brockenhurst,
Hampshire SO42 7XB, United Kingdom
www.bucklershard.co.uk
Photographic images © Chris Knox Photography
Design by 3 Men and a Suit - www.3men.co.uk

A CIP record for this book
is available from the British Library.

ISBN 978-0-9568092-0-9

James Darcy

This book is dedicated to those who lost their lives

in the early hours of Monday, 15th April 1912.

Chapter One

Archie Mullins lay in his bed watching the condensation run down the wall in front of him, fidgeting as he fought with the blanket slipping off his shoulder, an invitation for the bitter chill to join him as he buried his head beneath the itchy cloth, in darkness now, hands between his knees cursing the morning, cursing everything, not out loud, just a whisper under his breath. His mother in the room next door *listening*, waiting for the sound of his boots to hit the floor, the creak of the wooden floorboards twisting on the joists as he made his way to the door stepping over his brothers fast asleep both wrapped in horse blankets stolen from the Ironmongers on Oxford Street. Charlie and Will twitching in unison, it was their turn to sleep on the floor while Archie sunk into the stained mattress, it had lost its shape years ago, hollowed out down the middle like a casket of feathers, clinging on to its occupant as he struggled to leave, his legs swung over the cold metal frame, he sank further into the wire mesh scratching the bites now etched in blood; the bed bugs had found their way to Wickham Court and were showing no signs of leaving.

He loved the smell of sulphur and wasted several matches trying to light the old newspaper rolled into *candles*, twisting the lighter sticks buried beneath the coal, the flames licked into action hissing and spitting red hot splinters across the filthy rug, dying instantly on contact as though the effort to burn wasn't worth its while, the occasional back blow adding to the dreariness of the tiny living room that was his home. Archie always prepared the fire before leaving for work, his brothers would stir shortly and make their mother some tea, the wire guard in place he pulled on his jacket emptying some coins out on the kitchen table, sliding them into three piles distracted as he did, content to play *shove ha'penny*, marvelling at his skill in balancing them precariously on the edge, the *child* had returned but not for long, just long enough to administer the pain of necessity before returning the coins to their rightful place. The first pile was the money set aside to buy his newspapers; the second was his profit from yesterday which he carefully scraped together and off the table into a hand as black as the coal burning in the hearth. He placed the coins in an old jar on the mantelpiece, enough to buy some provisions, Charlie and Will would go together, it was easier in pairs, one would buy the bread and milk dropping the money across the floor, distracting the Storekeeper long enough for Will to relieve him of some eggs, stuffed in his cap, careful not to pick up any straw, an instant giveaway of the heinous crime. The final few coins he placed back in his inside pocket, stealing was one thing, being stolen from was quite another, he had no intention of ever confusing the two.

Archie closed the door behind him, pushing against it to ensure the latch had fallen, making his way through the arches, one eye on the open windows above spilling the contents of whatever lived under the bed, the other eye scanning the flagstones a pace or two ahead. The streets were full of *strays*, Archie smiled at the thought of it, you couldn't walk anywhere in a straight line without stepping over something, or someone, not down here, it wasn't the vision of him weaving down the alley that made him smile it was the thought of all the *strays*, after all he was one.

'If looks could kill' Archie muttered under his breath as he crossed St Michael's Square adjusting his step to fall in line with the cobbles underfoot, passing the huge church doors one slightly ajar, but enough of a gap for the priest to shuffle through, sweeping the entrance with more energy than was necessary, a cloud of dust kicked up around him as he took pleasure in frowning his contempt, peering over his spectacles perched on the end of his nose.

'Morning Father', Archie wasn't sure what to call him, it seemed the right thing at the time, he had never been in the place and wasn't about to start now; some *help* you can live without.

'Be on your way boy and remember god loves you!' came the reply in between dusting himself down, hitting his tunic like a carpet hung over a line, ensuring the filth of the streets stayed the *right side* of God's threshold, he wasn't biased, he included Archie in that.

'Morning Archie! Big day tomorrow! I can't wait! I've been down there twice already just to look at *her*! Have you seen her yet? Have you seen her? She's enormous!'

Archie strained his neck; he could hear the voice but for the life of him couldn't see where it was coming from.

'Where are you? I can't see you?'

Archie trying to follow the sound with his *eyes* as he took a step back off the pavement scouring each window of the Six Bells pub on French Street.

'Down here you plank!' came the reply as Samuel Fuller's head appeared from the cellar, clambering up the wooden ladder with a casket of ale precariously balanced on his shoulder and displacing his head contorted at thirty degrees, his apron catching on the last rung as he heaved the beer to one side of the open hatch before closing both doors shut with a thud sure to wake the neighbourhood from restful slumber.

'Hey Archie, I hope you're ready? I hope you're all packed? I've been packed for days but in truth I ain't got much so how long can it take?'

Archie knew the arrangements but that wouldn't stop Sammy Fuller from going over it again, he had made a mental note to go down the Back of the Walls this morning to avoid Sammy, but had forgotten. He liked him, liked him a lot, but how many times can you listen to the same thing?!

'Right Archie, now just so you're sure, we're meeting at 7.30 tomorrow morning at God's House, you know Winkle Street and not round the back, at the front opposite Town Quay ok? I hope you're alright with that Archie as I won't hang around! If you're not there by 7.35 I'm off, you'll only have yourself to blame if you miss the trip of a lifetime!'

Sammy continued to bicker in soft monotone as he locked the trap door, sliding an iron bar through the eyelets across the hinge, fastening it with a padlock worthy of the pauper's prison.

'I'll be there, don't worry, I won't let you down!'

With that Archie picked up the pace, waved goodbye and disappeared round the corner through West Gate into Latimer's, breaking into a trot, he was running late but some things just demand your attention and the Titanic wasn't about to be ignored.

'Oh my god, there's four of them!' He literally shouted that out as he ran across Queen's Park through the avenue of oak trees his heart beating faster and faster the closer he became.

'Oh my god! Look at the size of her!'

Bursting with excitement he could barely breathe, gasping for air with each stride, the four funnels now in full view towering over everything around them, huge and imposing, 46,000 tons of attitude stood majestic just a few hundred yards from his pitch, he could watch *her* all day, his last day, before joining as crew.

'I'll be with you tomorrow!' he shouted now running and waving his cap as he passed on by, glancing over his shoulder as if to make sure *she* hadn't left without him, navigating round a mother pushing a pram taking in the early morning air, 'Sorry Ma'am!' he said as he rushed past her over the dock gates, he crossed the road, jumping the train lines waving 'Top of the morning!' to the bell boys at The South Western Hotel all scurrying around the entrance, a hive of activity, their white gloves waving back in between humping leather trunks, suitcases and hat boxes the like he'd never seen; Archie laughed at the sight of *armless* white hands waving back like a magic trick better performed in the dark. This was it, this is what his mother wanted when she had asked Samuel's father to put a word in for her boy to get him off the streets. Samuel's dad knew everyone, the Six Bells was a popular pub, a docker's pub and when the White Star Line opened their doors for crew, Samuel and Archie were at the front, it was no coincidence a casket of ale had been left carelessly unattended.

The yellow packet spun in the air several times, Archie catching it with one hand like a cricket ball and he gave a little *jig* as his father used to do when he was drunk, Irish out of Ireland and all that.

'Thank you Drippin, you big fat slob! Why are you so late this morning? I don't think that horse will want to pull your ass much longer, look at the poor bastard, it hasn't stopped panting since it got here!'

Archie loved Drippin like his own, the friendly banter took place every morning like a ritual between friends, more than friends, blood brothers, in their spare time they would go fishing and in the summer months swim off Mayflower Park, all daring each other to go under the pier between the groins, a rite of passage, an unspoken entry into the *club*, they were inseparable, cut one and they both bled.

Archie took the yellow pack and took out a cigarette, ten Gold Flake, divided by the five boys Archie, Sammy, Drippin, and two of the Hotel Porters; they all chipped in and shared them. As well as delivering the newspapers around the town Drippin did what his parents had done before him, *Rag and Bone* on his cart, all manner of stuff he would buy and sell. He was off to the South Western Hotel, word on the street was they were dumping old mattresses before the *London set* arrived on the afternoon train, his mates on the door tipping him the wink, he was expected round the side gate at nine. By this evening a hand full of families would have something for their children to sleep on and the Head of House would be pissed on *free* Irish whisky delivered in a hessian sack.

Archie always ordered the same number of newspapers delivered in two bundles tied with horse hair string, he pulled them off the back of the cart while Drippin sat up front eating an apple before throwing the core off the wagon, seagulls swooping instantly fighting over the spoils like their lives depended on it.

'That's right Drippin, don't help will you? You just sit up there and watch!'

8

Archie delivered his sideways instructions with as much sarcasm as could be mustered. He was called *Drippin* because of his diet of dripping sandwiches, he loved them and it showed. Archie clambered up onto the cart and sat next to his mate, counting out the coins for the papers stacked by the side of the road; from tomorrow his younger brother, Charlie, would take his place. He knew the routine, the numbers and what was expected of him, but there was an awkwardness, Archie didn't need to speak, his friend knew what he was thinking, what he wanted to hear.

'Don't go worrying Archie; while you're gone no one will muscle in on your pitch. I will be down here every day checking on Charlie when I deliver his papers, if he's got any problems I'll know about it ok? If anyone gives him trouble, they will have me to deal with, you have my word on that; your kid brother is family, so piss off before you start me crying.'

The two boys shook hands, looking at each other they spontaneously hugged, patting each other on the back before Archie climbed down, walking along the side of the wooden cart tapping his fingers as he went, reaching the end he gave a couple of knocks indicating his friend was free to go. Archie took off his cap and waved it at Drippin smiling like the weight of the world had just been lifted.

'Thank you mate, that means everything to me, take care of my Charlie and I will be back before you know it!'

With a flick of the wrists the horse and cart moved off joining the traffic on Canute Road now bustling with activity; he didn't look back, enough had been said, Drippin raised his arm and waved goodbye.

Weight and balance, that was the trick as Archie carried his newspapers the 100 yards or so to the corner of Royal Crescent, a bundle in each hand, his arms throbbing with the weight as he shuffled up the street holding them adrift so as not to bash his legs, the string cutting into his palms bluish red with friction burns, his fingers numbed as the blood flow detoured, it would try again next time around. Panting softly in between the morning chorus of greetings 'Morning Mr Harris', 'Morning Mrs Smyth' as he passed the Fishmonger two doors down from the railway crossing,

'Morning Mr Campbell, cold again today, but I think we'll be busy!' he shouted across the tops of the flowers stacked into galvanised iron buckets set on a timber frame, all colours of the rainbow dancing in the early morning breeze.

'I'm going to miss you young Archie, you take care of yourself now, send your mother my regards!'

Archie nodded accepting his goodwill, he couldn't put the papers down, not now, he had built up a head of steam, his little legs likely to buckle under the strain, leather boots like weights on the end of spindles bought a size or two bigger than was needed, he'd grow into them but in the meantime looked like he had club foot, socks and britches and a jacket over a woollen sweater, rough and itchy, made worse by a cold sweat now developing with every step. The sheer joy of getting to the *pitch* pushed its way onto Archie's face, muttering something about 'The last time he would do that' stamping his feet blowing the kiss of life back into his hands, bringing them back as he slowly twiddled his fingers; he did everything but count them.

He crossed the street and disappeared down the iron steps to the side of the Greengrocers already set up for the day. Mr Fitzpatrick was old school, he had a military background and it showed, he would collect his produce while the rest of us were sleeping and would have them displayed on parade by dawn, all in neat rows, standing proudly to attention, boxes of fruit and vegetables, all local produce fresh from the ground delivered daily from the farms out Bursledon way and beyond. Archie reappeared from below carrying three plywood boxes he used for his stand, Mr Fitzpatrick allowed him to keep them there overnight. He liked Archie, everyone did, he would walk across to his pitch now and again and hand him a bag of *damaged* fruit, 'Something for you and your brothers, make sure your mother has some too!' Archie knew they weren't damaged, he would check them himself, but Mr Fitzpatrick had a reputation to keep, a man not to be messed with, the man Archie knew was as soft as a plum.

Archie set up the stand, cutting the string with his penknife hauling the first bundle of papers onto the boxes stacked one on top of the other. He placed his cap upside down next to the papers throwing in a few coins for change, by the end of the day his hands would be covered in ink and his throat sore from the shouting:

'Southampton Times! Get your Southampton Times!'

His legs aching with feet like blocks of ice, a stiff back from all the standing, but little did he know, in four days' time he would give everything, absolutely everything to be back there.

There was no escaping the excitement, even if he wasn't going there was a real buzz around the town. Near the docks the traffic had built up steadily during the day, a mixture of trucks and horse and carts ferrying all manner of goods. The trains pulling up to the hotel entrance hissing and spitting as the huge iron wheels ground to a halt, the glass canopy filling with steam and smoke, high pitched whistles as another train departed up town while those passengers inbound spilled onto the platforms, luggage everywhere, porters darting in and out of the hotel lobby identifying those more likely to tip. Cafés overflowing mainly with local people in town to enjoy the atmosphere, window shopping and gawping at the ship through the dock gate manned to keep out the undesirables until *her* departure at noon on April 10th 1912. In just 22 hours' time she will slip out of Berth 44 and head down Southampton water, waving goodbye for the very first time, and the very last.

You couldn't buy the view; Archie may be steerage but not today. He had the best tickets in town; if he squinted he could see people moving about on the bridge, the noise from the station up the street peppered with the occasional sound of broken china from the cafés. The smell of coffee wafting downwind mingled with tobacco and stale beer from the bars bustling with crew all laughing and joking in drunken banter. Pale Ale, Bitter and Guinness, local *women* enjoying the attention, offering *friendship* to those that could remember what *to do*, those with a *need* taken down by the side of the Barber's shop under the red and white pole while *gentlemen* enjoyed a straight razor shave finished with French cologne. All human life was there, the rich, the poor, young and old and Archie would spend the day observing

them in between selling his papers and thinking of
her.

Chapter Two

'No! Don't shut the gates!'

Archie shouted to Docherty pulling on the iron slip lock nestling in the road, kicking the base of it free with his size 10's.

'Sorry Archie, the Governor's told me I have to shut them, there's too much traffic coming in this side of the station, we're forcing it around Terminus Terrace. Sorry mate!'

Docherty gave a shrug of the shoulders as if acknowledging the effect on his trade, an apology in single movement. The two cast iron gates were slowly pulled together clanging into place, *kissing* before being wrapped in chains, padlocked and imposing. His work done, he skulked off to have a cigarette break sitting on the disused railway line hidden behind the buffers, out of sight and out of mind, the blue smoke drifted up amongst the brambles and nettles.

'No! Not today of all days' Archie muttered, his plans in tatters before him, in truth it was only a minor setback, he could still see the Haberdashery across the street, he just needed to peer through the iron bars, he would have to concentrate that's all, keeping *an eye out* between selling papers and rehearsing what the hell he was going to say given the chance to speak to her.

'Hello, my name's Archie, Afternoon Miss, I'm Archie from across the street', he hadn't got past the introduction when the first of his chances went begging. Archie gave the man his change allowing the coins to tumble from the side of his palm, 'Thank you sir, see you tomorrow!', the man smiled, took the paper and was gone, reading the headlines he manoeuvred around the oncoming obstacles his eyes flicking between print and pot holes, the balance of risk and reward.

Audrey Campbell had been in the street for almost twenty years. The Haberdashery was sat between a Confectioners on one side and a printing business on the other, she had seen many come and go but her reputation had kept a steady trade, subsidising her income teaching evening classes of dress making, essential skills for the young modern woman, replicating the latest fashions at a fraction of the price. Archie had never been inside her shop, at best he had looked through the window after they'd closed, holding his hand to the glass to shield the reflection, the cold pane flat against his face while he imagined her in there just yards from his pitch, drinking tea and chatting to Mrs Campbell. They'd laugh and joke at his expense when he dropped his papers or a customer's change, talking to himself out loud, both sides of the conversation, breaking into song while his feet joined in spontaneously, completing the public humiliation that was, Archie Mullins.

It was really the best sound in the world, his ears were finely tuned to the pitch, he could disseminate the tone from all those flutes and whistles around him, when the door to Mrs Campbell's opened he would be ready. Just nine newspapers left and that was it, he would have no more reason to remain, nothing but three plywood boxes and an empty expression, he couldn't just stand there with nothing to sell, he couldn't just pretend, if she didn't come out soon his chance would be gone and by lunch time tomorrow, so would he.

He was in mid-air when the sound reached him, jumping on the spot, he could feel his feet land gluing him rigid with the fear of Christ as the dark green door opened inwards to the inner sanctuary of everything good. Archie just froze, watching, waiting, he had stopped breathing temporarily like a distraction he could do without, the door wide and inviting *calling on him* to be strong, he had been through this many times before never quite having the courage to speak, but it was today or never and the pressure had settled in his stomach, his mouth as dry as Drippin's sense of humour. How long is a lifetime when you're waiting for it to pass? Nothing was moving, not even a shadow, he could hear voices amongst the traffic and see the rows of material all stacked in blocks of colour, Broadcloth, Velvet, Crêpe de Chine, Poplin, Wool Repp and Silk, they had everything. He could see the mannequin he had mistaken early one morning for an intruder, before his eyes had time to adjust, he had forgotten about that until now, reinforcing his vulnerability, reminding him who *he* was, as if his hands covered in newsprint wasn't enough.

When she stepped through the door Archie captured the moment, like time had stopped, watching as she adjusted to the chill, buttoning her coat she glided down the steps to the pavement below, her blonde hair tied up and twisted into something beyond his description, her blue top coat catching the breeze, boots fastened with a hundred eyelets, laces pulled tightly around her ankles, delicate and slender, she stood for a second with the grace of silence, she was beautiful and like real beauty she didn't know it. Archie had already talked himself out of the opportunity, citing numerous reasons beyond his control, pacifying his inner self that his time would come, maybe tomorrow? He had averted his eyes, not to be *caught* but this time a second too long, she was already half way across the street and heading towards him. Archie combed his hair with his fingers, he barely had time to pull on his coat-tails or brush off the remains of his lunch clinging to his tunic; he docked his cap and reached for a newspaper, folding it in half as much for something to do with his hands as anything, 'Afternoon Miss!' Archie did it! He got the words out in the right order, holding out the paper like an offering to the gods.

'Good morning Archie, I don't believe we've met? My name is Sarah.'

The two mannequins in the window had been joined by a third, the latest arrival busying herself dusting and straightening the clothes hung on the other two, darting glances over shoulders from across the street, *her* little girl chatting and laughing with young Archie like they had known each other a lifetime. Mrs Campbell content with the progress stepped out of the window and back into the shop humming a song of love as Sarah passed young Archie a flower she had made the previous week cut from silk and ribbon entwined on a short green stem, small enough to wear as a button hole or a token of something special to be hidden in his kitbag and taken out as he lay on his bunk, a reminder of what he had left behind, worthless but priceless to him. Rolling the small flower into a package of print, not a single word typed on that paper could have ever expressed what he was feeling at that precise moment, carefully slipping it inside his jacket pocket, patting it twice to acknowledge it was safe, wherever he went *it* would follow.

Never has a pair of scissors stopped so abruptly from what they were doing, Mrs Campbell's head spinning towards the door as Sarah returned to the shop, quickly gathering up the four yards of silk with enough white cotton to make a fine dress adorned with mother of pearl buttons and a black ribbon waist band she could hardly wait to see the finished article. Usually she would chat for England on the pattern, the cutting technique, sizing and finishing, she was never in a hurry but not today, quickly folding the material she completed the sale and opened the door, her conversation encouraging but polite, steering them toward the exit with all the skill of a shepherd rounding them up, waving them off the premises and goodbye.

Sarah had been employed at the shop for almost a year and while she wouldn't admit it Mrs Campbell adored her, she could see the child she never had, the child she would have wanted, she could see the child she lost all wrapped up in this bundle of energy now sat across the cutting room floor. Animated and happy, her face glowing with excitement as she told *her* story, stopping only to sip her tea, desperate to dunk her biscuit, she resisted the temptation, unwilling to let Mrs Campbell down, her lessons in table manners had not gone in vain. Sarah spent the next half hour telling her everything that was said, stopping only to catch her breath, her voice the whole time one octave higher than usual, speeding up with every new revelation as if time itself would defeat her.

Archie Mullins didn't know it, but he was a popular young man, every now and again Mrs Campbell would get up and walk over to the window, matching the image across the street with the tales of love emanating from *her Sarah* now in full flow, she had been watching Archie since she started working there, her first memory was of him picking up a child's glove, chasing the mother up the street to return it as he gave a little bow touching his cap with all the grace of a gentleman and running back to his stand anxious not to lose a sale calling out ahead to announce his arrival. Archie Mullins' life would always be like that, like so many he had been born one step behind the race, he had something though, Mr Fitzpatrick could see it, he could measure a footstep as sure as any drill sergeant with his pacing stick, he knew Archie would come good, Mrs Campbell could see it, she had known him from a young child paying his way in the only currency he had to offer, work.

Mrs Campbell returned to her duties, bringing a sense of order back to the shop while Sarah cleared the cups and saucers like props at the end of the show, little did they know the finalé was just a few days away.

****

Of course youth is wasted on the young and Archie was certainly that, just seventeen years notched on his card but like stray dogs running through the streets, some come with more of life's *experience* and Archie was testament to that. It didn't matter, not today, nothing could touch him as he ran back home from the pitch having sold the remains of his papers, replacing the plywood boxes out of sight, stacking them neatly up against the wall as if a subliminal message to Charlie *do as I do*, he would tell him anyway but sometimes actions speak louder than words, perhaps he was shaking off his youth after all. He didn't need anyone but wanted everyone, well at least to know he had made a friend, a *girlfriend*, she had spoken with him, teased him, laughed with him, taken a genuine interest in who he was, god she even knew his name, it was practically *official*.

He barely needed the air in his lungs, he wasn't using it anyway. Skipping and hopping his way up Bugle Street he dodged the cracks in the pavement, his penance on failure to return to the crack before the one he had stood on and start again. Smiling like a

Cheshire cat, whistling a tune only he could recognise skidding around the corner of Vyse Lane, the narrow alleyways oppressive and dank, the overhanging buildings just feet apart capturing the darkness of the shadows. Unable to escape they wouldn't catch Archie, his boots in full flight, they worked in tandem with the rest of him, dodging the rain water streaming down the cobbles, the remains of the *swill* swirled into dams of filth and brown slurry releasing veins of stagnant water down to the neighbours below, some things should never be shared. Will had arrived home just ahead of Archie, he was out back chopping discarded fruit boxes from the market, kindling gathered into manageable bundles and stored in the cupboard beneath the stairs, dry and combustible, a tinderbox beneath them as they slept, the danger lost in their *normality*.

Archie shared his news with the boys adding to the drama as he pulled out the flower from the inside of his coat, carefully unfurling the foliage not to damage the leaves, reliving the moment, ensuring he gave a fair account of events balanced with a dignified scoop of hope for when he returned. He would carry on later when they were all tucked up, a sort of bed time story, the main character believable and real, someone to look up to, someone who had always pulled them through, he would always be there, not on horseback slaying dragons or robbing the rich for the poor, Archie was no fable, he was everything to Will and Charlie, they worshipped the ground he walked on, hung on his every word, when Archie was around life was bearable. They could see a future, something beyond the four walls of Wickham Court, even in their darkest moment; the death of their father, he glued the family together, pulling his mother back from the brink of depression and hopelessness. He had dragged them all to the *shore* gulping back their grief, back to the present and judged by the standards of others, they were desperately poor, but it's not where you are it's where you began and Archie had taught the boys the power of a single word, *persistence*, and in time it would save their lives. On the stove was a cast iron pot, the thick gravy sauce full of green beans and cabbage bubbling away, a skillet frying bread in fat perfect for dipping, tales of Sarah and adventures that would soon begin, but for tonight they would eat well, talk, laugh and be one.

Chapter Three

Flores Mullins stood with her back to the boys, she was scraping the dried gravy from the pots and placing them to soak in the sink, she didn't need to see them, not with her eyes, she knew where they were as each of them chatted away, animated, excited and *full*. Her small frame lost in a shapeless black frock of heavy cotton cut to the knee over flat shoes that had seen better days. Archie sat with his brothers for a while listening to Will describe his day, he was still at school, at least for now, and *bent* the ear of Charlie about anything and everything. Archie laughed quietly at the sight of it as they nattered away, sometimes engaging, others not, sometimes Charlie wouldn't even listen, it wasn't about that anyway, not all conversations have to be heard to be understood! Flores moved gently around the kitchen placing the remains of the vegetables back in the pantry for tomorrow, they would have the same but with butterbeans instead, Will and Charlie's favourite. It wouldn't make up for *his* empty seat, or fill the silence when conversation drifted, but she knew it was her turn again, her turn to drive it forward and *take the wind*, she was quietly thinking as she placed the cups upside down to drain, in and out of the candlelight her frail torso lost against the darkness of the room, wiping down the table with a cloth where Will had missed his mouth as he tried to eat and talk at the same time, unaware until the morning when the stains down his front would give him away.

Archie heard it first, three loud thuds delivered with all the skill of a debt collector, the boys looking at each other to open the door, their mother fearing the worst of everything as the knocking bounced off the walls, they had nothing, but down here even that was worth protecting. Throwing a cloth over the back of a chair they stood behind her as she grappled with the lock. Archie stood the closest feeling the anxiety like the devil himself was paying a visit, pulling the wooden door open and peering slowly through the gap, the hinges creaked and groaned in time with the boys' heads all craning to catch a glimpse of *trouble*. No one would walk these streets at night, not without a purpose, not without *authority* or something to hide, when the door opened the answer stood in front of them.

'For Christ sake, hurry up! I've been stood out here for ages, now get out here Archie and give me a hand!'

Drippin smiled at Archie's mum, docked his cap and apologised for using Christ's name in vain, tucking his shirt into his trousers as his stomach fought against gravity while his braces destined to *fly* the other way held *it* all in place as he dragged the first of two *new* mattresses off his cart, stamped down the seam was *SWH* in blue ink, careful not to let them touch the ground, pushing past the *gathering* stood dumbstruck at the front door, scanning for prying eyes or shadows in the darkness, the kind with tall hats, truncheons and no sense of humour. With both mattresses lugged up the stairs Archie thanked Drippin, paying over the money they'd agreed in a handshake, ruffling his hair, an unspoken gesture of friendship that would carry the moment beyond words and into the memory of Drippin as yet to be called upon.

****

Archie watched Charlie breathing, his mouth gaping open catching flies, he didn't have the heart to wake him, not yet, he could have another half hour while he made the fire for the last time.

He crept past Charlie but in truth nothing would have woken him, he could sleep through anything given the chance, it really was like *waking the dead*, stretching a little as Archie walked by lost in the moment as he travelled through that *place*, the place that bridged life and death itself. Downstairs Archie did as he had been doing, stoking the embers from last night and shovelling to one side some of the ash making way for the timber and coal to start the fire. The small room would soon be warm, the water hot for washing, stripped down Archie stood in the kitchen, the iron bath swilling with enough water to tickle his ankles, crouching, a block of carbonate of soda flew across the kitchen floor spinning to a halt in the corner of the room; Archie forced to retrieve it, tiptoeing the cold flagstones, cursing as the puddles gathered beneath him. With his hair washed he rinsed away the soap and grime and poured the grey remains into the back yard disappearing into the cracks, absorbed forever like *he* was returning to his rightful place and leaving *something* behind. With frayed cuffs and collar he pulled on his shirt, it was old but clean, his mother had washed his things and packed them in the small leather suitcase now resting on the table, he would pack his wash bag last and that was it, one pair of boots and they were on his feet, he was ready.

Both boys sat around the kitchen table drinking tea with bread and some jam from Mrs Hoskins on Blue Anchor Lane, she had delivered it to the family as a *going away* present, the boys grins registering their approval as Archie scooped another dollop spreading the *pleasure* across his bread with all the flair of an artist. Charlie nodded back and forth as he ate and snoozed, struggling with his eyelids like the shutters on a shop window not quite ready to open. Archie knew she was there, his mother wouldn't say much as she passed them heading for the sink, her hand running the length of Archie's shoulders and squeezing the top of his arm, love without words, registered by them both with a simple glance, nothing more needed to be said, he would soon be gone and she would be back holding the fort. Charlie knew his time had come, he was the *man* of the house now, he was the breadwinner, staring across the table he watched his brother finish his breakfast, kicking back his chair and pulling on his jacket in a single movement, 'I'm off! I've got work to do!'

Archie smiled and acknowledged what had really been said, it was nothing to do with selling papers or getting to the pitch on time, no, it was much more than that, it was a statement of intent, it was Charlie *stepping up* and announcing everything was safe with him, he was releasing his older brother to another life, a life outside Wickham Court. Flores Mullins watched as the two boys hugged at the front door, both of them close to tears but too afraid to show it, like emotion was a visitor that had lost their address. Archie waved as his brother reached the end of the street, stopping as he looked back; he held up his thumb, smiled and was gone.

She didn't turn around, just rinsed the cups from the breakfast table but Archie knew she was in tears, he could hear the soft sniffles as she coughed to hide her feelings, gathering herself back, she would be strong now, strong for Archie, strong for all of them, she wanted a *life* for him, this was his chance, she knew the sacrifice, their whole lives had been a compromise, the currency of which would be the wrenching pain in the pit of her stomach, fighting with the smile as she turned around to face him.

'Go and get your case. Don't forget your wash bag and make sure you lock it properly.'

Archie stayed out the way for the next half hour, there were no words that could fill the emptiness now welling up inside, the further away from each other the closer they became. Archie sat at the table quietly waiting for his mother to return, spinning a fork in circles like a compass charting his passage, the squeak of the door stopping him suddenly as he stood and brushed himself down.

'Are you ready Archie? Are you ready for the adventure of a lifetime?'

She could barely get the last words out without the whole of her sentence consuming her, holding the cheeks either side of her face, framed in Archie's memory like a picture.

'I'm ready mother and I'll be off now. I will be back before you know it. Charlie will be here for you, kiss

Will goodbye for me and thank Mrs Hoskins for the jam.'

He didn't rattle now, Archie had counted out the last of his coins and a couple of notes, he had paid his *way* with Drippin, smiling to himself at the sight of the boys faces when they settled down last night on their own mattresses, eyes wide open, listening to Archie talk of Sarah, both lying under blankets, propped up with an elbow, chins resting in palms, their heads getting heavier as the tale unfolded. He wouldn't need much money his food and board were included, while his mother was upstairs he had taken what he had and put most of it in the jar keeping a few *coppers* for himself, what he didn't have couldn't be stolen, a simple act that belied Archie's years but gave him away, exposing the reality of his life, straight from the streets, thinking ahead, thinking of every possibility and making harsh decisions before they were made for him.

He placed his leather suitcase at the front door and returned for his cap and gloves, stopping for a second to look around the room, his mother in the doorway an old cloth in her hand doubling as a handkerchief, woven through her fingers, she was unaware how upset she looked. Archie knew her, knew what she was going through, he would take the lead one final time as he picked up his bag,

'Mother, I've put some money aside. Charlie knows what he has to do and Will has been told to be a good boy. I'll be back as soon as the ship returns to Southampton, I'll work hard and whatever the cost was for Samuel's dad to get me this job I'll repay. I will not let you down.'

It was all just too much. Flores Mullins threw her arms around him clinging on to his head pulled flat against her chest as she stroked his hair, a tear bouncing off his face as she wept, her body stricken with emotion, every conceivable thought, everything was there, all spilling out of her and onto the floor captured in droplets that could never be returned, she wiped her eyes and forced a smile onto her face, 'Get along with you young Archie!' she forced passed her lips. Holding him at arm's length she took one last look at her *boy*, a final inspection only a mother knows how, a gentle touch under his chin as Archie stepped out onto the pavement and into the fresh morning air, underlining the reality of his departure and those he would leave behind. His boots moved off first, as if they knew best, carrying him with them walking into a better life. He heard the door close and the latch come down behind him, competing with the squawks of the seagulls carried on the wind up from the river calling Archie to the waterfront as if his past and his future had just been introduced.

He didn't need to see Samuel's face he knew it was him from a hundred yards away. There he was stood with his bag at his feet pacing up and down spinning on his heels back and forth like a caged animal, watching and waiting for Archie to arrive, practicing what he would say if he was late, muttering to himself louder as he made his point, 'The very shame of it, the first day and we never even got on board and....'

'Oh Archie, you're here! I was just thinking what a good time keeper you are and that you wouldn't let me down!'

Archie knew Samuel would be worrying himself senseless, he worried about everything, always on edge, always thinking the worst but you couldn't help but like him, he had a heart of gold and would fret over every conceivable thing and Archie loved him like his own.

'We've got plenty of time Sammy, they haven't called the muster yet, I think that's at eight, so there's no need to be worrying. How long have you been here?'

Sammy stopped what he was doing but only long enough to answer Archie before re-checking his papers, in and out of his jacket pocket like a cuckoo clock, the joining instructions as if he hadn't read them a thousand times before, his look gave him away, sheepishly dropping his head, avoiding eye contact, he returned to his bag for comfort nudging it with his boot as he skirted around the question, his arrival confirmed at 6:30, padding out the *confession* with 'He couldn't sleep anyway'; the subject changed to Charlie who he had spoken with earlier on his way to set up the stand. Sat on the bench against the huge stone walls of God's House Tower, flicking ash from a cigarette passed between them *binding* them together, *what's mine's yours*. The morning breeze off the river, cold and sharp, swirling around East Gate carried a few pages of newsprint with it picked up and dropped in a gust as it passed them by, yesterday's news and for Archie, yesterday's life. To their left the sun was making an appearance adding to the drama of what sat across the street, the red glow rising slowly behind *her* peering up over Calshot Spit, the perfect silhouette of their new *home* waiting patiently for them, a cabin, a warm bunk, hot running water and three meals a day. Archie finished the cigarette and flicked the butt into the street watching as the remains burnt down to ash, the embers giving up with a final puff of smoke signalling the *end* and the *beginning* in a single gesture.

The pair of them bookends from behind, Archie on the left closest to the roadside, small leather suitcase in hand, Sammy on the right, side by side as they walked up the street, Sammy swinging his case around and chatting a hundred words a minute, stopping only to catch a breath before continuing the tale, desperate to ensure Archie was *on board* in more ways than one. Sammy reeled off a list of *do's and don'ts,* all the things he had read, sort of laying the ground rules for him to acknowledge, ticking them off his list mentally and when he was sure Archie had *registered* the information, he was happy to move on. The two boys didn't stop talking all the way down to Dock Gate 4, Sammy covering every subject from signing on to where they would meet on board, likely shift patterns, the work they had signed up for, France, Ireland and New York, the evils of drink and how not to get turned over in a card game, Archie was exhausted just listening but he knew Sammy would have to get it off his chest, he didn't mind, he would let him continue, he could see the contentment it gave him as he made each point.

'Do you understand Archie? Have you got that?'

Archie's head never stopped nodding as if to emphasise each instruction, tucking them away like gems passed down the generations, it was like walking with his father. Sammy, old before his time, watching over his friend as they made their way across the junction and onto Platform Road, the huge Post Office building a hive of activity sorting the mail that would travel with them, hundreds of sacks bundled on the back of trucks all literally heading in the same direction. Up the street and away from them, turning right through the two brick pillars and beyond, the boys would catch them up, there was no rush and nothing worth getting indigestion for as Sammy pulled from his tunic a *doorstep* sandwich of cheese and ham his mother had made before he left, wrapped in paper now unfurled at the corners evenly cut in two, held out before him like an *offering* and carried with it the obligation to eat properly at all times. Sammy was concerned at the britches gaping around his friend's waist as he pulled them up every few yards, suitcase in one hand, trousers in the other, he had run out of hands, stopping to take the *gift* that would fill him till lunch time and take away the *growling* noise he had long stopped noticing.

'Make sure you eat properly Archie, that's heavy work you'll be doing, it's important. Now here, half each, eat your breakfast.'

The two boys stood to one side and tucked into the huge white loaf wrapped around a wedge of cheese and roughly sliced ham, it was a meal in itself, he didn't notice Sammy watching him eat, Archie's eyes closed the whole time he devoured the sandwich, savouring every mouthful and savouring his friendship. This was it, this was the beginning for them both, beyond the gates, just a few yards away now and they would have to part, Sammy had already briefed Archie where to go and who to ask for beyond the dock gates. The excitement they had both felt since opening their eyes had gone now replaced with something else, something they both felt but couldn't express, they hadn't noticed but they had slowed down, walking at snail's pace, dragging out the inevitable as they passed across the threshold. Within half an hour they would step off the shore and the realisation had just hit them. As their papers where checked both boys pointed in the direction of their muster with a friendly 'Get a move on' adding to the urgency. Archie broke the silence, it was as if Sammy had spoken so much and for both of them all the way down here he had nothing else to say, nothing that would do the moment justice.

'Let's remember this Sammy, let's just take a second and remember our chat and *breakfast* this morning. If we don't get to see each other on board, I'll see you as arranged in New York.'

The two boys shook hands and wished each other luck, leaving in separate directions to sign on. Sammy looked back over his shoulder and watched as Archie walked away, tugging at his britches as he had done all morning, he couldn't help but think how fragile he looked he disappeared into the distance, he was hardly built to be a trimmer but that was all he could get and Sammy was already feeling a huge pang of guilt and regret for asking his father, yes it was Archie's mother who had asked the original *favour* but she wasn't the one shovelling the coal, all 8,000 tons of it. Sammy knew Archie would do his best, he always did and that just made it worse.

****

It was the smell that he noticed first, Mr Fitzpatrick would have been in seventh heaven Archie thought bringing a wry smile to his face, there's something about a warehouse full of fruit and vegetables that can't be described, just something comfortable as he entered the huge structure along the dockside. Archie was in awe of everything around him, he had never seen anything like it, each warehouse the size of a football pitch led into another as he walked the length of them, zigzagging he dodged his way through the mayhem now in full swing, men shouting and bawling at each other at the tops of their voices, loading flatbed trucks with boxes piled high with all manner of goods, horse and carts disappearing out the huge open mouthed hanger doors at the other end, clip clopping their way up the dockside next to *her*, indifferent to her beauty, blinkered from everything as they chewed on the bit pulled deep into their mouths, muted from offering an opinion, content not to look beyond the next meal now hung in hessian sacks off the side. Archie watched as an old *hag* pulled away in front of him, a few boxes swaying with the momentum spilling some apples across the floor with one finding its way into Archie's pocket, Sammy would have been proud of him, he could hear him now 'You have to eat your greens you know', he chuckled to himself as he continued down the warehouse but fruit was no longer on his mind. He couldn't quite work it out; it was as if he was being teased as he walked the length of *her,* catching glimpses as he passed the doors and windows that ran the length of the shed. Every opening was completely filled with a *black* background consuming the entire space; an imposing solid wall, cold, still, and to him, uninviting. He knew it was *her*, he didn't need an introduction, he had been looking at *her* for days, watching from his pitch studying *her* lines, the curve of her bow, the precision of those port holes running down *her* side like buttons on an overcoat ready to be opened.

Archie would meet *her* soon enough as he continued to the end of the last shed. The muster station had been set up with tables and chairs and an old wooden bench covered with papers weighed down and fluttering in the breeze, he could taste the salt in the air as it settled on his lips, it was cold down there as he watched others rush around outside. The berth covered in boxes and crates bundled up in huge rope netting, some dangling from cranes precariously above, shouting and swearing carried on the wind, thick ropes strained and twisted with the movement of the water as the swell from the tenders came and went, it really was a sight to be seen, *she* just sat there, motionless, while all around pandered to her every need. It was enough to feed a small town and judging by the manifest soon to be complete, it would have done so and more.

She would be there all morning at the *table*, the list of supplies endless, but never enough and Archie's mind wandered back to Wickham Court and his mother's small pantry, a few items would be in there but not much, what there was would be sat on the shelves spaced out to make it look more, but tonight she would make a special effort for the boys, they would eat properly, a hot meal, they would tuck in and she would watch them as they chased around the last of the vegetables. Archie was *there* now, sat with them across the table, he could smell the fire, his boots drying out on the hearth, it wasn't that far as the crow flies, less than a mile from his home but right now it felt like the other side of the world.

He hadn't noticed his name called the first time, much to the irritation of the man stood behind the bench, his handlebar moustache twitching to register his annoyance.

'Mullins! Is there an Archie Mullins amongst you?'
'Matheson! Is there a Tully Matheson amongst you?'

He didn't try to hide his impatience as he called the names again, looking up and around the shed for movement like an auctioneer waiting for a sign, a noise, a shuffle, a wave. Archie pushed his way forward and walked to the front of the line, his arm raised as if to share some of the *blame* weaving in and out of the crowd now gathered in front of him, 'Coming through!' he shouted, clearing a path as he jostled to the front.

'Morning sir, I'm Archie Mullins!'

The man didn't look up; he just ticked his name from the list and nodded to his right for Archie to stand *over there*. Archie picked up his bag and moved away, he could *feel* the man's eyes boring a hole in his back as he gave a loud sigh, muttering beneath his breath but loud enough to be heard, Archie knew what was said, he had heard it all his life, he wouldn't respond, not *like that*, he wouldn't give him the satisfaction and that, in itself, was the difference between them.

Archie had signed on, he was now officially *crew*, he was on the payroll, he was a member of *The Black Gang*.

Archie sat out the way as he was told and watched the chaos unfold as people came and went, signing on before being directed into small groups allocated into their roles and separated like cattle at a market. He couldn't help but think the only thing missing was a prong as each *huddle* headed to a part of the shed ready for embarkation. You didn't need signs, you could guess what type of job each group would do, catering, waiting staff, chamber maids and stewards all in their cotton uniforms of black and white starched to the point of discomfort as they minimised their movement, another group of men and women suited and booted, clerks and bookkeepers would work for the Purser's Office and the like, able seamen sharing cigarettes wrapped in heavy boat coats and tilted hats. Archie's group boasted a half dozen men, oblivious to their *standing*, it was like they hadn't got a care in the world, that was for others, they knew who they were and what they were there for, there was no need to pretend or stand on *parade* and that alone made them different from the rest. The name didn't help, *The Black Gang*, as if they never washed and judging by the distance they had been given, never had!

Archie noticed these things, he could see they were the subject of conversation, fleeting glances directed at them, *nods and winks*, the occasional snigger, but only if they couldn't be seen, or thought they couldn't, but not much got past him, he was used to people talking out the *side of their necks* in low whispers, like the plague had just arrived, straight off the streets of St Mary's or Holyrood, containment was the best policy as the Firemen, Stokers and Greasers chatted away, like Archie, for some, it would be the first time, but a few were old hands like Isaac and Docherty, they had been on the ships all their lives, you could see it in their faces, their skin etched with a dull wrinkled texture like old leather worn and tired, drying out with the passage of time, engrained with oil and coal that no amount of scrubbing would remove. He was staring at the *future* and as he did caught the eye of Tully Matheson sat across the circle now formed around a few empty chairs, he was staring at them too and Archie knew what he was thinking as he watched the men lost in conversation. Tully nodded to Archie across the floor like they had been friends for years, they didn't need to speak, they both knew what they were staring at, nodding back and acknowledging the observation like the penny had dropped, this was where the real work would be done and these are the men that would do it. Archie couldn't help but notice he wasn't exactly built for the job, even Tully was stocky, he didn't get time to ponder, a few minutes later and they were on board.

'Listen up! May I have your attention?! All those men now signed on and working the engine room and services welcome to RMS Titanic!'

He was a breath of fresh air, smiling and cheerful, the man gathered up *his* group and made the obligatory introductions, they would be bunked in groups of four, six or eight over decks E and F and allocated as per the plans now being waived above his head, at least that was the intention before he dropped them much to everyone's amusement watching him chase them up the dockside before securing their return, apologising as he shook out the lists that had settled in puddles, ink runs adding to the challenge he squinted through the next few minutes. Archie and Tully's names had been announced as they had been when signing on, now joined by two others Harry Price and Albert Hemmings, their new home and quarters, E deck, midships between a boiler casing and port side, welcome to Scotland Road.

Chapter Four

'Not long now Archie!' he had been saying that all morning as the excitement grew, Canute Road now as busy as he could remember it, bustling with tourists hoping to secure their vantage point and wave *her* goodbye. Several shop owners had already been out onto the street checking *she* was still there, synchronising watches before returning inside content not to have missed anything. Charlie watched from the street corner his pitch in full swing, from a distance he could have been mistaken for Archie as he stamped his feet and waved a paper in the air, calling out the headline of the day, the front page photo, *bow on*, **Southampton Does Her Proud** in large print across the top, a spare paper folded and ready tucked under his arm, Archie had taught him well. He was enjoying the attention, everyone knew his brother was on board, Drippin had been down with the papers earlier and had brought him a buttered bun, his parental instinct and promise to Archie already evident, watching out for him while everyone else was watching *her*.

'See that young Charlie?! See that flag they've just run up?! That's the pilot's that is! Not long now and your Archie will be off down the river and gone.'

45

Mr Fitzpatrick spent the next few minutes stood on Charlie's stand pointing at the mast awash with flags all flapping in the wind explaining what a pilot was, how he would have control of the ship until leaving, returning by tender when the job was done. Charlie tried to look as though he understood but in truth it was lost on him, his brother was on board and that's all he needed to know, he was never going to suppress the excitement, he didn't try, you could *feel it* in the air, there were people everywhere, milling up and down waiting for that moment when she would slip her lines to the sound of sirens that would carry East down the shoreline signalling she was on her way, her guard of honour stood waiting, those that could only dream, caps and handkerchiefs, waving goodbye while Archie stood on her stern watching as the huge ropes were gathered in, her path defined by the silt and salty foam extending back to the dockside.

'See you Charlie, take care!' he shouted bellowing it out at the top of his voice cupping his mouth with his hands *willing* the sound to make its way across the docks and beyond the roofs of the sheds he had walked through earlier that morning. He imagined Charlie jumping up and down waving frantically desperate to be seen. Mrs Campbell would have closed up and she and Sarah would be there peering through the iron gates, faces in the crowd, unrecognisable from a distance but there all the same, he didn't need to see them but it didn't stop him trying as he climbed up on the railings balancing precariously with his knees wedged in the gaps holding on for dear life as others jostled and pushed for a better view, Archie working out in his mind where they would most likely stand, straining his eyes at the *shapes* off in the distance convincing himself he had seen her blue coat waving back at him. A personal drama but unaware the ship was having one of its own as the SS New York broke her lines and drifted toward them, the drama avoided by the skill of the pilot pushing her off with propeller wake and she passed safely. It would be a while before calm was restored, another of those nine lives used up, Titanic was getting through them at an alarming rate; the death of a worker at her launch, the fire still smouldering in the starboard bunker of boiler room six, the coal strike that threatened her maiden voyage, the list was growing but Archie knew none of it, all that mattered now was that the dock was shrinking in the distance as the ship steamed out into the Channel, Archie stayed until he could no longer see his home, the excitement had now been replaced with regret, if he could get off now he would.

****

'Hey Archie! No point looking back, there's nothing there for you now! Come on let's have another wander around and get our bearings.'

Tully Matheson had come topside to find him, he had spent the last half hour walking the corridors and reading the signs, the enormity of the task hampered by third class passengers and crew scampering in all directions doing the same thing quite literally *lost at sea* as every passageway led to another, Tully mapping his way through decks E, F and G, he had nailed most of it, the toilets, the washrooms, the Engineers' Mess, all that was left was the Orlop deck and the Tank Top and that would come soon enough. He and Archie had been allocated their shifts and Tully would start at four till eight, Archie eight till twelve port side boiler room five, he would make sure Archie knew his way around, knew where to get a proper meal before he started, he couldn't help notice how skinny he was, he seemed oblivious to what lay ahead, he was part of the Engineer's Department, all 325 crew with one simple task, to steam this huge ship across the Atlantic, back breaking work in horrendous conditions, 825 tons of coal a day, every day, Archie's reality would start in six hours' time.

'You'll freeze to bloody death out here Archie! Come on we've got some exploring to do!'

Tully beckoned him across the wooden deck, from a distance it looked as though he was fanning his face as he waved his hand, summoning Archie over to him, his actions slowing down the closer he came, spinning his cap on his head in a gesture of friendship, cheering him up. He could see Archie was lost in thought, he was *back* home or at least wanted to be, selling his papers, talking to his regulars, sharing a cigarette with Drippin, watching in silence as his brothers slept and then there was Sarah and then he was gone.

'Cheer up mate, think of it as an adventure, before you know it we'll be in New York. I promise if we get a chance we'll all have a beer, you, me, Harry and Albert they won't know what's hit '*em!*'

Archie smiled at the thought but more at the effort Tully was making to snap him out of it, they were like old friends with Tully taking the lead, he was almost 19 years old and counting the days, he couldn't have planned it if he'd tried, the very next day they arrive in New York, he would celebrate his birthday, reinforcing the pecking order as Archie followed him through the heavy doors and down the stairs to E deck.

'We get in on the 17th Archie, and the following day is *me* birthday, so make sure you cheer up by then!'

Archie promised he would and added Samuel to the list, they skipped their way down the stairs three at a time, skidding around the levels before descending again, laughing and joking as they went, their voices louder and louder as they competed with each other to make a point, their sound left floating in the air, diminishing from the boat deck down to the hatchway they clambered through joining the thoroughfare that was Scotland Road. Archie and Tully were off now *ten to the dozen* as they headed up the corridor back towards the mess, Tully had arranged to meet Harry and Albert at three o'clock, it would probably be their only meal together this side of *the pond*, they had drawn the short straw and would work the 12 to 4 shift, so they would be last to go. In an hour's time Tully would be down below, just like those there now, he was determined to enjoy his lunch.

'Just a bit more, thank you' as the second ladle of gravy washed over the mountain of mashed potatoes, sausage and greens piled high on the plate, swilling off the edge as the ship swayed to one side burning Tully's fingers as if a reminder when to say enough, licking them individually he sat down plate first to join the others.

'Let's eat boys, we're gonna need it', swinging his legs under the table and shovelling in his fuel in a single motion; Harry and Albert didn't wait for the invitation, they were already tucked in while Archie stared at the plate deciding where to begin, it was enough to last him a week or so he thought, dipping a sausage in the gravy and relishing the moment, it wasn't the food, he'd eat it soon enough, Archie was consuming everything, the whole experience had finally caught up with him, he was on his way to France, to Ireland, and on to New York, his bunk was clean and his alone, Titanic was indescribable, it was all those things, but none of them, what mattered to Archie was much more important, by now his mother would have found the extra money he left this morning when she was keeping out of the way, it wasn't much but it would make a difference, enough to stock the larder for a week, enough to ensure the boys had food on the table, coal and timber in the yard and enough to make her cry when she found it.

Just for a moment Archie could feel his mood darken as he thought of her holding the jar, she would slump in the chair, the money in piles on the kitchen table and sob at the thought of it, she would know what he'd done, there was no way he could have saved that much selling his papers, Samuel had mentioned the *tradition* of getting an advance on the first week's pay, like a seafarer's perk or something, but to Archie an opportunity not to be missed. He had queued at the White Star Offices and explained his circumstances like others had done before him, he would be paid the monthly *rate* of £4-10s-10d, and receive the six day signing equivalent rate of £1-17s-11d and would get an advance of ten per cent, he left the single note and coppers with a message.

Stay strong for me mother, kiss the boys goodnight.

Archie x

He didn't see them coming as they flew across the table spinning and twisting in rotation before hitting him clean in the face!

'Oi, Archie! What did I say about cheering up; you've gone all serious on us!'

He almost fell off his chair, he was leaning back, balancing on the two rear legs when Tully's gloves caught him head on, his cap flying behind him skimming across the polished floor much to the amusement of Harry and Albert now bent over with laughter at Archie squinting through one eye and rubbing the end of his nose, taking the sting out of it but trying not to let it show. New found friends finding their way and Archie was a part of that, he smiled, laughed and joined in the moment calling Tully a few choice words and questioning his parenthood before returning the gravy splattered gloves having landed on his empty plate, Tully catching them to the applause of the table enjoying the afternoon entertainment and the small insignificant acts that would bind them together.

'Ok boys, me and Archie are going to finish the tour and then I'll be working my ass off shovelling coal, keep the noise down later.'

With that Tully and Archie pushed back their chairs and left to the sound of Harry shouting out across the mess floor 'Hey Tully! Keep in touch with yourself!', the friendly banter had begun and as if to acknowledge it Tully became the focus of attention as others stopped to laugh at what had been said, knives and forks suspended before gaping mouths anxious to hear a reply, they did everything but clap, Tully now playing to his *audience* took off his cap, bowed and was gone.

'Ok Archie, I haven't got long so concentrate, we'll do this deck first and then down alright?' Tully explained what he would find on each level, pointing out anything of interest along the way, the Quarter Master's office, the Barber's, the Steward's Mess and then down descending to F deck and the home of steerage, as if the congestion didn't speak for itself, heading up towards the Engineers' Mess with Tully in full swing.

'We were lucky Archie, most of us working the boilers and engine rooms are on this deck', adding

that the four of them were born within the *city walls,*
'Well, almost, Harry coming from London Road, but
we'll forgive him for that', laughing at the thought,
as if it were a thousand miles away, Christ he was
almost a foreigner. Archie had long stopped listening
as another sense was now *pulling* him along without
the need for maps or directions, the smell of baking
bread wafting up the passageways somewhere up
wind, his nostrils savouring the sheer joy of it as he
spontaneously closed his eyes to inhale, transported
back to Mrs Sullivan's on Albert Road, her bakery
tucked between two pubs and The Atlantic Hotel,
and, as of yesterday, full of third class passengers
eating her *famous* pasties straight from the oven so
hot you had to flip them from one hand to the other
in between bites. Archie was back there now with
Charlie and Will sharing one between them for
lunch, payment for their help moving some furniture
for the Immigrants' House.

'Watch the steps Archie! It's a bit dark down here.'
Tully disappeared into the shadows of the narrow
stairwell before opening the door at the bottom,
shards of light flooding in and creeping up the stairs
guiding Archie's feet down to the Tank Top, the
noise now intense as they came closer to her
heartbeat, huge coal bunkers ran two thirds of the
ship with *open* third class to the stern packed in like
sardines, men, women and children, making a space
for themselves and in five days' time making a *life.*

'That's it Archie, I'm off to start my shift, you're on at eight ok, don't be late!'

Archie climbed the stairs back to E deck having watched Tully's head disappear into the gloom below; in four hours' time he would follow him but for now he would rest and try to sleep, his eyes already heavy from the lunch now settled in his stomach, full to bursting his smile had returned.

Archie skipped up the stairs and played the game he and his brothers would on the walls by Catchcold Tower, the forty stone steps worn over time, low rise and tiring *climb one step, then two, then three at a time and four, jump back down the ten steps and do it again.* By the time he reached E deck he was panting his face glowing red but it didn't matter, just for a moment he was *home* and running down Latimer Quays with the boys to the shore line, skimming stones across the water and counting the bounce like life itself depended on it, lost in the moment and now lost in the present as he reappeared, reading the signage in front of him, numbers and arrows and cabins pointing in both directions, to his left the master at arms and hatch number 2, to his right endless cabins would take him to the stern of the ship and the storerooms, the assistant purser's cabin, the potato storage and washer and then amongst all of his confusion it jumped out at him, *the Scullions and Plate*, he could barely contain his excitement, the very fact that *he* might be working on the same deck after all and not far from Archie's quarters, just further down the corridor and that's where Sammy would be. Archie made his way back to his cabin imagining Sammy at work, making lists of everything he was told, his notepad already covered in lead, full of *do's and don'ts* that he would follow religiously, the White Star Line didn't know how lucky they were to employ Sammy, he was born in the family pub and had worked there as soon as he could make a contribution, his father insisting on teaching him all there was to know from an early age and with that knowledge came confidence and Sammy had it in abundance. Archie smiled all the way back to his door, a small white plate at eye level (04/17 E Crew) met him on arrival and for the first time today he felt at ease, Sammy was up the corridor and even though he might not get to see him, the very fact that he was there somehow made everything ok, he had made three new friends and an older *brother* in Tully, that role was usually Archie's and he liked the feeling of shedding the responsibility allowing Tully to take the lead, happy to be part of the pack, no longer burdened with the worry that had become Archie's life, he was two thirds the way across the English Channel with 2,227 souls on board and hundreds of them from back home, mostly crew, and all trying to make their way.

Archie closed the door behind him, the tiny cabin empty and quiet, the sound of the water rushing past and running the length of the hull, waves breaking into white horses as the spray showered the sides, the ship slicing its way to Cherbourg with Archie straining to see through the port hole and the film of salty water that had dried across it obscuring his view before settling on his bunk content to hear his way there. In just a few hours or less he would be in French Waters, Southampton may be fifty miles off in the distance but Archie was already feeling her presence; for fun over lunch they had renamed Scotland Road to *Queens Terrace* and their cabin was now *Merchants House*. Archie stared at the ceiling counting the rivet heads from left to right, he could almost touch them from the top bunk, Tully couldn't be arsed to climb up, but in truth Archie wanted it anyway, placing his leather case on the grey blanket when he first arrived and pulling back the clean white sheets at one corner to signal it was taken, this was his space and for the foreseeable future this was Archie's home, this was Wickham Court.

The agreement over lunch to keep the gangway clear at all times was coming home to him now, Archie kicked off his boots and pushed them to one side with his foot, coming to rest up against the wall next to his leather case, both now taking up valuable space on his bunk, Tully wasn't daft after all, his own bag neatly tucked under his bed out of the way, freeing up the opportunity to stretch out unrestricted. Archie smiled at that, like a lesson had materialised without a word being spoken *things aren't always what they seem!* He chuckled to himself and stretched out anyway; he was short enough not to be affected so in his eyes they had both won. As he settled down, rubbing his back into the soft mattress, his crisp new pillow wrapped around his head, the company logo stitched into the fabric, the flag with a split trailing edge, a white star on red background, a reminder to Archie, even in his slumber, who he worked for, *he* was theirs now as was the pillow case and every other item he came across, the cutlery, the cups and saucers, plates, bowls, dishes, the towels in the washrooms down the hallway, everywhere you looked a *message* was conveyed, depending on your *standing*, to some a simple company image demonstrating affluence and strength and to others these belong to *us* and should remain when you leave, Archie assumed the latter. His eyes were heavy now and the sounds washed over him as he slowly drifted off, he could hear people walking up and down the corridor outside, laying on his side watching the shadows under the door as they passed, listening to the conversations, catching the gist of them and filling in the blanks, quietly whispering to himself the *endings* as he snuggled his knees into his chest, slowly drifting, Archie closed his eyes, his breath heavy with the rhythm of the sea, rocking him like a baby to sleep as the water passed him by, twitching, his eyes fluttering in hopeless resistance, and then slowly, very slowly, he was gone.

A dream at sea:

The hand, palm up, held the black leather book out in front of him, muttering as the pages were turned from right to left, flattening the page and pulling the silk marker out from under the sheet placing it down the centre so as not to lose his place, the page covered in ink, black and blue, with entries running the length of it, scored out here and there, acknowledging mistakes, optimism that failed to deliver, alterations, missed payments circled as if to emphasise the risks involved, the life of a debt collector held out before her. Archie watching as he walked up French Street turning right down Vyse Lane, he could see the man stood at their door, leaning on the frame with a cocky arrogance, his black hair slicked back in oil, clean shaven in his heavy woollen suit, leering at his mother who stood arms folded across her chest, like a barrier between right and wrong, caught in the middle and balancing her replies as he took the pencil from behind his ear totting up the columns slowly, revelling in the numbers now encased in brackets, confirmation of her debt, his eyes flicking up and down her, *eating her*, suggestions without words but words that would never come as he all but fell into the hallway in anticipation.

'You will get your money, I can pay another shilling today and the rest over the next four weeks.'

Flores Mullins delivered the rebuttal with all the force of a shovel across the bridge of his nose, much to the enjoyment of Archie as he overheard the conversation, interrupting the last part, 'And the outstanding balance', Archie opened his jacket and took out the 15s/14d enough to clear the account in full and for him to remove the vermin that preyed on the vulnerable. With the account closed, Archie ripped the page from the book while his mother went inside pulling the door ajar behind her, his receipt tucked in his waistcoat; he gave a long stare, nodded and said 'Goodbye'.

'Archie! Wake up Archie! You'll be late!'

If it wasn't for the twitching Harry would have sworn he was dead, shaking Archie's shoulder his head now face down in the pillow, 'Come on Archie! I've seen more life in driftwood!' Harry persisted until signs of movement made way for the occasional groan. Archie squinted one eye skywards and acknowledged that he was coming around, stretching to a compliment of yawns like a fog horn across the river. Archie sat up and scratched his head, more in disbelief that he had slept as long as he had, undisturbed despite all the activity in his absence, he was back now, with a half hour before his shift and he had missed everything.

'What time is it?'

'It's about 7:30 Archie, you've got half an hour and you better get down there with ten minutes to spare, start as you mean to go on!'

Harry jumped back on his bunk, while Albert lay in the bunk below, hands cupping the back of his head, craning his neck around the mattress above, the wire mesh now creaking with Harry above, fidgeting and talking in unison his legs swinging over the side, feet dangling like a pendulum clock swivelling at the ankles with the excitement of it as he filled in the blanks for Archie sat opposite Harry like a mirror, plus or minus ten years.

'It's all been going on, I can't believe you've slept through it?!'

To be honest neither could he, Archie sat rubbing the sleepy dust from his eyes, while Albert's head rocked back and forth with the rhythm of the story, Harry animated and in full flow, edging out every detail determined to give a fair account of it, balancing the drama with the limitation of twenty minutes or so remaining. 'Well, first of all mate, you've missed France! We'll soon be steaming to Ireland!' That was the introduction, the headline to set the scene, before offering an abridged version of the comings and goings that Archie had twitched his way through. Harry would do his best to make it sound as exciting as possible but in truth it was nothing of the sort, they didn't steam up the Seine or visit the Moulin Rouge, they didn't even get a look at the town from the dockside or wave at the locals, it was more about what didn't happen. Titanic arrived an hour late docking in the Cherbourg Roadstead at 6:30 pm, the ships draft too deep and the port too small to accommodate the huge hull that would shortly be pushing 20 knots or so West, indifferent to the reception it had received, the French hadn't disappointed, they were nothing if not consistent.

Harry and Albert had gone topside for a better view like so many others with the same idea, mingling on the stairwells now bottlenecked at the exit and out into the fresh air, they had missed the arrival of the first tender although that small detail wouldn't ruin the story, was it Nomadic with the first and second class passengers or Traffic with the third class and a thousand sacks of post? It would make no odds to Harry, he would embellish the tale to suit, describing the toffs in their finery and the women in low cut dresses waving to him, in his dreams, before disappearing out of sight while he hung over the side watching as they boarded *her* escorted by stewards who would take them to their cabins to freshen up and cocktails before Dinner. Harry was lost in the thought, his description so real even Albert was there reinforcing the drama, chipping in as if the truth needed bending any further, as they teased Archie now balancing on the edge of the metal frame, eyes wide open and awake waiting for the next line.

'I'll tell you the rest tomorrow Archie, now get downstairs and shovel some coal!'

Four feet was all that it took to change the mood.

That was the distance Archie would fall when he pushed himself off the top bunk, landing like a mosquito on a pond, svelte like he barely registered a ripple, spinning around he straightened his bed brushing the creases from the blanket and puffing up the pillows as if someone would mark him if he left it untidy.

He was quiet now, this was his turn, Tully would almost be finished, stopping off in the washrooms before returning to the cabin and some well-earned rest, Harry and Albert would spend the next four hours sleeping, they've had enough excitement for one day Archie had thought as he sat on Tully's bunk tying his boot laces and trying to look as confident as he could, the sinking feeling in his stomach reminded him why he was there and for the first time today he was nervous, not just of the unknown or the back breaking work for someone of his size, it was more personal than that, he didn't want to let his friends down.

'Archie, when you get down there go and report in, tell them you have never done this work before ok, make sure you take a break and drink plenty of water!'

Harry got off his bunk and opened the canvas bag hung over the end of the bed, Archie couldn't help but notice how old and worn it was with the toggle broken and held together with a draw string pulled at one end, an old checked shirt lay across the top keeping everything in place, the sides bulging with all manner of things as he delved into the unknown, his wife had packed it for him the night before, like a child incapable of doing it himself, lost without the bag and lost without her.

'You better get on now son, take these with you, you're gonna need them.'

Harry passed Archie a pair of strong canvas gloves placing them on his chest as he gathered them up, his face registering the gesture with all the grace of a *boy* twice his age, half smiling through his sadness, the realisation of who *Archie* was came home to him in that single gesture and the lad's quiet dignified reply.

'Thank you Harry, that's very kind of you, I will take good care of them.'

'Don't worry about the gloves, take care of yourself.'

Archie closed the cabin door behind him and made his way to the stairwell, descending down the four levels to the Tank Top and into the belly of the ship.

Harry folded the clothes he had taken out of his bag to find his spare gloves, re-packing them now, pushing down with one hand while pulling on the cord with the other, neither he nor Albert had spoken a single word since Archie had left, the click of the cabin door closing still hung in the air. Harry sat down on Tully's bunk wrapped in a blanket of silent reflection, both men were thinking the same thing but neither needed or wanted to say it, if either of them could have taken his place they would have, they had done this work for years, they knew what Archie was about to face, the heat, the suffocating airless existence, the pounding noise so loud it will make him sick to his stomach and then there's the coal, 825 tons of it each day, every day, Titanic had an insatiable appetite and if Archie wasn't careful it would consume him too.

Albert broke the silence, his softly spoken voice was almost a whisper, coughing slightly his throat coarse and rasping with years of coal dust or just the difficulty in getting the words out? Harry assumed the latter.

'Don't worry, the kid's small but he's got his wits about him, he'll be ok.'

****

Tully put his hand in the water, breaking the thick film of coal dust settled on the surface as he searched for the plug wedged in the hole at the bottom of the basin, the chain having been borrowed on a permanent basis, Tully cursed the perpetrator and made a mental note not to use this one again. Stood in his underwear he leaned over the sink dunking his head in the water and washing his hair, spiky, blond and cropped, shaven at the sides, if you didn't know him he looked the type to avoid, how wrong you would be from appearance alone. Rinsing the soap off his head with his cupped hands like a ladle, he watched the water run away, the steam rising from the bowl as he topped up with piping hot water, a wedge of soap to remove the grime, washing away the last four hours. Singing quietly he dried himself with a towel, spinning it rope like to make the task easier as he dried his back lost in the thought of supper, his stomach already in full conversation.

'We were sailing along on Moonlight Bay
We could hear the voices ringing
They seemed to say you have stolen her heart
Now don't go away
As we sang loves old sweet song
On Moonlight Bay'

Tully stood staring at his reflection in the mirror, blurred from the steam, wiping it with his hand just made it worse, he buttoned his shirt and sang the chorus to Moonlight Bay, thinking of home and thinking of Beth and what she had said to him before he left. He would buy her a present in New York, nothing fancy but something that she would cherish, a keepsake, something of his that she could wear, something that made an *announcement*, he couldn't take the smile off his face, just the thought of it made him happy, he didn't need the mirror to tell him how he was feeling, he had finished work and was clean again, he was hungry and supper was calling, sending him an invitation carried in the air, the aroma filled the passageway stretched out before him as he made his way to the mess.

It's the *tone* he felt first when the ship started to move. For the last two hours they had been at anchor, motionless through the breakwater, the ship barely moved at all, the hum through his feet as she steamed had been replaced with the sense of eerie silence, like the ship's *voice* had been muted but now back on song as the huge propellers churned up the water, slowly but gradually getting faster as the power was increased moving *her* out of the bay, all lights ablaze, Titanic's silhouette filled the early evening horizon, she was on her way to Ireland. Tully didn't need to look out the window or go topside, he could see everything sat in the dining room as he watched the salt and pepper pots dance, the bowl of broth joining in as the vibrations travelled up through the decks and settled on the end of his spoon, shaking with anticipation, teasing Tully with the challenge now set before him, mouth or shirt? Pulling the bowl toward him, he wasn't about to take a chance.

He hadn't noticed it earlier in the day, the brass clock hung above the galley serving hatch now a hive of activity as others queued in line for their supper.

8:30 pm and Titanic was on her way to Ireland, they had prepared as much coal as they could, taking advantage of the two hours or so sat in Cherbourg Harbour, in truth Tully's first shift was relatively easy as the ship lay at anchor, but his thoughts were already elsewhere, distracted only by the red flag on the inside of his bowl re-emerging as the level of his broth fell with every mouthful, like a shipwreck back from the dead as the tide ebbed away, half submerged it rose out of the *water* surrounded by *dumplings*, symbolic of something *menacing*, sat motionless and proud above the surface of his soup but all too subtle for Tully as he sliced the dough in half with the side of his spoon slurping what remained of his meal, soaking bread to wipe the bowl clean and fending off indigestion as he thumped his chest in apology for eating too quickly. Tully had cleared his bowl with all the grace of a spring tide and would feel the effects of it later as he lay on his bunk, but for now he was back downstairs thinking of Archie, half an hour into his shift, full on as the ship sailed West and later up into St George's Channel and Queenstown, the overnight sailing would cover the three shift cycle and for the first time be a taste of what was to come.

Working in teams Archie had been paired with Lyle Benson, they would supply coal to boiler room number five, one would fill the barrow and the other would wheel it up the tunnel to the Stokers and Firemen working the furnaces, all 159 of them. Archie could see Lyle's disappointment when his name was paired with him, they had never met, it was nothing personal but Lyle was six feet or more and built like the *side of a house*, bending over in a permanent hunch to duck under the hatchway doors and stood by his side, nothing less than a mismatch. Archie straightened his back in an effort to look taller holding out his hand with all the confidence he could muster, 'Hello, I'm Archie Mullins!' he shouted, the noise deafening as he tried to be heard but this wasn't a place for conversation, anything that needed saying was by gesture as he pointed to his ears and summoned Archie away from the boilers, the hissing sound so loud they struggled to communicate. Lyle didn't wait to be asked, he took control and suggested Archie load the barrow, it was easier than wheeling the coal up the tunnel and left Archie in the darkened bunker, a mountain of coal from floor to ceiling, up to his ankles in it with every movement as the ship lurched its way to Ireland. This was it, no excuses, both *men's* feet on the *plate* and both on the payroll. Archie would fill the spare in rotation and would swap in half hour slots when the heat, noise and the pain was too much to bear. Stripped to his waist covered in sweat and coal dust he did his best to keep up as Lyle spun around the corner dumping the empty barrow and disappearing into the darkened tunnel, his shadow dancing on the walls as the faint yellow lights flickered on and off, the *dead* weight piled high, balancing the load as he struggled to keep from spilling the equivalent of two Archies in every trip. He claimed not to have noticed the time; it was almost an hour before he *allowed* Archie to take his place.

'Not like that Archie, bend your knees and keep your back straight. Don't lift the barrow too far off the ground, keep it low and take your time.'

Lyle demonstrated how to move the barrow, correcting Archie's posture before he moved off, calling to him as he headed up the tunnel wobbling with the weight of it, his sinewy arms outstretched looked no bigger than the steel handles he clung to, his borrowed gloves from Harry oversized, perhaps something he would fill in time.

'That's it Archie! Keep it like that and you'll be fine!'

Lyle bellowed up after him, wiping the sweat from his brow, the black salty runs irritating his eyes as he rubbed them with the back of his hand, sweat dripping off the end of his nose and onto the coal as he returned to the shovelling.

You could never prepare for this; you could never have imagined the enormity of the place. Archie pushed his way up the tunnel doing his best to keep the load on an even keel as the ship listed to port, nothing much but enough for Archie to correct it by adjusting his hold, forcing a dull ache across his shoulders like a knife plunged into his back, his arms pulled on their sockets like they would *pop* any moment under the strain. Sick to the stomach with the noise piercing his skull the high pitched shrill of the whistles blowing off steam; six boiler rooms housing 29 boilers, they stood fifteen feet tall and each weighing a 100 tons producing steam (at 215psi) forced into two huge triple expansion reciprocating engines driving port and starboard with a third middle screw low pressure Parsons Turbine; in total some 76,000 of horse power and each and every one of them was riding roughshod through Archie's head. His whole body convulsed, bringing bile to the back of his throat, the fire like hell itself licking the open mouths of the furnaces, all consuming as they cried out for more, the heat burning into his body, Archie was sure his flesh was dripping off him, mixed with the sweat that sizzled as it fell to the plate floor instantly evaporating on contact, he was slowly disappearing before his very eyes. Dumping the coal for the stokers, he returned down the tunnel, the glow from the fires on his back and followed him into the darkness *calling him* like Satan himself, 'Come back Archie Mullins!' laughing at him as he made his *escape* back into the gloom of the bunkers, his eyes adjusting to the darkness. Archie stopped and put down the barrow, mid tunnel he stood alone holding his face into a welcome breeze cooling him down like his mother mopping his brow, breathing deeply he closed his eyes as a chill ran the length of his spine, 16 compartments, 15 transverse bulkheads, 12 watertight doors, down below sea level but the *breeze* had found him, it had searched him out, passing through him as if to remind him of something better to come, not just for him but his whole family, like no other breeze that had touched his face before, this one came from somewhere neither land nor sea could claim.

He was back in the bunker shovelling coal when the bell rang, the continual clatter like a bell ringer's breakdown unable to stop as the piercing racket travelled a tone or two above the boilers competing for attention, the sound reverberating as it bounced off the walls. Archie had finished his first shift and was struggling to stand up straight, his back in a permanent hunch, bent over the shovel he rested his arms and head using the handle as a pillow, catching his breath while he waited as Lyle returned from the tunnel, flipping the barrow up and over onto its bucket he threw it upside down on the coal stack, *legs* in the air as the wheels spun slowly to a stop as if time itself waited for the final revolution. Archie rubbed as much of the pain out of his lower back as he could and pulled off his gloves stuffing them down the front of his trousers and wiping his brow with his shirt sleeve, the whites of his eyes accentuated against his skin, a black grime of coal and sweat etched into his face but couldn't hide his smile as he realised what he had done. They didn't hang around, Lyle put his arm across Archie's shoulder and pushed him towards the stairwell, an unspoken *nod* and with it carried the authority of any command that would receive no resistance as the two men headed up the stairs, the sound of their footsteps returning like a dull thud as they climbed away like something was given back to them, a sign to mark their return it would take a full hour for their ears to adjust as they continued to shout making their way to F deck, Lyle was one floor below, stopping to say 'Cheerio' as they reached the exit. 'Thank you for helping me today' Archie offering his hand to shake, Lyle looking down noticed Archie's whole arm was trembling with the *weight* of it held out before him exhausted and grateful, that he didn't hesitate as he shook Archie's hand and gently thumped his arm, he didn't need to say much but what he did say was enough for Archie as Lyle headed down the corridor.

'Get something to eat and get some rest, I'll see you in eight hours' time.'

'Like ships in the night', the very expression seemed to conjure up all manner of thoughts as Archie stepped over the lip on the door and out onto Scotland Road, stretched out before him this was the place to see the true size of the ship as the corridor disappeared into the distance narrowing as both walls gradually converged, an unbroken view but for a steward carrying bed linen, white folded sheets starched into submission, his chin resting on them as he peered over the top, moving down the track the deep varnished hand rails glinting under the lights as he made his way, the irritation of the linen cupboard door squeaking as it gently swayed on its hinges, banging open and closed muttering to himself he stacked the bedclothes onto the wooden slats, glaring at Archie over his shoulder as he passed him by, like the coal dust could be carried in the air, tarnishing his efforts now heaped into bundles of comfort, he quickly closed the door, slamming it unnecessarily to emphasise his point. Archie never bothered looking back; a *stain* is a stain from both sides of the sheet.

It had gone midnight but you could still hear music seeping through the decks as it cascaded down the stairwells, the syncopated off beat rhythm of the *Parisienne* mellow and warm adding weight to Archie's eyelids as he scrubbed himself clean. Overnight the ship would break free of the English Channel, the excitement of the first evening on board witnessed by laughter and the sound of glasses *chinking* somewhere above him. Archie buried his face in the towel and listened in silence, a dripping tap, *keeping time* filled the washroom as they danced the night away, oblivious to what went on below as the brandy swilled in glass balloons, hand rolled cigars *cut* with delicacy, their origins discussed into the night, in the smoking room the gentlemen debate the merits of blend and capa, brightly coloured ring bands flouted like a symbol of *taste* nestled in their top pockets *label up* and worn for all the world to see, a heinous crime to go *unnoticed*, as if that were possible. Empty wine bottles *neck* down in silver ice buckets, napkins soaking up the watery dregs and in the ballroom *colour* swirled around the floor like paint on a canvass as silk dresses swished and swayed below waist bands in need of sustenance, deprived for *the cause* as if anything else would do. Archie dried his face, and made his way back to the cabin, the faint sound of *Melancholy Baby*, the finalé of a good night and in the morning the women would nurse sore feet bathed in salty water. They will *take a turn* with their husbands on the boat deck, look out across Queenstown Harbour and watch as hundreds of Irish immigrants board the ship leaving their home shores forever, broken families that will flee the starvation of a nation in the hope of a better life. Yes, tomorrow is a *big day*, the sail away party from Ireland and that all important decision *what to wear*, life can be cruel sometimes.

Chapter Five

Drippin had spent the morning in St Mary's making his way from Northam he would work the length of the street, round the back of the Chapel to the Immigrants Houses on Albert Road, buying and selling as he made his way down, an old wooden box on his cart spilling over with old clothes destined for a life as rags to be used in the factories or sold on if they had *life in them*, old bones and potato peel for glue, he would sell the scrap iron in St Denys and clear out houses before the bailiffs came, a last stand of defiance as if it mattered anyway, *you can't take something from nothing* but that wouldn't stop them trying.

'Aneowraganbooon! Aneowraganbooon!'

Shouting his arrival he watched the curtains twitch as he passed on by, chatting to the kids sat on the edge of the pavement, scrawny white legs lined up like a picket post, filthy and stained, the grime partly covered by knee length socks, unwilling or unable to stay up, throwing stones across the street, stopping only to allow *Spike* to clip clop past, patting his neck and jumping back as he shook his head and nibbled at their sleeves, stained yellow teeth in better condition than their own.

'Top of the morning to ya! Top of the moooorning to ya!'

It needed work, but Drippin had time before he got back to town and Wickham Court, he still had a couple of stops and the inevitable bartering with the Irish travellers buying bits and pieces before the journey that would *follow* Titanic across the Atlantic, like a conveyor belt of poverty destined for *hard labour* and more of the same, the accent might change, but for most the outcome had already been decided. Drippin would get to them soon enough, he was in no rush, he never was, besides *Spike* would dictate the pace as he pulled the cart, creaking timber with makeshift repairs, twisting and groaning the flatbed wagon, a reluctant accomplice, its faded paintwork long gone, burnt off over a decade or two in the sun, stripped back to blackened timber all bar the kick board worn away into two generations of boot marks, literally following his father's footsteps as he pushed against the board and clicked *Spike* into something resembling a stroll, he was old but strong, well fed, well watered, and Drippin adored him.

'There's a goodin.'

Drippin muttered as he moved off, *Spike* twitching the length of his back, swishing his mane to deter the midges practicing the art of *duck and dive* and safety in numbers, a lesson to us all perhaps as they returned on mass, his brown heavy coat yet to be trimmed, his smell carried in the breeze and up the street to the slums opposite the church, now competing with the stench that hung over the place, *Spike* was a breath of fresh air in comparison; they made their way through it, rounding the graveyard on the junction and following the flint wall down to the level crossing and over the bridge to the Arches, *Spike* speeding up voluntarily as they passed the slaughter house, there was no need to tempt fate, not today, besides, he hadn't had his lunch.

He was missing *them* already, it was only a day but he felt like time had stood still, his routine had changed as a result, there was no need to drop by the pub this morning and park the wheel of his cart over the cellar door, trapping Sammy down there, banging on the inside of the hatch cursing Drippin at the top of his voice but secretly laughing at the *craic* both boys enjoying it for what it was, friendship. He wouldn't see Archie later for a cigarette and a natter, sat in the sidings so he could keep an eye on his stand while *Spike* took a breather and slurped from a bucket, washing away the foam from his mouth now floating on the surface of the water; no, Drippin was already making adjustments and he didn't much like it.

'Honestly, would I lie to you?!' came the reply from Mitch (Taffy) Evans shouting up to Drippin from

the side of the road, leaning on the wagon with one
foot on the running board, the other firmly planted
on the pavement, keeping his options open just in
case.

'I didn't know that iron was stolen honest! I heard a
rumour that's all, a misunderstanding, nothing more
than that, a *white* lie at best.'

Drippin had heard it all before, and explained to
Taffy a few home truths; it may have been a *white* lie,
but he wasn't colour blind and he'd be wanting his
half crown back by the end of the week, a few cheap
mattresses was one thing, iron bars borrowed from
the goods yards of South Western Railway quite
another; he never raised his voice, he didn't like to
spook the horse, besides they'd keep it between
them, it was better that way.

The rest of the morning would pass slowly as if to
reinforce the fact that Drippin had been left behind,
Sammy and Archie had already been to France and
in an hour or two would be somewhere off the coast
of Ireland, not that they would see it but that wasn't
the point, they were there. It wasn't as if he could
have gone, how could he, who would ride the cart
scraping a living as his father had done, his days now
spent coughing up blood in between cigarettes,
forcing himself out of the armchair when they came
back to the yard, slapping *Spike's* arse with affection

and casting an eye over the spoils as he rummaged through the items, a small brass statue, some old blankets, an iron gate and some children's toys that had seen better days, there wasn't much but what there was would be sold soon enough, his father disappearing back inside the scullery his chest wheezing as it recovered from the fresh air, glancing back at Drippin he closed the door behind him and left an uneasy feeling, a knowing look that you could take either way, the type that would have you filling in the gaps for the rest of the day. Did he think he was skimming or not pulling his weight? Drippin would never know what went on behind those eyes, did it matter anyway? He would do his best and that's all, it would never be enough, he knew that, like pleasing the dead and in many ways that's what he was trying to do.

He could smell the sea now as he zigzagged his way across the cobbles and into Royal Crescent, the vibrations shuddering up through the wooden wheels as he watched his sandwich dance on the bench seat beside him, settling in the corner nestled up against the lip, cowering under a blanket of grease paper, its life expectancy already extended beyond 9 o 'clock, unheard of for Drippin, as if proof enough that this was no ordinary day, there would be no absolution as he devoured the crusty loaf smeared with fat, bread in one hand, reins in the other he would make his way to the Atlantic Hotel and talk to the back of *Spike's* head, offering reassurance, he had no intention to leave, and no desire to be elsewhere, in truth you couldn't prize them apart, but he was missing his friends, it was the only *family* he had.

There's something about a full stomach that made him want to whistle, his mood had changed as he pushed *Spike* on, before you know it Sammy and Archie would be back, they would all meet down on the quay, exchange their stories and exaggerate at every opportunity, they would share a meat pie and cigarette, their legs dangling over the pier watching the tugs and ferry boats up and down the river, all those ships, some would leave this week, others delayed as the coal strike came to an end, but leave they would, taking with them broken friendships that could never be replaced. Drippin felt a pang of guilt as he turned onto Albert Road pulling to a stop across the street from the Immigrant's House, he watched the children playing hopscotch outside the main door, oblivious to the future, three floors up a head appeared through an open window, curtains flapping against the brickwork as a mother shouted down to a child her words lost in the breeze or selectively ignored as the boy continued to play; ending the *negotiations* the sash window creaking to a close, clattering against the sill, *mouthing* something through the glass pane and with one final stare she was gone.

What price for a smile? They were positively wealthy if only that were the currency, Drippin thought as he jumped down from the wagon, loosening a strap around *Spike's* girth. He wouldn't stay long, in truth he didn't have much with him, just some old clothes that would pass and some children's shoes piled into a box for sorting. He would watch the mothers rummage while he smoked a cigarette, nodding the occasional agreement as they matched a left and right, holding them up to the light to make sure of a pair, pulling on the heels and placing them sole on sole, the final test slapping them together, a *sign* for Drippin to collect. Distracted, he watched some boys huddled in a circle on the pavement, mesmerised with a starburst of colour as the final blow was delivered, the crack of glass marbles scattered in all directions, reds and blues, oranges and emerald green, the same green as the luggage tags now tied around the handle of their suitcases back in their rooms. Within a few days they too would be *scattered*, America, Canada, Australia and beyond, carried on ships whose names bore nothing but deception to the life most would fulfil, few would see *Regal or Majestic Resplendent*, instead most would live hand to mouth, crammed into filthy tenement buildings three families to a room, New York, Philadelphia, Boston and St Louis just some of the destinations that would consume them for what they were, desperate. One more game, that's what *she* had mouthed through the window as the young boy picked out all the blue ones and carefully placed them in an open handkerchief, a new game had begun but not for him, he would do as his mother asked stopping only to take a boiled sweet of cherry glaze from Drippin as he skipped on by, 'Thank you mister!' he shouted, disappearing inside and through the heavy doors, his *colours* chinking as he climbed the stairs. From *pavement* to *sidewalk* in the space of a week, he would carry his childhood in a cotton cloth unfurling it thousands of miles away, checking the glass balls for damage while he waited in line for others to check him for disease and lice. A chalk mark on his jacket giving him the all clear, at the same time that *mark* would take something away, he didn't know it yet, it would take years to resurface, waiting patiently for a *hairline crack* to appear, it would manifest itself into a hundred little traits that he would *carry* with him, just like that handkerchief full of childhood hopes and dreams, but painfully flawed on closer inspection.

He liked it here, he liked the feeling he got just being amongst them, it was difficult to describe, maybe the sense of belonging, the closeness, most were strangers to one another and yet they were family, bound by circumstance, past and present accounted for, it had brought them here to this tiny street, just a few hundred yards from the water's edge and the dock gates. They would walk in Archie's footsteps on the way to *Majestic* and step *off the edge* of this life for another, a leap of faith that could never be undone, but not unnoticed presenting their third class tickets, stained in sweat and crumpled from the journey, the type set *One Way* completing the story, lost in the pages of a manifest, but unlike Titanic this manifest would hold no further interest. It would not be printed in newspapers around the world or posted on bill boards for grieving relatives, no one in the US Senate or Board of Trade picking over it, their names scrolling the page, already the lucky ones, the hand of fate working for them as the children played in the early morning sunshine. For them their time would pass in a haze of games and laughter, speckled in the shadows of the poplar trees now crawling the facade of the hotel and pubs that ran the length of the street. It was a moment that's all, but one that Drippin would savour as he gathered up the unsold goods lobbing loose shoes into open boxes on his cart, *Spike* scuffing his hoof, it was time to go, and they would soon enough, down to the pitch to check on Charlie and up to Wickham Court and Mrs Mullins. He would get there around eleven, about the time Archie would arrive in Ireland, and sit on her doorstep slurping tea wedged between the frame while she darned socks in the pantry and talked to the back of his head. Where was Archie? What was he doing? When would he leave for America? Drippin's tea would be cold by the time he finished talking but he'd drink it anyway and drop off the potatoes now starting to sprout. Yes this morning he would do all those things, leaving the children in Albert Road, screeching with laughter as they played *your it* , they were glad to be there, in truth, they were glad to be anywhere, and three floors up their parents would watch them from the windows planning their future, planted elsewhere, in time they would put down their roots, some would grow and prosper, others would perish, it was no different here, they would all live by the same rules and Drippin was no exception.

He had learnt something today, it had never really *sunk in* before, he had never thought of it like that, after all this was the first time he had been separated from his friends, but he knew now and he would never need reminding, you don't need a surname to be part of a *family*.

Chapter Six

Hunched over the bench like an aged fruit picker his *round shoulders* would give him away; the silence of the room broken only by the occasional hum as the foot pedal spun the wheel, driving the mechanism, the spool of white silk thread dancing to his tune, spinning evenly to the demand of the bobbin guiding the shirt through the *feed dogs*, their appetite suppressed by a lifetime of experience, as the old man stopped to draw on his cigarette. He was in no rush, not yet, not until the morning when the *emergency* alterations arrived and the tension would move *up a notch* just like the tension carried from wheel to needle, he would feel it beginning to appear in the back of his eyes, a dull ache that would develop through the early hours in anticipation for what was to come, but for now he would sit in the dark, his bench light throwing a glow across the table and spilling off the edges as the smoke settled like early morning fog, draped in his tape measure the inch markers running down his chest, forcing a smile as he inhaled the other pleasure that shared his life, like a mistress to his first love, the love that would *go* with him when his time had come, the love of *cutting*.

Yusef Gans had been in the business for fifty nine years and it showed, from the age of fifteen he had been working the cloth, man and boy it was a standing joke that the tape measure had already *sized him up* and as if a permanent reminder it would hang off his neck everyday counting the inches to the patterns strewn out before him, marked in cross sections and sides, tailor made with all the love and dedication that a cutter could bring to the table, his fingers yellow from his affair with nicotine, cupping *her* into his palm for one last drag, an act of defiance in the face of *shortening* odds like those inches remaining on his tape and, in time, they too would be used up and there would be nothing left to measure, nothing that you would need a tailor for.

His tiny workshop on F deck nestled in between a boiler casing on one side and the Turkish Baths on the other, strangely quiet, almost eerily he would work through the night. On the back of the door hung a dinner suit yet to be altered and from the corner of his eye kept him company as he chatted to it, waiting for a reply that would never come, it didn't matter he knew the answers to the questions anyway but like the rest of us the search for approval had not diminished with time. Yusef unfurled the black and grey fabric from the roll allowing enough to hang over the edge as he bellowed air beneath it, watching it run the length of the yarn, settling back down like a giant wave coming to rest, the chalk mark sufficiently aligned, he would take his scissors and slice through the material carving out a straight line as would Titanic as it *cut* a path overnight from Cherbourg to Queenstown Ireland and in both their wakes, *separation*, but unbeknown to them the type only time would attempt to heal. Yusef could repair almost anything but what was coming would require more than a *stitch in time*.

It was six thirty when Archie opened his eyes, well, just one eye, preferring to let the day in gently as he squinted and contorted his face now buried in his hands.

'Where did that go?' muttering to himself, softly, so as not to wake Harry and Albert both sleeping, Albert's arm flailing off the end of the bunk and resting on the floor like a cantilever to stop him rolling out, the light flooding through the port hole bounced off the top of his head and into the cabin, the torch like beam weakening as it washed away the darkness, reflecting off the poster Tully had hung on the back of the door, Egon Schiele's model standing nude, stared over her shoulder as she struggled to hold on to the sheet slipping off her bottom, like a troubled soul she was used to awkward moments and would take no offence when Archie drifted back to sleep.

Yusef Gans had kept the darkness company; he preferred to work at night and always alone, now resting in his armchair the only other item beside his machine he would not leave behind. With his bench light off he sat in the shadows and listened as the water rushed by, his mind lost in the thoughts of Hulda and her last few months before she was taken, he could still smell her perfume on the chair as he rested his head against the frayed material, his temple covering the shinny patch that played witness to a decade of naps taken in his workshop on the estate, his wife *in service* and a lifetime together, before his notice to quit a week after her death.

There was just one deck that separated Archie and Yusef but they would never meet, kept apart by steel and seven decades of a life already lived, quietly both men listened as the sea rushed past, the sense of speed transferred through their feet as the ship pushed on, twenty knots or more, conveyed to them in a message that each would receive marked *addressee only* delivered as a narrative they would both embrace, their stories set before them to shape, Archie like a sponge soaking up everything, excited at the opportunity to earn some money to help his family and then there was Sarah; in a week he would walk the streets of New York and with the passage of time, came the future.

Yusef closed his eyes and let the sense of melancholia wash over him, in silence he scratched the back of his hand splitting the skin, fragile like an Autumn leaf too long in the sun, bruised tissue of brown and purple trauma gently seeping blood beneath his finger nail as he marked time, rubbing the wound to the rhythm of the waves, he was seventy four years old and still working, they were both on a journey and for now they were heading in the same direction, carried in the belly of the whale, Archie looking forward, Yusef clinging on to the past and the life he had with Hulda left in his wake. On the surface they had nothing in common besides a lifetime of struggle made easier by the love of those around them but, as with most people, look a little deeper and perhaps their lives weren't that different after all.

You could feel the pull to the left like a magnet drawing them out into the North Atlantic, crossing the Celtic Sea and up into St Georges Channel, lines on a chart the only source of separation, flapping in the breeze through an open window to the bridge.

Archie found a table and quietly focused on staying awake, watching his tea swirl around the cup, slicing the yolk of an egg with the side of his fork, he burst the *yellow balloon* and watched the contents escape around his plate, circling fried bread island before cutting the landscape into manageable pieces. He couldn't hide his tiredness as he quietly watched others join the morning breakfast and wondered did he look as bad as he felt? Allowing the steam from his tea to warm his face, staring over the brim at those in the queue, slowly shuffling forward in a line of dark blue uniforms and polished shoes, but they were not enough to capture Archie's attention, lost between thoughts of home and a starched white bow, tied off in the small of her back, the ribbon wrapped around her slender waist like a Christmas box placed in a shop window never to be opened.

Within the hour he would be down on the *plate* shovelling coal that would take the ship to Queenstown, his second shift would renew the grime that had resisted all attempts to be removed despite his efforts to scrub away the insecurity that came with it. Magnified the white crockery background teased him with a contrast as he poured himself more tea from the urn, his hands etched with a message in blackened filth soaked into his skin like a drunken tattoo, no amount of regret or remorse could ever remove. Archie already knew the message, it would occupy his thoughts long before resistance would falter into submission, he finished his breakfast and watched her across the dining room, sat alone, content in the solitude of the morning, unaware of his thoughts and unaware of him.

****

An hour earlier he had jumped at the chance, anything would be better than humping flour and groceries from the store rooms on G deck and a chance to work in a kitchen or cellar, he didn't much mind as he stepped forward his arm raised.

Sammy made his way up from the pantries on G deck wedged between hatch number 4 and the huge engine casing that spanned the width of the ship, dominating everything around it but Sammy's enthusiasm to enjoy the experience. Pushing his way onwards like an early spring flower he forced his way out onto E deck, breaking through he emerged with all the optimism that Bluebells can bring, glancing back down the stairwell as if to ensure winter didn't follow him through. It was like he had been released for good behaviour underlined by the smile on his face and the irony of the stairwell housed between the potato washroom and store, reinforcing the stereotype as he made his escape, hampered only by the full length apron restricting his legs, the sound of brushed cotton following him up the corridor to the Engineers' Mess. He didn't look around on first hearing, it was like tempting fate, almost to the border only to be picked up and returned back to the drudgery that was yesterday. He would help prepare and serve breakfast for the crew, just like back home, helping his dad in the pub, opening early they'd serve fried eggs and mash washed down with mugs of tea for the Dockers and anyone else within an ear's length of their banter, peppered with filth and crude stories tempered only by Sammy's father when *his* boy cleared away the plates.

He wouldn't come easy but the voice following him up the passage carried with it an air of determination, etched in contradiction as his soft Italian tone washed away the anxiety and with it Sammy's resistance to ignore it anymore.

'Excuse me, Excuse Me?! You dropped this towel! Please make sure it goes straight into the laundry and is not used again, thank you.'

It was relief more than anything, as Sammy quickly acknowledged his request, delivered with friendly confidence and expectation.

'Yes sir, right away.'

It would play on his mind for the next hour or so, in between grilling sausages, bacon and huge plum tomatoes splitting as they were browned off beneath the flames, placed face up in steel trays next to scrambled eggs, mushrooms, black pudding and at the end of the serving hatch baskets of bread for toasting and dipping; yes, the White Star Line may well work you to death but you wouldn't die hungry. Sammy was in his element as he stirred the contents of a pan, a clean cloth thrown over his shoulder, cheeks puffed and red with the heat as the perspiration ran down his face. Sammy was *home* as was Archie, well, at least *at home*, like returning sons they were less than fifty miles from Ireland and back to a place neither had been before, back for the first time and back for the last. Emptying the dregs of the urn into the sink and placing the steel canister on its stand, carefully counting spoonfuls of tea scooped with all the precision only he could bring to the task, watching the steam disappear on the breeze of an open door and carried across the dining room its final act to draw attention, a last desperate plea before dissipating forever into the ceiling rose above his head, Sammy placed the lid on the urn and watched his friend from the kitchen.

Archie sat alone his leg twitching beneath the table like a nervous *tick*, his stained hands cupping his mug, an offering yet to be taken, the contents danced to the tremors as he fidgeted in his seat, he was unaware of how he looked, unaware of the stares from those around him and unaware of Sammy close to tears. It wasn't Sammy's fault Archie was shovelling coal, but it may as well have been as he watched him finish his tea.

Samuel Fuller was a sensitive soul, he would worry constantly about everything and everyone, his mind would race ten to the dozen, fussing over the smallest detail, over and over until he could worry no more. He had never stopped thinking of Archie since they said their goodbyes at the dock gate, in truth he never thought he would feel so awful but the reality of him sat there before his shift had changed all that, the thought of Archie in those conditions, *trimming* coal, port and starboard in equal measure, an even keel and all of that, while Sammy *trimmed* fat off the bacon magnified every emotion he was feeling suppressed only by the happiness in seeing his friend. He wouldn't have long, he could see Archie was ready to leave, his cap in hand *kneading* it like a dog seeking attention, lost in a moment of affection he closed his eyes and clawed at the cap and in that moment, Archie looked like he needed all the friends he could get.

'Archie! Archie! Over here, Archie!'

Sammy waved the ladle above his head and shouted across the room, stopping only when tomato sauce ran up his sleeve; waving at Archie with the other hand licking the bright red trail as it rounded his wrist and disappeared.

'Archie! Archie!'

'Sammy! Oh my god, Sammy!'

It was only a day but you would never have known it, beaming smiles and laughter both talking over each other to get a word in, Sammy ruffling Archie's hair and play punches between hugs of affection, they were back, well two thirds of the gang, 'Where was Drippin when you needed him?' Both boys fell into chairs, Archie sat round the wrong way resting his chin on the back, out of the way they spent the next ten minutes catching up, Sammy careful not to gloat, Archie careful not to sound dejected, they would meet up again when their shifts allowed, maybe the 15th on the Monday morning if Sammy was back in the kitchen, it was a plan, at least something like one and both boys shook on it. Sammy caught the glances of his boss now deteriorating into glares as he threw some dirty pots into an open sink determined to make as much noise as possible.

'I've got to go Archie or my life won't be worth living, I'll see you as planned ok?'

Neither boy wanted to leave; they could have chatted for hours about everything and nothing. The clock was pulling Archie downstairs below the waterline and into the darkness; Sammy scowled back across the dining room and gave *him* the look of a thousand daggers as it took away his friend.

'Take care Archie, there's nothing to prove, just do your best and stay safe.'

Sammy watched his friend make his way to the door, stopping to wave goodbye, captured like a picture in the doorframe, grinning back he flipped his cap onto his head and waved, pointing over Sammy's shoulder and laughing at his boss, and through that he laughed at him, he held up his thumb and with one last smile he was gone.

Chapter Seven

It was always going to be her fault as he held the door open out onto the boat deck, he watched his hat swirling above him before descending like a stone into the foaming wash, for a moment he stood frozen, dumbstruck like a statue unsure whether to laugh or cry, he chose irritation as he snapped at his wife like she had thrown it herself curbing his anger as a couple passed them by. They would take the morning air before breakfast and plan the rest of the day in silence, broken by clipped conversation when the moment demanded, their façade intact, the mood mirrored by the bitter sharpness of the chill running the length of the ship, sliced into high pitched whistles as the wind cut through by a hundred stays and shrouds supporting the masts and funnels drilled into the deck like a maypole of cold industrial steel, worthy of a Belfast shipyard and worthy of their marriage.

He would sulk his way to Ireland and battle with pride and stupidity, mellowing in time for supper and the etiquette that would answer to no one. Titanic was waking up, in less than four hours the ship would be at anchor off Roches Point, the smell of breakfast was carried in the air, a door hatch clattered caught on the breeze while cigarette smoke competed with the burners driving the ship to

Queenstown, with Archie's sweat nine decks below, soot ladened smoke settled on the stern, a testament to his efforts, and in the distance the sound of the ships bell jolted him back from the person he had become, back to a country church where he waited for *her* almost twenty five years ago and remembered why they were there on this ship and on their way to New York. He held the door open while she walked beneath his arm held aloft and holding the weight of the sprung loaded hinge, like a guard of honour she had stepped through and into his life, he wouldn't wait for dinner, his pride replaced with embarrassment and a foolishness reserved only for men, he followed her through as did the freshness of the morning. It was up to him to make amends and salvage the day destined to be as raw as a northerly wind, softened by the smell of coffee and breakfast as he led her up the corridor, stopping at the dining room doors wedged open like a welcoming friend, he lifted his coat slung over his arm, looking beneath it, swivelling on his feet, he checked the floor around him, feigning badly to over emphasise the point, and with a childish grin that could roll back the years of any face, he broke the silence.

'Have you seen my hat?'

They would *cover* ten miles or so over breakfast and Archie would cover the blister now bleeding in the palm of his hand, his neckerchief tied around it to help with the pain.

Ten layers from boat deck down to the Tank Top and Ten layers of life interwoven like a patchwork quilt, each reliant on the next, every shade, every colour, clinging on to something or someone, a life, a future, a marriage, it was all there to be seen, laid out for the scrutiny of the thoughtful, but oblivious to most. Walking the decks and passageways, exploring the ship like excited children on a paper chase, their enthusiasm curbed only by the invisible boundaries never to be crossed, painted in blocks on stairwell walls and bulkheads *No Third Class Beyond This Point*. It would filter through to the first and second class, its emphasis changing by degree from limitation to confirmation as they made their way from breakfast, each dining room careful not to *blend* and with that came a comfort not limited to those who would dine this evening in the À la Carte *Ritz*. Louis VI splendour and confused opulence of walnut veneer, gilded swags and festoons beneath crystal chandeliers, their natural motion robbed forever muting voices that will mirror the diners who will sit beneath them, black linen starched, a humourless acknowledgement to the conversation, rigid in their seats and in their lives.

It would make no difference to Archie, his morning would be spent the wrong side of inch thick plate, doubled up and held together by three million rivets, trapped in the hull of a ship or trapped in a life of expectation, either way there was a price to pay.

Lyle Benson had been watching Archie for the last half hour, slowing with every trip to the furnace and stopping to adjust the cloth around his blistered hand, he would compensate by piling loose coal to one side dragging it off the pile into manageable heaps ready for scooping, *getting ahead* and leaving Archie with enough coal to load without the backbreaking work that would see him wince in pain with every shovel. He would work the tunnel for the rest of the morning and resist Archie's offer to take his turn.

'I need to move me legs Archie, if you don't mind I'll carry on *ta*.'

That was all that was said about it, but Archie knew, he would watch Lyle back and forth up and down the tunnel, sweat dripping from the end of his nose, down his forehead and into his eyes, smeared across his face, and for the next hour or so his friend *carried him* all the way to the end of their shift and all the way to Ireland.

****

Hagan O'Dalaigh rested his hip against the side of the galley hatch and stood legs apart to keep his balance, he would ride the shallow waves at the bow singing gently to himself as he gutted the fish, there was nowhere else he wanted to be, his life mapped out before him, thirteen years old and as salty as the sea bass staring up at him from steel buckets washed in salt and brine while the entrails of blood and guts dissipated in the wash. He would see *her* first, the huge funnels spilling out her black calling card, in silence she would announce her arrival, slicing through St George's Channel with all the precision of a straight razor, Hagan offering homage, slicing the fish from gut to jaw in a single motion as good a straight line you will ever see and worthy of the new compass upgraded on Titanic that morning.

Barely three miles away her hull steaming towards them, Hagan jumped up onto the chain locker steadying himself, he clung to the foremast his arm wrapped around it, the other pointing furiously southeast and the horizon, yelling the length of the deck to the men hauling the nets off the starboard side and his father at the open helm guiding *Ballyfouloo* into the tide, holding her position with a stern wind while they gathered in a livelihood yet to be realised.

'Do you see her?! Do you see her?! Look at the sight o dat!'

In less than ten minutes Titanic would be *on them* and for a moment they would disappear, lost in her shadow, the huge hull of cold black steel eclipsing the sunlight as it passed them by like morsels at the feet of the vulture, vulnerable they would scurry away, *Finny* barking his orders to the crew as he steered the fishing boat downwind watching his son waving with all the passion and excitement only youth can muster, his spectacles filled from rim to rim with a wall of darkness and then without warning or direction to a man they fell silent as *she* passed. Finny clung to the wheel and *brought them about* waiting for the wake, he watched the men dumbstruck, each stood still as a *mourner*, bleak lifeless expressions behind dead eyes, they stood before the village priest as he scattered soil into the open grave freshly dug and filling with salty water. Finbar O'Dalaigh closed his eyes and gasped at the sight of it, the cold air hitting the back of his throat he coughed his way back to the present circling his shoulders to chase away the shiver running the length of his spine gnawing at the marrow like a dull ache etched with despair, it would seep from his flesh every time he recalled that moment, the moment *she* passed, he would take it to his own grave and would never speak of it again.

'Get back to work na!'

That was all that was said of it, the *congregation* broken, the men returned subdued to the net swinging on the boom, their morning haul glistening in the sunlight, gasping mouths that would draw their last breath given up to an early death out of the water, the irony of that lost on them all.

It should have been something special, something to tell the grandchildren kind of moment, but it wasn't, there was something wrong and each and every one of them felt it in their own way.

They would drag the nets once more this morning. Moving northwest on a flowing tide and later when the light was fading land their catch and listen to the talk of *her* spilling through the windows of the ale house next to O'Faolain's the Fishmonger, the stench blended with stale beer and cigarettes that no one would notice, laughter and stories would fill the saloon while old men listened from the *snug*. Weathered hands around glasses of stout would see the evening done and tales of *the beautiful one*, her black cloak furled around her body, leaving flashes of insignia yellow and white, completing her *livery* teasing them as she *walked* away, the promise to return hung from *her* lips, an empty pledge in a moment of passion, lost in the haze of intoxication; she had captivated their hearts blurring the truth beyond recognition.

Across the stone floor Finbar would sit alone and stare out the window, he would watch the faces distort as they passed the circled balloons blown into the glass, a single candle flickered on his table warming the back of his hand, his whisky swirled into submission while he waited for the water to breach the top of the grave. Head in hand he wiped the sweat from his temple and pinched the bridge of his nose, scrunching his eyes to focus on the shape floating in the water, breaking the surface and the greasy film shimmering beneath *white light*, he lifted the veil and shuffled slowly to the side of the grave, falling to his knees skimming the water he peered into the darkness, and through the eyes of a young mother clutching her baby, he peered into her soul.

She left them in her wake, disappeared into the distance and like all bad news travelled fast slowing only to adjust the approach; Dalon O'Dwyer's voice was lost on the wind, shouting something about the 'Size of her ass!' She didn't look back, not even a glance, glinting in the early morning sun, and for those who would make her acquaintance the sound of silk brushed over flesh as she swayed in the cross wind and at the *altar* white horses lapped around her thighs as she waited for the pilot from the Daunt light ship, he would take her hand and guide the rest of the way. Myrtleville on the bow, the compass slowly backing to pick up a bearing, gliding gently past Fennell's Bay and Kilcolta to port, Finure drifting off to starboard, but she would disappoint once more, a cruel tease to those waiting patiently on the dockside of Queenstown harbour, held off like distant strangers she would drop anchor near Roches Point, *lying* elsewhere, the *deliverance* of a finalé not even she could have imagined. Titanic stood stage front, and worked the crowd, in just two hours' time she would leave them, leave them wanting more.

It nearly split his eardrums when it went off, right above his head the sound so loud it made him wince, hunching his shoulders and covering his ears, the red flashing light picked out his silhouette in the darkness, Archie could barely make out what Lyle was bellowing up the tunnel.

'It's a drill Archie, don't worry we're alright, stay where you are they're closing the watertight doors!'

The last words trailing as Archie stood alone the *right side* of boiler room five and through his feet a deafening thud as the huge steel doors came to rest, stamping their authority on the proceedings as if it was ever in doubt, and nine decks above the lifeboat drill had completed, a handful of crew dispersed like puffins as they struggled to remove their life jackets designed for maximum inconvenience and discomfort, it might save your life but not without irritation.

It was just part of the frenzy that would occupy the next two hours but it was nothing to the turmoil in the stomach of Mary Duggan. Piercing the space that occupied hair and scalp, her hat pin *probing* safe ground before plunging like a needle, there was no time for hesitation, no turning back, the day had arrived and so had *she*, her life and that of her children were about to change forever. With one final glance she pulled the tangled hair from the bristles and placed the brush back in her bag, looking over her shoulder at the three children sat on the side of the bed, washed and scrubbed, the sight of them had her crying again. From her sewing kit she held a needle and pricked her bottom lip watching the bubble of blood form pressing her lips top and bottom, smearing the edges before it dried, her lipstick was done.

The small stone cottages were tightly packed, three rows of eight each side of the main track winding out of the village and down to the quay and beyond them a sweeping green carpet that would carry the bitter winter straight off the hills that stood on either side, their *heads* decapitated as the mist rolled down the valley in the early evening, seeping through every crevice, it would settle in their lungs as they slept, their stifled breath broken by phlegm filled coughs.

'Yous be gettin darnstairs, it's time to go!'

She didn't need to see the horse and cart; it would appear soon enough and follow the sound that would grind a path to her door, through an open window, the screech of axles desperate for greasing carried on the breeze, syncopated through curtains that would flap gently delivering the *message* like semaphore from ship to shore. It was time and as if to underline that, the dust trailing his old rig would come to rest *coating* the morning dew that ran the edges of the cobbles and last year's grass, dull and lifeless it would wear the badge of mistrust and wait, content to second guess an April frost brought on by a false sense of security, a lesson Mary Duggan knew all too well.

'Gimme notice if yous gonna creep up on me!'

She heard one of the children say and for a brief moment it made her smile as she struggled with the buttons on her coat determined to *give her away* and through her fumbling fingers reveal the cold fear cursing through her veins. Gathering them at the front door watching as old man O'Shea loaded the bags and helped the children clamber on the back of his cart, fastening the tailgate with iron pins wedged into place, he would check it was secure several times more and wait for their mother, her shadow visible through the downstairs window, straightening the furniture and sliding a chair beneath the table. He had *watched* her grow up from a child and had insisted on taking them the three miles down to Queenstown and the White Star wharf, slowing as he passed the only shop and a final wave from Mrs Mcbay, sure to be waiting on hearing the cart back down the hill. With her back to the children she gently closed the door, tugging on the old metal latch, the distorted frame offering the usual resistance would irritate no more, pushing to check it was closed she placed the iron key beneath a large stone to the side of the step and kissed the black metal cross that had swung from under her coat.

'Tell me it was worth it *Annie Moore*, tell me what I'm about to do with my babies will give them a chance, tell me your life began at the gates of Ellis Island?!'

She didn't wait for a reply that would never come, instead she did what she had always done, take control. With a final brush of her coat she turned to Donald O'Shea and in a manner they both knew was not for their benefit made peace with a moment that would never return.

'Are you ready Donald to get us underway and on to a new life in America? Well then, let's be off!'

He wanted to help her, he could see the pleading in her eyes as she stared back at him, a smile etched with anxiety, her face lined with a lifetime of worry far beyond her years, the old man looked up from beneath his cap and clutched the leather reins resting in his hands, swivelling in his seat he turned toward her, looking down from the cart, he tapped the wooden bench beside him and wrapped in that gesture a momentary glance that would say 'It's alright Mary, it'll be alright.'

'Hold on now children, we'll be getting on our way!'

With clipped command best understood between horse and master, the old cart groaned into life, Mary checking on the children across her shoulder she watched as the house disappeared, rounding the bend approaching the fork to Mulligan's farm, it was all but gone. The old stone cottage off in the distance burning timber waterlogged from the recent rain, blue smoke billowing its intent carried on the breeze, an unspoken lesson, like stupidity it was difficult to hide.

'Look Mary! Out in the bay, she's waiting for you!'

The old man broke the silence and with it took away the crutch they had both relied upon. Skirting the woods beneath them the tree lined canopy obscuring their view, *her* shape broken by the foliage waving in a stiffening breeze. Through the gaps a hundred rooftops stretched out like stepping stones across a stream stopping abruptly at the water's edge like one step too far but beyond that last *leap of faith* she stood, motionless, a mile off the eastern edge of the bay, quietly resting and watching the mayhem as the morning unfolded into well-rehearsed chaos. The horse and cart clearing what was left of the woods it re-emerged into the sunlight and the houses that would line the rest of the journey down through the old town already bustling with excitement. Slipping on the cobbles they weaved their way through the traffic filled streets, the old man's mouth moving slightly as he rehearsed his *goodbye* flicking the reins with gentle encouragement turning on Sullivan Street, level now with the water's edge, they would *run* the dockside to the entrance and the wharf. Mary clinched her hands for comfort wringing them like washing before hung out to dry, she would take what solace she could and straightened her back, glimpsing past the lattice work of cranes, the four huge funnels, like fingers held aloft, one for each of them confirmed their arrival as they swung around the barriers and joined the queue. Watching those in front unload, gathering up their bags and cases, counting *heads* and straightening collars stood by the side of the road, checking papers flapping in idle hands overpowered by the desire to be part of something bigger, something only belonging can satisfy, the *comfort* of being amongst your own. Mary averted her gaze and kept a watchful eye out in the bay, distracted by the soil in the foot well no longer dancing having drawn to a halt, it was as if everything at that moment had come together, in a few seconds time she would climb down from the cart and leave the soil scattered there, her tiny footprints like a symbol of what she was about to do, and in less than two hours' time they would *step off* forever, the realisation *sinking in* as the dark shape fixed in the corner of her stare prodded for attention. It was as clear to her as the fear on the face of a mother clinging to her children's shoulders, tightly knit, their possessions in four bags circling their feet, they were ready like her to tread this soil no more, ready to accept their decision, and staring out across the bay, there it was, the future.

What little power he had was wielded with as much polish as the shiny buttons on his jacket, whistle in hand he beckoned them forward, shouting at a man on horseback to clear his line of sight.

'Get away man! he bellowed, arms waving frantically signalling them forward he pointed to the lay-by, as if invisible without direction, the sign *move off* adding pressure they could both do without. The clock was ticking now and Donald knew what he wanted to say and woe betide any man who would stop him from saying it, any man but himself. With the luggage off they stood to one side exchanging an awkward silence, broken only by the scowl from the *badge of authority* holding up the traffic that had formed behind them.

All the rehearsal in the world couldn't help him now, the words just refused to leave his lips, like denial, if he didn't say them it wasn't happening and in amongst the hustle and bustle of the dockside he looked like a lost little boy clutching his cap to his chest, he wanted everything to stop, the shouts and screams, the clatter of trunks in dust balloons hauled onto trolleys by hopeful porters, skilfully swerving around them with a wall of labelled leather, the detour underlining it was time to go. Mary didn't need his words and didn't wait for them as he rummaged in his coat for the sweets he had bought for the children; she threw her arms around him and held his head to hers.

'If I could have chosen a father it would have been you', she felt the warmth of his tears fall on the back of her hand as he struggled to compose himself, wiping his eyes and patting the tops of her arms he gently pulled away.

'Whatever sky you sleep beneath this will always be your home and not a day will go by Mary when you're not in my thoughts and prayers, now go on with you, there's a life out there waiting to be lived, a life for you and these children, gather your bags now and be gone.'

She knew there was nothing left to say and kissed his fingers slipping from her hand and in that fleeting second she glimpsed beneath his top coat and all the words he struggled with or couldn't find were there hiding in a gesture, he had worn his weskit over a clean white shirt, his *Sunday Best....* it was Thursday morning.

Chapter Eight

It took almost six seconds for the cigarette to hit the water, nudged over the edge from boot to soggy end, Archie watched it spin through the glare of the sun reflecting off the surface like shards of glass.

Strip washed and brushed up he had made his way topside and out into the daylight, the heavy set doors varnished to an inch of their life offered nothing but resistance as he squeezed through the gap and onto the open deck limited to those whose pocket book was light to the touch, steerage, immigrants and missing crew stealing a moment, like landlords in the winter, they would be difficult to find hiding amongst a sea of black, the wardrobe of choice for those with none.

He wasn't sure how long they would stay but he smiled at the thought of Sammy, safe in the knowledge that he would know, it was probably scribbled into his notebook embellished with trivia and a sketch of Roches Point. The wild Irish landscape captured in scratched lead and smudged for effect, the date in the top corner, he would initial his notes just in case there was another quite like him, Archie caught himself chuckle out loud 'There's only one like you Sammy' he said whispering to himself, his face lit up in a warm orange glow. The early afternoon sun warmed the deck as the ship swung gently on the tide, a delicate pirouette mirrored the axis of the breeze and followed the arc around her bow line anchored to the sea bed with movement small enough to go unnoticed to those who would *take the air*, while mothers grateful of the respite watched their babies sleep, lost in slumber as deep as the water beneath their open cots, Archie moved across the deck to the starboard side and chose to stay *upwind* of them, content that some things travel faster than sound.

Archie wished he'd asked the question, but he never had, in truth he had no idea which part of Ireland his mother came from, not that it mattered, he didn't need the name of the town or village he just knew it was the poor part, and that was enough.

Had she found the money in the jar? Had she bought some veg and potatoes and lashed it with gravy for the boys' supper? Had she stopped crying?

No, no, not here, not yet, he would have these thoughts and savour them in his own way, but not until he found somewhere to settle out of the wind and down towards the stern. Nestled between the hold and storage that stretched the width of the ship, crouching beneath a hundred ropes and cargo runners he crawled behind a winch encased within a barrier, out of sight to all but the most inquisitive.

Clambering across a huge canvas yet to be stowed scrunched up like a stiff blanket, he sank into the middle and pulled the edges over his legs propping himself against the base, his face washed in sunshine like the day was smiling on him, he snuggled down in his *den* and kicked out his feet in homage to the *secret garden* registering approval in short fire bursts of spontaneous reaction, tempered briefly to the sound of footsteps approaching from behind, tapping a rhythm of meander, their conversation peppered with laughter and tied in a bow of agreement. Planning the trip of a lifetime, he caught the words museum and St Paul's chapel while he waited for them to pass, counting the seconds before they came into view, following the *planking* caulked in tar and bound together just like them, clinging on to each other they skirted two bollards positioned for maximum inconvenience, arms linked like a chain never to be parted, their footsteps making lost ground on voices that had gone on ahead, reunited, Archie watched them disappear down the steps that split the levels of the deck, descending out of sight between rows of washing hung out to dry. He wondered whether the vision of them still clear in the back of his eyes summed up the future, as they walked between a sea of nappies flapping on the breeze, the railings turned into makeshift clothes lines symbolic of a life full of compromise, he would give it no more thought as he pulled the crumpled pack of gold flake from his pocket, after all, he had problems of his own.

She wouldn't know what he was doing, but she would know where he was, Drippin would make sure of that.

Eight hours before his next shift, Archie was determined to make use of the time, and finding this place, his vantage point, he would watch the comings and goings and enjoy the relative peace of it hidden amongst the chaos that would mark the next hour or so. Like a flea on a dog he was just a passenger, the bigger picture unfolding before him as he pulled the canvas closer to the edge and hung his legs over the side. It was like he wasn't there, just an observer rolling the smoke around his mouth and blowing it skyward in circles, one after another they left his lips each chasing the last in a vain attempt to keep up, as if safety in numbers. 'God this is a great place to be' he whispered, reinforcing his thoughts like a sign of approval as he stepped in and out of his mind, back and forth he would travel, dashing from one place to the next, his family back home, *the state of the larder*, Will and Charlie and the newspaper stand, how Drippin was coping without *them*, the flower pressed between his clothes and wrapped in tissue at the bottom of his bag and, when his mind started to drift, he'd concentrate on just ten feet, ten square feet of water right beneath his dangling boots. He watched the seagulls sat bobbing about on the surface, two at first and then another, like him waiting for something, and that was it, he was *back* sat with his friends off the pier in Mayflower Park, watching the seagulls, *waiting for something to happen* and now it had.

'For Christ sake give us some warning!' He shouted out loud, more in shock, as the horn blasted his eardrums, the sound reverberating down the deck, the piercing shrill louder than imaginable until that close. Archie held his ears and waited for the last blast, keeping his hands cupped and firmly in place long after the sound had dissipated, trusting his instinct in favour of anything unannounced cursing the timing as he choked back the black smoke billowing up from the small cargo boats beneath him, one at a time they would come along side ladened with all manner of goods, passed from deck to hold amidst shouts and hollers carried on the breeze, the men yelling blue murder in accents as thick as the lungful that had him coughing and spluttering. In the distance the sound of laughter from the decks above, broken by the chinking of glass layered over the music that would dominate the background of an early party, they were getting ready to leave, he could *feel* the excitement in the pit of his stomach, but it wasn't about leaving, not for him, god he'd only just arrived, no, it was about being *close* to his mother, close to the shoreline from which he came as rugged and beautiful as he would ever see. A rolling landscape of open countryside *green as envy* spread out before him, away from the shoreline the shallow gradient rising steeply from the water's edge and sat between the rhythm of nature, Queenstown, just a few miles as the crow flew, he could almost touch her, nestled deep in the mouth of the cove, the harbour walls of blackened stone offered shelter through the broken groynes and beyond the shallow breakwaters a quayside as busy as any he'd seen before played host to a handful of fishing boats landing their morning catch. Further down the wharf a row of cargo boats *doubled up* their bellies relieved by the dockside cranes as they tugged on spring lines fore and aft to get away, a blue haze hung in the air from the *smoking sheds* that billowed burnt wood shavings into the afternoon sky, while horse and carts ferried all manner of goods out from the dockside and onto ledger lines of accounts, their double-entry adorned in black ink, registered by clerks with precision hand beneath the flicker of candle light.

Archie rested his chin on the back of his sleeve and clung to the railings, pulling on a thread with his teeth biting loose a strand that had run, giving up he flicked the ash from his cigarette and burnt it free, pressing what was left flat against the cloth, the *housekeeping* done. He scoured the view *panning* up the incline to the houses cut into its side like an open wound, row upon row they perched, layered terraces one above the other, the buildings four and five stories tall with fascia's painted randomly in soft pastel colours, warm enough to take the chill from a bright spring day but not enough to ease the *conscience* that would dominate everyone from the hilltop. Prodding the *flock* in neo gothic proportions as they went about their business, the huge cathedral spire hung over the town demanding of attention and impossible to avoid, set above huge ramparts, Archie could clearly see the buttresses and gargoyles as the sun moved across the south facing walls, calling on him like an unwelcome visitor as if there wasn't enough to be done for the *locals*. Set in stone and set in prejudice some things are difficult to *shake off*, Archie averted his gaze back to the houses and the pallet of washed blues, earthen reds, bone and cat's paw, taking what comfort he could purged himself of thoughts of fairness and inclusion content to keep his own council and watched the first of the tenders leave the jetty. With slipped lines the single stacked steamer belched her departure paddlewheels grinding slowly into life kicking up the water and kicking up a fuss she left a wake of foam and smoke difficult to *ignore*, her decks loaded with immigrants she passed slowly through the darkened shadow thrown across the harbour from the church and just for a second Archie glanced back and was convinced that the *church* looked the other way.

'We'll be on the next one' she told the children.

Mary pulled them all together and wrapped her arms around their shoulders, pointing to the tender as it left the pontoon, the open decks filled with passengers all vying for a place to see and be seen as they steamed through the breakwater and out across the bay, *wind over tide* welcomed them aboard as the small boat rocked and rolled on the swell to the deepwater quay collecting mail sacks as they went.

Archie watched it all from his vantage point high up on the stern of the ship convinced he could see everything from there, but he wouldn't see the pain in Mary's face as she winced to the sight of her youngest child, his head pulled back like a rag doll while his eyelids were raised with a buttonhook, a *white coat* was his symbol and enough to hide a lifetime of arrogance as the doctor bellowed his gruff instructions to the boy trembling in his presence. 'Look up, look down, left, now right!' accompanied the cursory inspection that would find no swollen eyes, watering through red lumps and open sores, there was no Trachoma, duly witnessed by the yellow chalk mark scored across his coat, it was the first of many *labels* he would be asked to wear, publically pinned on him like a badge for all to see. But for now he was free of lice, third class and cleared to travel, waved to one side he waited for his sisters and mother to follow and watched the queue *processed* behind him, stretching out of the tent, its *doors* tied back for a purpose, allowing the canvas tunnel to breathe as one by one they were examined, *marked* and ushered to the dockside gate for boarding, all within the *blink of an eye* filled with nothing but childhood innocence.

He hadn't noticed the numbers increase lost in his own little world, Archie was consumed by the boats back and forth leaving trails of activity as the traders bought alongside Irish Linen and specialist craftware for the first class passengers to buy. It was almost instinctive as he plunged his hand into his trouser pocket and swirled around the few coins nestled there *just checking*, as if considering a purchase, he counted the money by feel and touch, the sixth coin *hiding* in the corner beneath his penknife and hankie caused momentary panic, the *black sheep* lost from the fold was gathered in and returned to safety unlikely to see the light of day, Archie patted his thigh a couple of times as if to acknowledge he and his money would not be easily parted. Tucked out the way and sunk back into the canvas he watched the numbers increase as more and more passengers made their way topside and onto the open decks, claiming their spot against the railings they would stay until the ships departure, enjoying the band that had struck up a tune just two decks above, a double bass, some violins and what sounded like an accordion would provide the entertainment, chosen straight from the *White Star Line* contemporary repertoire of three hundred and forty two *cheerful numbers* guaranteed to get the toes tapping as the first of the two tenders approached in the distance. The small flotilla followed like cygnets in the wake of their mother carrying the first of the passengers out to the ship, the open hatches along her hull waiting to receive them. Not long now he thought, it was as if the tension was being measured by the shouts and hollers down below, the billowing smoke from *America* as she lined up the gangway and came alongside pulled in and tied off, the gap spanned by a boarded platform, *run out* on rollers that would soon expand across her sister, the *Ireland*, shortly to leave the quayside and with her those remaining passengers from the 123 boarding today making up the manifest of 2,227 souls pulled on board at the top of the gangways, with a little too much enthusiasm by crew members keen to assist.

'Welcome aboard Titanic, please may I take your name?'

It wasn't as if he knew she had just one foot left on Irish soil, in truth when he said it he wasn't even looking that way.

'Poor bastards' Archie muttered to himself, dragging on his cigarette he resumed a *watching brief*, his gaze distracted by the cold grey walls that dominated the small island a mile or so in the distance, he didn't need an explanation, a prison's a prison wherever it is and Spike Island was no exception. Built in black and white the huge structure stood above the perimeter walls cold and imposing amidst a baron scrubbed landscape, the windswept wild grass swaying on the breeze, choking the life from the reed beds down to the water's edge, it was as if it had been built to face Queenstown Harbour and the brightly coloured buildings smiling back from the quayside like a harsh reminder of the life *they* had all left behind. He couldn't see the detail and would fill in the blanks but could make out the main gate, set within huge stone walls of facing block work, and beneath the archway, solid oak doors would be the end of one life and the beginning of another, *convicts* held for penal transportation to the colonies, and now a prison with all the charm of a wet Sunday afternoon, the small bore cannon centred above the entrance, a reminder, as if one was required, as to where *they* had arrived.

'Poor Bastards!' he said again, scanning the length of the walls, three layers of windows as small as a squint their criss-cross bars set back into solid stone three feet thick, rationing the daylight that would dare to enter, *their* cells cold and darkened as a contrast to a bright spring day. Archie wondered, could they see *her* out in the bay and just in case he waved back, reserved at first and then with a little more passion he jumped up and down, shouting and waving in the hope, a vain hope, that at least one prisoner might see him, and in that moment connect with the outside world and the past now severed like an artery, their will to return ebbing as the months fade into years, reaching out into the bay down the landing post and tantalisingly close to the mainland, teasing them from across the water like salt in the wound, their *crimes* never forgotten, punished like a boil lanced from society, a life in isolation as bitter as the weather that would eat into their bones when the winter came. Archie didn't know its name or for that matter its reputation, but unbeknown to him right there across the bay stood the brutality that was… Spike Island.

It all happened in a blur; she never had a chance to hesitate.

The iron gate was all that stood between them and the tender, its vertical bars a barrier to most, painted black and worn to the metal around the push plate, offered nothing but temptation to the child whose head was momentarily stuck.

'Have your tickets ready for marking!'

The clerk announced his instructions and opened the gate, slamming it against the receiving post with a clatter sure enough to wake any baby within a mile;

mothers cursed him with sideways glances, conveying their displeasure without a single word as he *winced* his apology.

'Move along please! Move along at the front! Straight up, keep your bags close by!'

Mary pushed the children ahead and followed them onto the tender, clinging on to the youngest. They navigated the wooden slats in a vain attempt to co-ordinate arm and feet movements as she pulled her case up the gangway, clattering over every rung.

'Children, go around to the right and sit on that bench over there' and that was it, she was on her way with not a moment to change her mind, it was over before it started, her ticket punched, she *stepped off* Ireland just like the rest of them and would never return.

'Christ, if you load anymore on that it'll sink!' Archie shouted across the bay. Packed like sardines the open deck swollen with a sea of people waving to loved ones on the dockside, the crowd *doing them proud* offered a wall of enthusiastic noise beneath swaying hats and handkerchiefs as the tender got underway and carried on the breeze testaments of love broken by the shriek of a steam whistle like nails down a blackboard it would get Mary's attention as she watched the commotion unfold.

Huddled together they squeezed on the seat their backs to the shore, there was no one there to see them off, no one to wave or shout their goodbyes and she was grateful for it, content to be lost in a crowd of strangers crushed together amidst a temporary congregation of *darkened cloth* and optimism. They clung to caps and bonnets and anything else in search of *sea legs* yet to be tested, stumbling back and forth, toe and heel, they danced across the bay with all the grace of a midnight drunk, before coming alongside. Archie watched the tenders raft together as passengers disembarked with what they could carry and in their wake a mountain of trunks, cases and almost 200 *Gunny* sacks filled with mail, shifted on hunched backs as the porters shuffled through the open hatch, hauling the *jute* into piles yet to be sorted and while on board the men would steal a glimpse into *her*, a fleeting moment but enough to tell a bedtime story to a child with sleepy eyes when the winter nights set in.

Archie snuggled his back into the iron upright, and watched those to his right leaning over the railings in the hope of a better view.

From where he sat, they all looked decapitated, their heads hung down, pointing to the first class passengers whose names and faces had been in the press for a week or more. Archie had no desire to join them, content to eavesdrop on the commentary from the young couple closest by and watched with amusement as a hapless reporter came aboard, grappling with his attaché case and pulling himself up the gangway. With one camera around his neck and another slipping perilously close to the edge of his shoulder, he looked like a *disaster waiting to happen*, an affable buffoon impossible not to like; he climbed to the top of the gangway and proceeded to trip off the end. Archie watched the drama unfold, captured frame by frame, suspended in mid-air with arms and legs flailing desperate to save his hat from a watery grave, he landed on the deck in slow motion, like a sack of Irish potatoes, his possessions scattered to the winds and for a second he lay as still as a predator and then, as if nothing had happened, he jumped to his feet smiling, gaffing and bumbling, a charmed filled apology, brushing himself down and straightened his tie to a chorus of cheers and laughter. Archie liked him immediately and chuckled out loud when he docked his forehead to acknowledge the crowd, *the village idiot*, he gathered up his things from the floor, and stuffed some papers into his bag, leaving Archie feeling a pang of guilt having laughed at his expense, but couldn't help wonder, had his clumsiness become all too familiar, the *entertainment* for others as he made his way in the world, like Drippin, he was somebody's disappointment.

Archie pacified his guilt content in the knowledge he would never see him again, he would rejoin the rest of the press on the officers promenade deck, taking photos of uniformed men with puffed out chests and stern faces, there was nothing in steerage to photograph, nothing but hope.

On every level you could feel the excitement building as the departure time grew closer, not least for the traders who would soon be asked to leave, their success measured by the *coppers* jangling in their pinnies. Selling tablecloths and doilies hand stitched with *Queenstown* embroidered into the corner, a memento captured in lace, the delicate stitch work woven into swirls of intricate flowers on white cotton thread, the old lady had set out her stall placing her best work across an open wicker basket, she took a pace or two back vying for the attention of the small crowd gathered around them, and for those, if any, who would take a second glance, the contrast was difficult to miss. Stood behind her work of beauty, her rough peasant clothes lay the background to clasping hands weathered and deeply lined, her leathered skin told a story and belied the exquisite tablecloth now held high in the air, the *gentleman* examining the work, with a keen eye, he inspected each artistic detail, his meticulous appraisal done solely for affect, like sipping wine before it was poured, he knew nothing about that either but would bask in his *moment* and purchase the cloth for

131

his wife now stood by his side. An item to brighten the parlour, and an investment into peace and quiet, in truth it was probably both.

There were people everywhere, strolling the decking lost in private conversation, enjoying the afternoon sun, arm in arm and wrapped in topcoats, the breeze as fresh as the lobsters on borrowed time, stacked into flimsy pine boxes and doused in seawater waiting to be loaded. Up above music tumbled down the side of the hull washing the lower decks with optimism and a sense of anticipation as evidenced by those leaning against the railings tapping out a rhythm to a *strange* sensation now firmly etched into faces that had long since forgotten the pleasure of a smile, they were starting to enjoy themselves, they were almost ready to *let go*.

Archie felt the vibration through the seat of his pants and craned his neck to watch the stacks billowing a mixture of smoke and effort only a few would endure. The increase in power as the engines were made ready, boilers fired into life, they coughed and choked on their own appetite as they devoured the coal in anticipation. He knew it was almost time, the temperature rising, while the heat distorted the air leaving the funnels, they were building up a *head of steam*, and so were the band as they finished with a crescendo. The last of the six/four notes falling into silent contrast before launching into Verdi's *Rigoletto*

La Dona, cheerfulness personified they banged it out above a cauldron of noise, shouts, screams and chatter, mingled with bursts of laughter. The luggage and post was hauled aboard carried on shoulders beneath boots of leather, clattering on gangways that strained like a ruler flexed in a teacher's hand, the *blow* delivered with precision and in just a few minutes time Titanic would be sent on her way her *lesson* as yet to be learnt.

'Those on F deck please go down one level and move around to your left, a crew member is there and will take you to your quarters, those on G deck continue on down.'

'Keep together and follow those with the red tickets!' Mary called to the back of her children's heads bobbing down each rung of the iron stairwell, itself pleased to finally be put to some use as the clatter of a hundred footsteps competed with the hum of excitement and keeping time, the thud of a trunk too heavy for carrying, pulled off the edge step by step, much to the irritation of those following behind.

'They should have left it like the rest of us' muttered under the breath of a few, intent to have their say, from the corner of mouths that would remain anonymous to the charge. 'Grab the end of it if you're that concerned!' came the reply, like a challenge they would have the last word on the matter as they waited for those disgruntled to *step up to the plate*, but they never did. Their annoyance registered they would remain in the shadows and follow the crowd as they zigzagged their way down to the first of the decks and the huge corridor that could be seen through the double doors, its signage as alien to them as any they would ever read, *Squash / Racquet Court, Swimming Pool & Turkish Bath.*

'Not this one children; we're going down further to G deck ok, keep to your right and stay out of everyone's way!'

Mary needn't have worried, the throng of people up ahead had all but ground to a halt, checking and double checking their tickets, they mostly waited to be pointed in the right direction, but it wasn't that holding them up, it wasn't something that could have been anticipated, there was no oversight, nowhere to lay the blame. In truth it was as tragic as it was funny and a moment that would bring an uncomfortable smile to those that witnessed it, not least the crew who stood and watched. Their backs firmly pressed against lacquered panels of polished wood, in crisp starched *whites* their brass buttons glinting beneath electric light, but their smiles would fade soon enough, replaced by something embarrassing, something that the innocence of a child would not consider, something that in their quieter moments they'd have preferred not to have seen. Witnessing it they did as the thirty or so families made their way to the third class cabins, through the swing doors and along the corridor, wedged against a boiler casing and dining room, their new home for a week or more awaited them but they would have to step over him first. *He* just seemed to stop walking, as if it was all too much to take in, and then without warning threw himself onto the floor and buried his face down kneading the fabric with his hands, dragging himself along on his tummy in rhythmic waves, flipped onto his back, eyes closed, he rubbed the side of his face and neck into the floor like a puppy, a young boy expressing his excitement in the only way he knew how, captured in an image as disturbing as the reason he was down there. Watched by the backlog of families and crew, mouths agog, unsure of what to do or say, they waited in silence while his mother awkwardly pulled him to his feet, caressing his head into her thigh, there would be no apology and none was expected as the reality of what they had testified sunk in. The spontaneous reaction of a child who had never seen a carpet, never felt its warmth beneath his boots and in that moment of childhood innocence there was nowhere left to hide, nowhere to go and nowhere else to look, a corridor full of strangers all staring at the same thing, the bitter truth of poverty.

She never knew the cause of the delay; it was barely a minute and would pass soon enough, her emotions in tact she had almost *made it*.

There is something nauseous about the smell of lead paint, and stood waiting on the stairwell it was difficult to avoid, but then so were others not half as subtle.

'Move on down children and follow the others through the doors!'

Mary clung onto the railings and onto the last of her breath rationing her intake to avoid a repeat of the previous experience still persistent in the back of her throat, she tried not to gasp as she gulped back a mouthful of *clean air* forced down the stairwell as the last of the hatch doors were pulled shut. The running lock of greased iron closed like interlocking teeth as the wheel was spun till it could turn no more, closing out the sunlight and the last of the seagull cries as the huge door slammed into position, isolated from the sounds outside she felt momentarily trapped, her hearing dampened as the lock sealed them inside, her sense of smell suffered no such interference.

'Welcome to G deck, you are now at the bow of the ship, your quarters are situated next to the first class luggage storage area and post office, please follow me.'

It was that brief rocking motion that would give it away, like a gentle nudge in the back when you're off balance, but for those *in the know* it meant the anchor was being raised and for Archie his lunch was a little closer. He had nearly completed his promise, there wasn't a detail overlooked from his vantage point, not even Sammy could match his observations of Ireland. The finishing touches to the collage overlaid in his mind as the two tenders cast off amidst a flurry of activity, while traders, pressmen and local dignitaries competed with the blasts of horns and whistles acknowledging their departure and through faces etched with a tinge of envy they smiled back and waved to the crowd lining the railings, several hundred or more, like ants around a jam jar lid they gathered on the stern of the ship soaking up the atmosphere as unique to each deck as those that stood upon it. She had promised herself to stay with the children, to settle them into their accommodation, their cabin or *open* quarters, she had said her *goodbyes* and Ireland was finished with them, the future was all that mattered now and the promise of something to eat, her children content to wait while Mary went in search of the third class dining saloon and the lunchtime menu, to choose a meal from the card, it would prove to be the highlight of the day and every day, until they stepped into a new life and pacified the biggest appetite of all, the future.

She couldn't wait to see the children's faces when she showed them the choice, the menu rolled like a scroll tapping out a tune along the wooden handrail interrupted only to step aside as several families passed her in the other direction. Tight units of emotion all talking simultaneously their excitement registered in volume as the children ran the corridors doubling back to encourage their parents along, tugging on sleeves to make a point they scarpered ahead before disappearing around the corner with a final hurry up, its urgency lost in the distance. They had no need for Mary's menu, no need to see the neat blocks of typeface set out in three servings, they could smell it down the passage, their pace quickening unconsciously to the aroma of roast beef and gravy with sweet corn and boiled potatoes followed by plum pudding, tea and coffee, pleasure on a plate and later on faces yet to be seen, flushed with joy that would run the length of galley style tables overlaid with white cloth, even for *them*. Mary almost made the stairwell, almost pushed through the swing doors and down to F deck while her *babies* sat patiently waiting for her return. She could have dealt with the visions of holy communal, an altar of food beautifully prepared in steel dishes as deep as her thoughts, the simmering stew yet to be tasted, held to her lips while an image of old man

O'Shea's *Sunday best* stared back at her in convexed reflection off the side of her spoon. Yes, she could have dealt with all of that, all those buried emotions just long enough to be on her way, her pale hand inches from the brass plate captured her tiny frame, the aberration smudged by those who'd passed before, the sound of footsteps diminishing as they descended on suspended steel, back down below, out of reach and the relative safety of silence.

It was just a bar or two, maybe a little more, a few notes, nothing really, but it had her frozen to the spot and the wrong side of the door.

It was as if the scene had been arranged, planned in advance like a prerequisite for what was about to follow. She was there under false pretences, the children didn't need the menu they could have gone straight to lunch, they'd be out of the way now like those families she had passed a moment ago. There was no perversity in her being there, no *Murphy's Law*, there was something far beyond the human factor or plain bad luck and as if to emphasise gravity the corridor had fallen as quiet as a prayer, emptied into doorwells recessed like secrets never to be opened, Mary's *advent* was coming and as if to make matters worse she strained to hear the sounds creeping through the gap to the exit out onto the open deck and the crowds gathered for the departure. Stood in silence she listened to the excitement of those outside, the noise charged like electricity it carried the occasional shout and burst of laughter, fused with a mixture of music and the party now well under way a few decks above while the band in full swing fulfilled their promise, but that wasn't what she *heard*. Yes all of those *sounds* were there, but that wasn't what she *heard* forcing its way to the forefront of her mind, stopping her dead, that haunting cry piercing her very conscience, a life laid bare, she strung the notes together, catching them like butterflies as one by one they left the *reeds* pushed through pipes, the bellows breath, before the *chanter* and her moment of truth.

As the melody left *him* two whole octaves of heartache found their way to her, gasping back a whisper, that would escape her lips, each note joining the next, there could be no mistaking it, the elbow pipes crying uncontrollably, its voice a broken tremolo of sadness as poignant as the reaction it would receive as the song gathered an eerie hush among those who would witness it.

'Oh I sigh for those hearts I see undeserving, on their own native lands left to stray, in the midst of a plenty some thousands are starving, neither house, food or clothing have they.'

With tears streaming down her face, she closed her eyes and crushed the beads in her hand pulling them through her palm as she sang softly to the sound of Erin's Lament, calling to her to come outside and say goodbye, to stand with the others, amidst a small crowd that would circle Eugene Daly while his fingers danced across the holes. Titanic's huge propellers churning up the water beneath them, they were on their way and the minor keys bore witness to the enormity of what they were doing, the sound, heart-breaking made worse as many of the passengers joined in. Quivering voices that would be heard no more on these shores, Mary pushed passed them and made her way to the stern of the ship, sobbing and singing in equal measure her bloodshot eyes filled with sorrow, she suddenly looked old, a solitary figure making peace with the past, like unfinished business not yet laid to rest, this was her moment, not just for her, but for her children, the moment she forgave *Ireland* for letting them go.

Chapter Nine

Archie made a mental note of the time; it was 1:30 pm.

He hadn't really noticed the cold, distracted there was so much to see, but he was feeling it now, the morning sunshine giving way to a blanket of grey drab, the bow swinging to the mouth of the harbour and St George's Channel. With vibration, the only gauge to *something* happening, the wait was finally over as the harsh landscape on either side gradually *bled* away merging slowly together as the ship pushed out into open water, her wake slipping from the *hands of grace* the view as rugged as it was beautiful offered nothing if not a bleak farewell. It would add nothing to the mood of those who had left the decks early in search of warm hands around a mug of tea, they were glad to be back inside and out of the bitter wind cutting through those that remained, their numbers slowly dwindling leaving the band to pack up their gear. Chairs stacked into small piles, music stands and open mouthed cases of red crushed velvet caressed instruments of maple, spruce and rosewood, their voices muted until this evening, while diehards watched the eastern edge of the harbour drift past before dropping off the pilot at The Old Head of Kinsale. The final formalities strangely subdued as *she* headed out toward the North Atlantic.

There was nothing left to see, nothing but a coastline in the distance.

What is it about looking back that makes you feel you're moving faster? Archie compared it to hitching a ride with Drippin, his legs dangling off the back end of his cart while *Spike* kept a steady trot. But this was no illusion, the ship was moving now twenty knots or more and for the first time Archie thought about New York and the three thousand miles or so that stood in the way and all that coal beneath his feet waiting to be shovelled, and in six hours' time he'd be down there again.

'Don't wish your life away Archie', his mother would continually tell him every time his plans included a compromise set in the future, so it was probably best the future stayed where it was, *unknown*. Passing over the graveyard of RMS Lusitania buried into sand and broken shell, ninety metres down back there in the distance off the *Old Head of Kinsale*, witness to a tragedy that would see almost twelve hundred passengers lost beneath its waters. In *her* wake she would literally follow a path, like a mirror into the future staring back from the *looking glass* that was New York. A reciprocal journey bound for Liverpool just three years and one month later, her *reflection* could have been seen, but not now, there was nothing there, nothing retrospect, not a single *image* of imitation, her fate unknown as she slipped her lines on the first of May, bearing that decision to shut down boiler room 4, her maximum speed reduced to 21 knots together with her chances and the coal consumption that influenced it. All that way and not for the first time, this was her two hundredth and second crossing, reaching Ireland seven days later, another decision closer to the day of reckoning, and forced to slow down in fog, the irony of that judgement as sensible as any a captain would make, well on the *surface,* but that's not where her executioner conducted its business. Despite the standing orders to steam at full speed through the *zone* they pulled back to fifteen knots, swinging the life boats as a precaution. With extra lookouts they proceeded gingerly, but like walking on egg shells some things are inevitable, nevertheless to rely on *convention,* perhaps not, her adversaire had no intention of *breaking the surface*, a blackened silhouette lost beneath the edges of the North Atlantic and the Irish Sea. She waited in silence, the *Unterseeboot,* as patient as death itself, holding her breath and holding her nerve, approaching at just nine knots, unannounced, her farewell kiss delivered from the depths of the human spirit. The airlock broke the silence as she closed her *eyes* and the torpedo tubes, watching the run from just seven hundred metres, as cold as a lover betrayed, she waited, waited for the moment of truth and a final act of retribution. Devoid of emotion, the hollow victory registered nothing to a lifeless face, her pain discharged she slipped beneath the covers of blackened silk, down below the echoes of death that would return beating the side of her hull, the shouts and screams muted with lungfuls of salty water. The secondary explosions as intense as a thunderstorm competed with the *splashing* and the cold fear of desperation, clinging on while others took a final gasp of life, surrounded; they died *alone*, their solitude witnessed through headphones that would haunt *him* for the rest of his life. Switching off the radio, he buried his face in his hands, rocking in his seat like a child; the U Boat's depth was just twenty four metres beneath the carnage when it slipped away, her revenge complete, unscathed to those whose pen would write it up amidst a national outcry that would reverberate around the world. The headlines reminiscent of what had gone before, but headlines just the same, one thousand one hundred and ninety eight perish, seven hundred and sixty one, saved. There was no mention of the broken wireless operator.

Just ten minutes and the future separated them; it was 1:40 pm when she sank.

****

145

'Don't worry Archie, what will be, will be.'

Pulling up his collar he clasped the lapels of his jacket folding them one over the other, held in place by a single hand while he twisted the fabric scrunched into his palm. Inside his head the faintest voice of his mother, softly she repeated her advice while the seagulls that had followed them out shrieked uncontrollably without warning, settling on the surface, their grubby white bodies lost momentarily in the foam, adding to the sense of foreboding that had settled between his shoulder blades. The screams as cold as a surgeon's knife, each taking their turn, calling from the depths of despair, like a widow just informed, they cried out, an omen full of dread, each voice raising the alarm, louder and louder the cries, like a prophecy each falling short they sank without trace and in the distance Archie watched the wake dissipate as the carpet of salt returned to a dull green, leaving a gentle *sobbing* that he could hear but couldn't place. Somewhere out there as close to the *future* as could be seen; it was as if someone had *walked over his grave* or he had *walked over theirs* as the goose flesh ran the length of his spine, a cold shudder as raw as his prospects descended around him, alone in the stillness, his heartbeat louder than a hush, he looked back down into the water and followed the *whimper* still clear inside his head, mingled with his mother's words 'What will be will be' and down below him,

146

the sea as green as the emerald isle itself and not a single seagull to be seen.

'Archie! Is that you Archie? I thought we'd lost you over the side!'

'I've been looking everywhere for you, god there aint a nook or cranny I haven't been, I was seriously giving up on you, you'll catch your death out here mate!'

Back in the *present* Archie spun on his heels to see the beaming smile of Tully Matheson, his flushed cheeks beneath a mop of unruly hair refusing to co-operate, bounding across the deck he spat into his palm and had one last go flattening what he could behind his ear.

'I almost missed you tucked away up here, it was only cos you moved I noticed someone behind this crane, you finished your shift almost two hours ago!'

'I've been saying hello and goodbye to Ireland, I promised my mother, I've been wrapped up in this canvas watching the world go by, anyway you were sleeping when I came into the cabin.'

The two boys spent the next few minutes trading friendly banter, and comparing blisters, Tully pulling on some loose skin in a vain attempt to match the *corker* on Archie's thumb.

'God, that's the size of a penny Archie! I thought I told you to pace yourself; you'll be dead by the time we get there and not much good that will do you! Now come on with me out of this cold, I'm starving, let's get a mug of tea before I keel over.'

He couldn't resist Tully, it was his boundless enthusiasm and his ability to see the good in everything, it never much mattered how he arrived at it, sooner or later he could turn any situation into a positive, he wanted to tell him what he was feeling, the seagulls, the sense of dread, he wanted to be told he was imagining it, to pull himself together, in truth Tully would have just laughed at him and that in itself would have been enough, instead he said nothing.

Archie never knew what to think, as he watched the coastline fade over the horizon, he had never seen a country *slip off the edge,* perhaps that was it, perhaps his feelings were just an illusion, his mind was *back* on board, but he couldn't explain it, it was like holding two conversations, one with Tully the other with something or someone else, talking over each other to be heard, each sentence mixed with the next.

'I'll get the teas in, see you down there!'
'One thousand five hundred and twenty three lost,
Seven hundred and five saved!'
'Do you want milk and sugar?'
'Not enough life boats!'
'Mug or a cup?'
'Women and children first!'
'Don't be long or it'll get cold ok!'

Archie shook his head, and scratched the nape of his neck, his mind searching for something, anything that would make sense of how he was feeling, he was on the *edge*, like scraping back the soil, he knew whatever it was offered nothing but heartache, but still he wanted to see it, wanted it finished, behind him, like slipping a foot in the wrong shoe, you don't need to go *all the way in* to know it doesn't *feel* right. It just didn't and that would be the best of it, the circumstances were yet to unfold, and neither tragedy accounted for, but in three years' time a *paradox* will stain the hands of Charlie as the headline ink screamed out the truth. The *vision* that Archie can feel but can't see, *Lusitania Sunk, losses on the scale of Titanic.*

Charlie blew the edges of the paper opening the flimsy sheets with a little help from moistened fingers, the grainy newsprint and photos dominating two whole pages of misery.

It had happened again, as if once wasn't enough, yes the circumstances were different, but 'For Christ sake! Do we ever learn?!' Charlie would shout as he read the opening lines, unaware his mutterings were loud enough to be heard by passers-by. There at the top of the page a photograph of each ship, they were invincible, unsinkable, they stood like goliath with equal arrogance, posing for the camera, their huge bulk beneath four funnels, five hundred and seven metres in length between them, but that's not what Charlie would see, his eyes darting from one picture to the other, both ships captured leaving port and that was it, they both shared that look of substance, edging away from the dockside while crowds lost beneath the shadows, waved and cheered goodbye. Soaking it up, they would revel in the moment while Seneca and Kodak pocket cameras blinked, catching them hopelessly unawares, staring back from the page, demanding of attention, Charlie would have none of it, he'd see nothing but pride before a fall.

Commercial reality, human error, stupidity, it was difficult not to make the comparisons. Both ships lost, inclement weather, one steaming too fast the other too slow, both ignored advice, both would go down by the bow, their sterns high in the air, the crow's nest on both ships sounding the initial warnings, issues with life rafts that would cost hundreds of lives and on each occasion ships in the vicinity would fail to come to their aid. But back in

Queenstown the numbers wouldn't lie, the corpses laid out in rows along the quayside gawped over by the locals, while survivors dazed and confused looked for loved ones amongst the dead as more and more bodies were brought ashore or washed up on the beaches. The final reckoning, *the butcher's bill*, would seep out soon enough, spreading through the town in low level hush, quiet dignified whispers as the makeshift morgue overflowed, forcing those unidentified to be buried in mass graves in the old church cemetery. And in contrast children would play pirates in discarded life rafts, tied off to the quayside wall. Yes, all of that would happen, and in just three years' time the hot type face will run the lead copy, column upon column inch, lining the plate while the numbers flagged and underscored carried the *story*, the inevitable comparison to what had gone before, the mighty had fallen and straight to the bottom, the newspaper stands posted headlines mercifully smudged in the early morning rain, tears of salt water, as if there hadn't been enough.

It was nothing, not really, not even a premonition, just a strange feeling that he couldn't explain, couldn't put his finger on, an intense emptiness, like someone had pulled out the plug, *his plug*, and he drained away.

'Pull yourself together! Christ the cold's got to you!'

Archie told himself off, he had never been to sea before, yes that was it, he was nervous, uncomfortable as he watched Ireland slip away in the distance. It was only natural, he told himself several times, climbing down from the crane, catching the seat of his britches he stopped momentarily to unhook them, straightening his jacket at the same time and tugging on his shirtsleeves from beneath his cuffs. 'God, here you are sailing to New York, on Titanic, you've got great new friends, a mug of hot piping tea waiting for you and six hours to eat and sleep, what a prat you are sometimes Archie, now get downstairs out of the cold.'

Nothing else needed to be said; besides he was the only one listening and even he didn't understand it. 'I'll get Harry to read my tea leaves' he laughed, 'He can tell a story that one' he said quietly passing through the swing doors glancing back for just one last look, there was nothing there, well, just the horizon and the faintest change in colour as sea and land merged together, the ultimate gentleman's agreement in knowing when to stop.

His final thoughts were saved for the men on Spike Island and what they would give right now to be in his place. How *lucky* he was just to be there, it was hard work but how many would get the chance, not least to New York, 'Make the most of it Archie, make the most of it' he said again nodding his head in agreement, both sides of the conversation, he was used to that. It was like being on the stand, he would discuss the morning headlines, debating for and against, and just the thought of that made him smile. The thought of Sarah watching him from across the street while she drank her morning tea, the thought of her *flower* pressed beneath his clothes at the bottom of his case, lunch with Tully and the next hour or so *chewing the fat* and then there was Lyle, he'd never complained, not once, didn't even show it when he was paired with Archie, preferring to *take up the slack*, 'Do your best mate, no one can ask any more', that's all he said and as long as he did, Archie knew he would be alright.

She was moving now, twenty knots or more and nothing in her way but space, the vast open space that was the North Atlantic, intimidating, unpredictable and in front of them.

They would correct it soon enough, the listing to port blamed on the coal fire in boiler room six and the over use of coal from the starboard side. 'Get the trimmers to sort it out man! It's slowing us down!' came his bark, the young officer petrified scurried away while elsewhere others that had noticed would compensate. Their lunch extended, a nap before dinner and later a dance to Herman Finck's, *In The Shadow*, high heels caught on silk dresses, spilt wine from crystal glasses and laughter, the night was young and the problem ..... well, c'est la vie.

For the most part it had been a traumatic day that would continue through the evening when contemplation was best. With supper over and the children asleep, Mary sat in silence on the edge of her bed and watched a tiny mouse scamper across the floor, stopping abruptly on hearing a noise, it froze, undecided whether to continue on, or turn back to the relative safety from where it came. She could see its heart beat, its chest pounding and then a dash, a *leap of faith* to the *other side* disappearing beneath a door and whatever lied beyond. 'You see, you made it' she said softly, gently pulling up the covers around her youngest, 'You made it, and so shall we.'

For Mary it was everything, a new life, a new beginning, a future. For Archie it was an opportunity to visit the birthplace of his mother and for Yusef Gans it was another day closer to being with his wife.

Chapter Ten

He left it to the last moment before making the decision, flicking, the message for *Spike* to go another way, the cart swaying momentarily as the old horse adjusted his step.

'Gently does it *Spike*' he said, as if the horse had any say in it. Crossing the railway tracks and sidings some thirty feet beneath them, over the bridge and down toward Terminus Terrace, the hotel and station dominating the skyline. Huge stone buildings, their edges lost in the distance as the steam engines belched across four platforms engulfing the steps to the ground floor restaurant now barely visible it emerged through an amber glow, the hefty lanterns either side of the doors offered the only reference as the throng of passengers passed by, *chancing it* they disappeared into the fog that welcomed them to the London and South West Railway. It was busy for a Thursday, Drippin thought, while he waited for a space to clear, backing *Spike* up a little as a coal truck made a meal of it clipping the curb and spilling a bag or two of the *black stuff* onto the pavement. Clambering down to clear up the mess the driver acknowledged the cheers and laughter of the workmen gathered outside the sheds waiting to sign on for a day, navvy types with pickaxes and shovels. 'Pick up the coal and be gone' Drippin muttered beneath his breath steering *Spike* between the carriages and railings that ran the perimeter of the station. 'Easy boy, gently does it', he would give them no reason to cheer and laugh at him, no one would be questioning his parenthood, besides, he rarely took his own advice.

Drippin tied off the reins and came around the back of his cart relieved to see the driver with nothing more than a broom to hand, acknowledging him with a shrug of the shoulders and a purse of the lips, nothing much else needed to be *said*.

There wasn't much worth stealing but that didn't stop him shifting a few things around before he left, eyeing those with *time* on their hands he *clocked* the noise stood next to the *Bothy* and the *urchins* outside the Telegraph Office. In fact, anyone who wasn't moving was fair game for a stare.

'Back in a minute *Spike*!' he said, a little louder than usual, as he tucked the packet down the front of his jacket and headed off across the courtyard to the main entrance. Boxes and crates stacked too high for comfort, wedged up on timber slats, as precarious as could be imagined in contrast to the industrial flagstones that supported them. Black stone cut from the face in blocks, ten slabs to a block laid end to end covered the entrance to the station and the gap between the hotel. Its dreariness broken by splashes of colour, he stepped over the rotting tomatoes splattered beneath unsuspecting feet and running in the grooves soapy water raced the incline to the gutter having swilled the gent's toilet floor. A galvanised bucket and mop propped diagonally across the entrance spared the red clay tiles drying beyond the door, a sign by implication diverted several midstream who saw it in advance, checking pocket watches their footsteps quickened with an urgency magnified by the shriek of whistles and cries of 'All aboard!' that ran the length of the platform. Slamming doors and raised *paddles* would see her depart with or without them, and Drippin missed none of it. It wasn't just the smells he loved, the steam and choking clag, it was more than that, something deeper, a connection, like being part of *something*. He felt it every time he came here like an occasion, a sense of excitement on his doorstep, the noise, the crowds, roasted coffee and stale beer carried on the breeze, hot air from the bakery ovens Archie had discovered pumped through the vents down the alley, warming their hands on a cold winter's day, sharing a cigarette and watching the brakemen uncouple the coaches, huge chains linking them together and that was exactly how he felt when he was down here, a *link* in a chain. He had a purpose and for now that meant fulfilling a promise, to check on Charlie, a big brother sort of thing, just for a couple of weeks until Archie came back, watching out for him, yes he felt like he was part of

157

something, he *belonged*. Reaching the turnstile gates he joined the queue, glancing back across his shoulder to the wagon and *Spike* scuffing at the ground, he waited his turn while the merry-go-round counted them through with spring loaded satisfaction and a sound as comforting as any as he pushed the bar and it pushed him from behind and onto the concourse.

Drippin made his way across the station, past the ticket booth, and the shoe shine buffing the toe cap of a well-worn brogue, the young boy adding as much drama to the finalé as possible. A frenzied action of *to and fro* culminating in a flick of the cloth to indicate he was done and he was, or at least that's how he felt, staring down at the coin pressed in his hand. Drippin watched the expression on his face as the old man gathered his paper and walked away. He didn't need to lip read, there was no interpretation required; a *tight bastard* is the same in any language.

'Back in a minute!' he said, passing the entrance to the hotel, the porter laden with luggage smiled and kicked the swing doors, disappearing into the lobby like another world, his back washed with a warm glow from the crystal chandelier. Dewey Hine looked at home anywhere, always immaculate, he carried himself with a confidence far beyond his *standing*; softly spoken, his easy going style belied a work ethic that was matched with a quiet ruthlessness to get on. Drippin wouldn't hang around, he'd *collect* from outside the kitchen and later this afternoon sell the cotton sheets *soiled* to the lodging houses down on the waterfront while Dewey looked the other way, stock control and poverty made uncomfortable bedfellows.

****

He could see him now, newspaper in hand another stuffed beneath his arm, stood in front of the upturned boxes weighed down by the print and for a moment it was Archie, calling out the headlines.

He'd never expect him to walk through from the station, it would be a surprise, Drippin choosing to creep up on him avoiding the usual route, taking a moment to watch as he finished a sale. He bid the young couple 'Good day' with the doc of his cap, and stuffed the coin into his pocket, folding another he waited and prodded some change in the palm of his hand running his thumb over the spine of each newspaper left on the stand, counting his profits. Drippin watched his lips twitch as he stared up to the sky looking for help or divine intervention, like work in progress, he had more to do.

'Afternoon Charlie!' he shouted. 'God I thought you were Archie standing there!' and from the corner of his eye, Drippin came bounding toward him, a smile as wide as the estuary enhanced by rosy cheeks flushed and set to happy, his belly wobbling as he stepped off the curb to greet him. 'Charlie, I thought I'd creep up on you, how's it going then?'

He didn't give him a chance to answer, throwing an arm around his shoulders and pulling him tight, ruffling his hair and *cupping* the back of his head.

'Anything you need Charlie let me know, I'm here for you.'

The next five minutes or so were as good as any he'd spent laughing and joking with Archie's younger brother, ending with a promise to drop in on his mother when he left town later that day.

'See you in the morning Charlie. By the way, Archie would have left Ireland by now, he'll be on his way out into the North Atlantic, lucky bugger!' he laughed, waved and was gone.

'Sod it!' he said as he untied *Spike* from the railings, 'I knew I'd forgotten something', pulling the lump of bread pudding out from his jacket, 'I'll leave it with his mother, the boys can share it.'

He didn't need to stop at the junction, the traffic for the docks much less than yesterday when *she* had gone. He could see through the gates as he passed the main entrance, slowing as another horse and cart pulled out ahead, and through the brick pillars, berth 44 as empty as a pub after closing sat deserted. The quayside cranes swung dockside, lifeless, their skeletal frames disappeared behind the open sheds that ran the length of the quay, empty now, Drippin could see through them to the water beyond, like a light at the end of a tunnel snubbed out by the walls of the Post Office building he had come alongside, stealing his view and with it a momentary feeling of emptiness.

It didn't last long, the afternoon sunshine would see to that, streaming full on into his eyes he pulled down his cap counting the prospect of a few shillings from the lodging houses, always ready for a *bargain*, in truth he could have sold them clean, the price was the same. He had learnt some time ago by *marking* them they would sell as *seconds* but for the same price as new, he would rub the sheets against the wheel of his cart keeping one set clean, just in case, add a few *bob* and *discount* the dirty ones. It never failed to amaze him, but Drippin was quick to learn, he created the bargain and sold it, the ultimate *mark up* straight from the streets and in this case it was, quite literally.

Both fed and watered he spent the next hour, working the doors heading over to Wickham Court, past the pub and in time to find Mrs Mullins, moving the furniture, such that it was, re-arranging the parlour, lifting the chairs and lifting her mood, 'Idle hands' she would say.

'Afternoon Drippin! Have you come to tell me where my boy is?'

'I have Mrs Mullins, but I'll be quick, *Spike's* on his own at the end of the lane, I'll stand here if you don't mind and keep an eye on me wagon.'

'Can you believe it, he's already been to Cherbourg and Ireland!, and right now, maybe an hour past, he'll be on his way across the North Atlantic, like I said to Charlie earlier, he's a lucky bugger your Archie!'

Chapter Eleven

It wasn't an unreasonable assumption; you could smell it from one end of the corridor to the other, rising up from the stairwell it had made its way to E deck. Stronger in places, the pungent odour hung in the air, up from the Tank Top or thereabouts and the coal fire still burning in the aft corner of boiler room six.

'No the ship's not on fire son' the man explained to the young boy asking questions *twenty to the dozen*, barely stopping to take a breath between salvos, the questions kept coming falling short into open ground where parents hide in the world of muted response, the kind that never satisfies.

'So, if we're not on fire why does the bow of the ship smell of sulphur?' he said, craning his neck with reindeer eyes fixed on his father doing his best now to stare up ahead, ignoring the sound from by his side as they walked back from the dining room on F deck.

'Why is it only at the bow? Why couldn't we smell it at lunch?' he was *warming up* now just like the coal down below, smouldering it showed no sign of stopping anytime soon, much like the boy, still going as they pushed through the double doors passing

Archie who'd stood aside to let them through, had they known they could have asked him, he'd spent the last four hours trying to put it out.

Twelve of them had given it their best shot, but it was still burning by the time Archie's shift had ended.

In truth he wasn't part of the twelve man crew chosen to put out the fire. Dousing the coal stacks with hoses and buckets, soaking the top of the pile, the drenched coal as black as a Welshman's hair glistered in the glow of the wall lights flickering above them. From the *foot plate* they watched the water run top to bottom, as real as any river it found its natural path, weaving round the boulders and on, hissing into vapour as it ventured closer to the heat. The hot coals warmed through from those smouldering cherry red, buried beneath a heap of trouble, dry to the core, the coal stack shifting as it burned while the men stood amongst it cooling the soles of their boots in blackened slurry. Shovelling the coal into *barras* their sweat evaporating into nothing which is exactly what they had all been told to say on the matter, nothing, not a word of it. Determined to contain something if not the retched smouldering that had Archie and Lyle working next door in the bunker of boiler room five shifting burning coal straight to the furnace, away from the heat transfer through the watertight bulkhead. Hot to the touch, marked up with bearable lines, palm down mind, scored on the wall by the previous shift, a notch or two added by Lyle before the bell had sounded noon.

Archie hadn't really noticed much about the boy pestering his father, standing aside to let them pass, he was elsewhere, thinking on the conversation struck up with Lyle, he listened intently as he shared his news, as excited as could be imagined and for the first time Lyle looked as vulnerable as the rest of them.

'You see Archie, there wasn't a choice, you know how difficult it is to be *picked up* dockside, it's all about who you know, the family thing, and I ain't been down your way for long, so trimming was all I could get but I'm missing them bad' he said, as if that wasn't clear enough.

'I hate being away, but what's to do, we need every penny, she made me swear this'll be *me* last trip, I can't stand the thought of it again, he's just six weeks old, Christ if anything happened to them while I'm away, what use am I then...?!' Trailing off he finished the rest of the story in private, lost in his own thoughts, Archie could see his mind working overtime weighing up the options back and forth as he balanced it out, unaware he had picked up the pace of his shovel and *taking it out* on the coal. He'd move a ton or two in silence riddled with anxiety and compromise eating at him from inside, and when he was done, when *it* was all back where it needed to be, he slowed down as if to mark his return like the lines etched on the wall, his pain forced back by reason played second fiddle to guilt as he caught Archie trying to keep up, watching him run the tunnel his tiny frame disappearing into a wall of darkness smudged in amber, back blow and ash, waiting for Lyle to *give the word*, waiting on him, waiting for a chance to rest.

'Take a breather Archie, sorry mate, I got carried away, rest a while, you've done enough today.'

He didn't need asking twice, the barrow upturned before the words had chance to fade, steadying himself he leant against the steel wall picking at the rivets like a nervous tick, wiping the sweat from his brow he wedged his back into a cross ridge strengthening the door panel, his shoulders settling on whatever comfort could be found. Archie had played witness to Lyle's *recovery;* he would need the end of the shift to help find his own.

They hadn't expected to sit out the remaining ten minutes or so to the end of their shift, but sit them out they did, chatting about home and the lives left on the dockside. Lyle's two children and the new born, his wife Kathryn *his Kath*, her culinary disasters, described nothing but affection. Tales of kitchen catastrophes that would have them in stitches, 'Lost to the oven', 'Taken in its prime' he said, his grin as wide as the door. Archie could almost smell the charred remains as Lyle unfurled the tale and *shared* a moment, like a secret with a friend and in amongst it, drudgery and the same life he was living himself. Lyle up and out every morning looking for work, his belt tightened to compensate, unions and the inevitable backlash that was brewing, strikes and lay offs that could see them under but for the charity of others and there it was, the dilemma, he was lucky to be working, lucky to have something to burn.

'Talking a burnin, nip next door and see how that coal fire's doing Archie, if we don't get it under control they'll be bringing the New York Fire Brigade on board when we dock and that'll go down like a lead balloon, Christ I can hear it now, heads will roll you can count on it!'

Archie looked startled at the thought of losing his job, he'd worked his ass off, they all had, the bloody things been burning since the sea trials two weeks ago. Spontaneous combustion is one thing but you can't make a scapegoat of that, the press will have a field day he thought, *Maiden voyage, passengers put at risk, Titanic left Southampton on fire!*

Archie disappeared forward to check on progress next door, contemplating the White Star statement, the bit that would follow, 'We took swift action' and laughed at the irony of selling more newsprint as a consequence, but there was nothing good that would come of it and he could see that etched on the faces in boiler room six. 'Still burning' he said returning to find Lyle brushing down his jacket held aloft like it was carrying something contagious, beaten coal dust free while they waited for the bell to sound. They didn't know it but on the bridge the navigator marked his chart, 386 miles covered since they left Queenstown, his dividers swivelled like a giant's footsteps arcing the cross section, recorded by careful hand, the graphite lines and side notes registering their progress, in contrast to the *graphite* down below, on fire and, as yet, still burning.

It was distracting him now, his thoughts drifting off from where he wanted to be, back with Kath and the children, his lunch repeating he rubbed his chest, cursing the sausage, mash and greens that were threatening to *return*.

Stubbing out his cigarette, Lyle sunk into his pillow, holding *it* to his face he could almost touch her, with his eyes closed she was next to him, captured in time, the small block of soap, her smell tied in a handkerchief of lavender and a longing to be home. Distracted momentarily Lyle pushed his boots beneath his bunk, his hands rough and blackened were old before their time, like Archie, seventeen going on a hundred, a decade bridged by similarities that Lyle had not considered before. The *breadwinner* lost, Archie would carry the burden now, he was on his own, no wife to share it with just the unspoken responsibility, settled in a knot between his shoulders, made worse when time allowed for ponder, Lyle hadn't been to Wickham Court, in truth the French Quarter offered nothing but misery. Beyond his own existence, frequented only by circumstance or birth, the narrow streets played refuge to necessity, shaping lives with poverty its favoured son, like Lyle's indigestion burning to the heart of the matter without respite for most, Archie held his own antidote in his palm, the only possible way out for him and his family, take your medicine and any opportunities that may come along. That's why he was there, living with compromise, just like Lyle, he was for all the world a *grown up* amongst the men of the Tank Top, bound by something greater than his years could divide, amongst his own and those that recognised sacrifice.

He couldn't sleep not yet, not with the noise outside, the constant whirl of the fans and clatter from the bakery, his cabin wedged aft of the third class galley, served a constant stream of hunger as it passed by his door. Instead, he'd read a while, and finish the letter almost done, ready for posting on arrival, sending word back home, Kath would read it to the children snuggled in bed beneath horse hair blankets and candlelight and touch the very letter he would finish now, signing off, the pencil pressed firm against the page underlined the sentiment, his hand held steady swirled a quick flurry of lead, underscored, it read;

My dearest Kath, see you soon, your loving husband.

Lyle x

Archie held the carafe in the air and watched the shapes distort through the water.

It was good to rest, to be out of there, his back throbbing from the last four hours, tinged with pain he settled into the slatted bench of the third class general rooms. It was busy when he had arrived but clearing now, the Captain's chairs strewn like obstacles surrounded unwitting tables of darkened wood dressed with beer mats and plain glass carafes of drinking water, the upturned glasses glinting from the ceiling lights set in military precision ran the width of the room. With six hours left he could relax and enjoy a moment, doodling on the ships' newspaper, such that it was, a bulletin style single sheet collage of headlines, menus, stock prices, horse racing and gossip, set beneath the grand banner *Atlantic Daily Bulletin*. Archie smudged the ink into his fingers and enjoyed the sight of it, 'Couldn't print a comic' he said, laughing to himself, as if selling newsprint made him an authority, but it did something, it made him smile, and that was enough.

His stomach full there was nothing pressing other than sleep and he would do that soon enough preferring to sit a while, people watching and the crossword as yet to be mastered, his thoughts wrapped in panels of pine finished in enamel white, it was something very special, like therapy painted on the walls. The thing is, it was always different, every time he walked *the circuit*, a route he had devised to walk the length of the ship avoiding the working decks, he'd seen enough of them for a lifetime, this was how he passed his time, walking the length of Scotland Road. He'd start at the stairwell by hatch number five and explore bow to stern, down to the Interpreter's Office and the stairs to F deck, doubling back, he'd do it all again, just because he could. A constant stream of faces coming and going, killing time like him, ambling along, it made no difference, he'd wind up back here, scribbling notes and drifting off into day dreams when childhood was allowed. Trolleys down Bugle Street on discarded pram wheels, courtesy of Drippin's old man before he turned ill, lolly sticks woven into triangles for throwing, *walking the walls*, fishing and dad's penny whistle pulling him back, back from the *man* down on the foot plate covered in filth. Old before his time, back just a few years, the same years that Charlie will lose, stolen years scribbled on the newspaper, an aeroplane with push prop, driven by elastic band, like the one he saw earlier carried by the young boy, the one *he* wanted, a chance to fly free, down the runway, pulling up, it disappeared into cloud, Archie drew the aeroplane untethered, unlike him, and looked at those around the room, staring back at the page he scrawled a line across his picture and landed with a bump.

He could feel his face blush as he awkwardly turned the page, flattening the paper on the table pretending to read the news.

Did *she* see him, could she tell what he was thinking, the girl sat with her parents bickering over who would take charge of the child, her gentle smile softened those around as she caught his eye, curling her hair around a finger, she placed a foot upon the strut of a chair and pulled it toward her. Unsure where to look Archie jotted illegible notes beneath a photo of the Café Parisien, scrolling the menu he ticked his choice and wrote a mishmash across the page, his hands occupied he did his best to look away, shuffling in his seat, her glances weighing him up, averting her stare momentarily to acknowledge her father, taking the hand of a toddler unsteady on his feet, picking him up she bounced the bundle on her knee and accepted the *summing up* and the decision he made for her.

'There, it's settled, Alice will take care of the child while you rest.'

Archie would never see the Café Parisien or pass beyond the shuttered gates through to B deck or grace the wicker chairs set beneath tables overlooking the ocean. The walls adorned with intricate French trellis work entwined in Ivy, the young plants keen to seduce had little time, the white card placed upon the table cloth, its down stroke hook of flourish and swash in blackened ink, delicately announcing his arrival. *Privé Réservé,* there'd be no champagne, not today, his *choices*, oysters, roast duckling and salmon, pâté de foie gras and, for desert, peaches in chartreuse jelly would remain hidden beneath silver domes held down by white cotton gloves and through a *sea* of faces they took their pleasure, smirking in silence as he was *politely* shown the door. A life of grime, Archie's life, betrayed by the coal dust that trailed the restaurant floor.

Archie took a slurp of water from the glass and wiped his chin; catching a *run* he smudged it into his face.

He'd tried not to show it, but there was nowhere to hide, his insecurities laid bare for all to see, made worse as he tugged on his shirt and felt his cheek with the back of his hand. It was all in his mind of course, but that's all you are, what you feel, and it wasn't good. Archie returned to his paper and scribbled something across the menu, making peace with it he'd regained what composure he could and finished reading the *news of the day*, his ruffled feathers smoothed into place, the *ice* broken as the ball bounced towards him.

'Could you, please?', she said, pointing under the table in front of him, Archie clambered on all fours and picked the ball from the floor, clumsily spilling it from his hand, doubling back, he used the opportunity to collect his jacket and newspaper from the table where he'd sat.

'Thank you, that's very kind.'

'Not at all Miss' he said, unsure of what else to say, placing the ball into sticky hands the child clasped his wrist, gently pulling free. He docked his cap and headed for the door, his paper, a *dog's breakfast* of scribble covered type face, rolled into a tube, a makeshift trumpet, he *played* it as he left, his youth clear to see, blowing aimlessly he struggled for a tune before stuffing the paper in his back trouser pocket, capturing the contradiction of child and man perfectly. Disappearing into the shadows of the passageway and the sound of laughter and shrieks of happiness echoing the length of the corridor, the third class children, lively to the point of irritation, played unfettered as they explored every nook and cranny. The boys, swung on baggage cranes unable to resist doors marked Danger or Private, their rite of passage called upon in the interest of mischief, girls *helped* their mothers, dressed rag dolls, read, skipped and all manner of good things, passing time, they made the best of the adventure. Upstairs they'd play while their governesses watched them, deck quoits, spinning tops, jumping jacks they played, their books set aside to let off steam, the type that wouldn't offend the sensitivity of others, like enjoyment on a Sunday. God's day, limited they would play *Noah's Ark,* the only game allowed, its biblical name carried the approval of respectability, nothing so tasteless as to watch a child have fun. The name *Noah's Ark*, pretentious, it would prove as unpalatable as the salt water yet to be swallowed, waiting for them, more than half the two hundred children would never see daybreak on Monday or any other day, their toys stored beneath their beds, out of sight, they'd wait forever to be played with again.

He'd judge their direction from the racket *flooding* the passageway and the dull thud under foot, like a stampede, it accompanied their shouts and hollers, child's play, a haunting sound, second only to silence.

Fun and games would see more than the children entertained while Archie slept, not yet back on his bunk, he avoided the noise and headed down the companionway on the starboard side, off the beaten track, a sense of trespass magnified by solitude followed him down, his anxiety soothed by the delicate aroma as sweet as his first *kiss*. Jasmine, Eucalyptus, Lavender, Chamomile and who knows what else filled the corridor void of all but himself as he read the sign on the door, Turkish Bath. He didn't know the detail, what was involved; it was enough to know it existed, having heard it spoken of along with the swimming pool. Whatever it was it smelt expensive. He hadn't noticed but he'd taken off his cap, clutching it in both hands like he was in the presence of something and perhaps he was, an experience not for the likes of him, reinforced by the poster behind a glass frame, *The ship*, sailing full steam, cutting through the waves beneath the banner, *The New White Star Liner RMS Titanic, The Largest Vessel in the World*, the advert set inside a coiled rope wrapped the two photos of *Vinolia Otto Luxury Toilet Soap,* ideal for those with sensitive skin and delicate complexions, the perfect indulgence, There is no soap more delightful it went on, opulence for the *worthy,* the advert signature said everything and more in just a few words: *London and*

Paris. Archie hadn't heard the footsteps from behind, a polite cough enough to indicate he was stood in the way. Stepping to one side, the man acknowledged him and went through, holding the door ajar momentarily, long enough to peek inside and watch him cross the mosaic floor like a chess board, blue and white alternate squares set with four leaf inlay, carried him to the smiling face greeting his arrival. Picking up a ticket blown back in the draught, number 438 entitled the bearer to the use of the Turkish or *electric* bath for one visit and the price for this indulgence $1 or 4/-. 'Bloody hell!' he said, shaking his head, weighing up how long that could feed his Ma and the boys, three days or more if they were careful, just to sit in some steam, 'Christ they could come downstairs and work a shift or two'.

Archie wouldn't get to see inside, the extravagance limited to those in first class, its beauty shrouded in mystery, but through the inter connecting doors, steam baths, hot, temperate, and cooling rooms awaited. Portholes hidden behind a Cairo curtain, intricately carved into mystical shapes distorting the light into *eastern* promise as the patterns washed up the walls. Tiled from dado rail to gilded cornice, the huge blue and green panels like the ocean itself called you in. A broken message in red tessera, setting the background to the *furnace* as the lighting from Arab lamps hung from ornate cast iron brackets. Shadows swaying gently to the rhythm of the ship, as one rested in the cooling room, reclining on low slung chairs, drinking tea and coffee, the obligatory cigar and the company of a good book. Your Damascus table beside you as if there was any other way.

It truly was beautiful, from another time and place, its Arabian style offered a sumptuous luxury few would enjoy but he had seen it, well, at least from the outside, it was something else to tell the boys when he got home, a bedtime story, they'd drift off to sleep bathed in candlelight and take a *Magical Flying Carpet Ride* with Archie, a *Thousand and One Nights* of adventure, back through the ages of mystical escapade to enjoy. Archie took one last look at the advert of the Turkish Bath, smiling at the thought of Charlie and Will captivated by the tale. Heavy eyed it would wait another night to finish, with so many stories, where to begin, *A Genie in a Lamp, Ali Baba, The Seven Voyages, Sinbad,* he'd thought of them all as he climbed the stairs, reappearing by number two hatch opposite the master at arms, a short skip back to the cabin and his *circuit* complete.

He'd sleep now, a few hours or more, blissfully unaware of what was to come, his future like the *lamp* held in his hands, three wishes not to be wasted may well have been different to those made from the comfort of his bunk.

Childs play it was and today was as good a day as any, Archie grateful the din from F deck hadn't followed him up, he'd settle down for a few hours *kip* while the cabin was empty, not long now before Harry and Albert were finished.

'Looks like a laundry' he said, picking up some clothes fallen from a makeshift line, careful not to get a face full of socks and pants, he climbed up onto his bunk and kicked off his boots. Another shift done and by this time tomorrow almost a thousand miles covered, his confirmation to rest the clatter of boots hitting the floor, and three empty bunks with skew-whiff blankets pulled over coal stained sheets and pillows, moulded by a previous visit they waited for the indentation to be filled once more.

'If you closed one eye you can see it' he said, convinced the listing was no better, scrunching his face he practiced what he preached before settling down to rest. A gentle hum its source indistinguishable, competed with gurgling pipes by his head, rocked to sleep, the sounds as comforting as any, *porting* him from work to rest. He'd leave others to finish the day, fun filled and suitably diverted while his friends passed like ships in the night, work, eat and sleep, their routine established offered little time for anything else. But up on the boat deck a shilling or two would change hands and right about now at three o'clock any child using the gymnasium would be asked to leave, the moustachioed men in flannels rode electric camels and horses pushing static bicycles as others stretched and tried in vain to find feet and toes unseen for a decade. Huffing and puffing this new fandangle thing called *exercise,* the gymnasium washed in natural sunlight, bouncing off the floor reflecting back from the atlas and the ships diagram resting beneath a glass frame. The Piece de Resistance positioned proudly on the floor, to *practice* the art of *rowing.* The two machines lined the middle of the gym, running board tracks carried leather seats between two sets of oars, for an aft they were as real as any could be, oh what fun and games, plimsoll clad they *rowed,* keeping the rhythm, faces flushed in blood pressure bloom.

'Keep the time, that's it, easy does it, heave one two, heave one two, and again, heave one two...'

Yes, what fun it is to *row.*

Everything in life comes to those that wait, *rowing,* done, if only it were that simple.

Chapter Twelve

He'd be downstairs shortly, just twenty minutes before his shift, long enough to gulp some air and ruin the cigarette hung off his lips.

Strange as it was, despite the work, Tully was starting to enjoy himself. Today of all days there was something in the air or in *his water* but something right enough, the weather helped, it could have been pissing down, instead the bright sunshine threw angular shadows across the deck, deceiving those who'd ventured out late afternoon, the chill, colder than church steps, kept coats and jackets fastened in a westerly breeze. It was as if the ship had come alive, you could feel a sense of excitement, call it what you will, people were starting to relax, they had found their bearings and depending on where you were in the *food chain* it surfaced in many different ways. Down in steerage there was a sense of momentary relief from everything that had brought them here, a chance to rest and prepare for what was coming their way, a new life, a new country and for most an awful lot more of the same, but today those things were buried, like the side of a fork splitting dumplings in two just an hour before in the third class dining room, more food than you could eat, clean sheets, and something only three thousand miles could bring, hope. Tully watched the families

181

closest to him and wondered where they would all be a year from now, hand to mouth, make do and mend, they kept going, you could see it, feel it, that steely determination faced with whatever came their way, they'd have a go, just like Mary and the children, a one way ticket punch holed in faith.

'Does he bite mister?' the young boy asked.

Tully almost ready to leave, wobbled on the top of the railings, his feet wedged around the bottom bar, it was all that kept him from tumbling backward into the sea, as calm as the duck pond on the common.

'No son, it's a *she* and no, she doesn't bite'. It was a good job, as the boy didn't wait for an answer. Cupping the dog's head in each hand and with too much enthusiasm for a first encounter, pulling the dog's jowly face, kissing her slobber ridden muzzle, the dog, a mastiff of some kind, peered back through droopy eyes and shook her head, the reverberations down its spine fizzling out through a stumpy tail *docked* to an inch of its life. Bandy legs bowed beneath a chest Archie would be proud of, the white freckled splash against a shiny brown coat; she was out for a walk, stretching legs too long idle. Loved or loathed, beauty is in the eye of the beholder and for one little boy his new best friend may well need prizing away. Tully watched them playing tug of war, a piece of old rope its sole possession clamped between jaws, her chiselled bite soaked in saliva, held the sodden *prize* never to be shared, a canine lesson to those around, 'I'll be leaving with the rope if that's ok with you?' Tully laughed as the steward disappeared around the corner, his arm outstretched the dog pulling him on, with bucket and spade in hand it was the last thing he saw, he'd use his imagination for what came next.

Yes, it had been a good day, a day for fun and games and later that evening in the wireless room when the radio would fail, not quite what they had in mind, a different kind of fun and games but all the same there was more to come.

The heavy jacket hung off the back of the chair, eight brass buttons set two abreast visible from the door, a Marconi uniform cap threatening to fall off a pile of papers strewn on the desk, messages, ADVISELUM, the onslaught of passenger communications yet to be sent.

'Cup of tea old boy' he said, placing a mug on the desk, a writing pad doubling as a coaster to the leather inlaid top, the huge desk four drawers across, three each side, couldn't have been more imposing if it tried. The dark varnished mahogany, decorated in half moon brass handles worn like medals on its chest, puffed out it demanded attention, dominating a room no bigger than a very small cabin, its panelled white walls, cold and clinical, the background to a raft of strange equipment that looked capable of delivering pain. Like an operating theatre, its gravitas reinforced by that which is unknown and a faint smell of burning peculiar to the corridor, as yet unexplained.

'Happy belated birthday! I put two sugars in and half again for luck; you can stand your spoon in it!'

'Thank you, anything I need to know?'

'The usual I'm afraid, I've spent the whole shift sending trivia, why the hell they can't wait till they get there god only knows, I had cleared most of it but more has come through I'm afraid, do you want me to stay on and help?'

'No, get some sleep, you look tired, I can deal with it from here. I see we've had further ice warnings? How many is it now, ten, eleven or so? All logged *process-verbal*? First Officer and the Captain informed? OK fine, I'll drink my tea and get on with it, there's steak pie in the canteen if you're hungry?!'

With *modus operandi* established they, like everyone else, fell into the routine of it. Mundane *chatter* back and forth broken by established procedures well-rehearsed, both men had commissioned the equipment, fine tuning it over the weeks leading up to departure, taking a short break after the sea trials ready for the off, a quiet confidence born from constant use and final testing that would have them *working* Tenerife and even Port Said more than three thousand miles away. The latest five KW synchronous rotary spark, as good as it gets, five circuits direct from the ships electrical mains regulated into high powered radio oscillations sent packing into the atmosphere beneath a gentle touch. Tapping away they'd make sense of it, the telegrams piling up on one side, outbound drivel would take time to process passed beneath the Telegraph Keys, *dit* and *dah* punched out like bullets from a barrel, hundreds of messages to decipher and type onto telegram forms, sent back and forth to the Inquiry Office by pneumatic tube. Incoming carriers announcing their arrival falling into the wire mesh tray on the desk, handwritten messages stuffed inside the *twist tops*, a constant stream of work and revenue, striking a balance with the Purser's Office at the end of the day, 12/- 6d for the first ten words and 9d a word thereafter. This was it, they were ready, rested and both back on board by the 9th April; Jack Phillips, the Senior, aboard three days earlier to check the spares, as if it could go wrong, it was new after all but that wouldn't stop it failing and, in a moment or two, Bride's steak sandwich was about to be interrupted.

'He who pays the piper calls the tune' he said softly, scrolling through a manual, the White Star Logo emblazoned across the front, neither man actually worked for them, they were *charged out*, trip at a time. Marconi employees and proud of it, separate from the rest and not directly responsible to any of the ship's crew, with limited exceptions to the captain, they were obviously different, their uniform of white shirt and tie, black suit with double breasted tunic, Marconi emblem buttons with matching cap badge, their sleeve insignia the final touch, it sent out a message, as did they, no doubt interpreted differently by those that would *receive it*.

'Christ that tea's strong', he said, slurping the brew and blowing cold air on the tips of his fingers, the steam rising from the cup disappeared into the huge brass lamp hanging above the desk. The softly lit room strangely eerie to the uninitiated spoke in clicks, high pitch squeals and low tone *Shhhh* depending on who was talking. Each background noise identified, they maintained a *listening watch* round the clock, their shifts pattern, 2000-0200 - 0200-0800, and during the daytime they'd arrange to suit each other, the workload having the final say. It would speak again soon, testing them both through the night and into the early hours of Saturday morning, searching for the problem that had caused the main radio to fail, the ships communications limited to the auxiliary backup, it would have to do, well for now, but other issues would soon be pressing. Amongst the endless messages of congratulations, warnings that had been repeated during the day, all along the North Atlantic shipping lanes, bergs, growlers and field ice, not uncommon for April but already causing significant problems navigating a course. Earlier that day the French steamer Niagara had stopped surrounded by ice, initially calling for assistance only to cancel the request. 'Food for thought' he muttered under his breath, softly, like someone was *listening* or reading his thoughts seeping through the *cans* strapped to his head, his disquiet out into the wilderness and the public domain. Finishing his tea, he gathered up the pile of papers marked *sent* and took the clipboard off the wall, adding them to those already trapped beneath the spring loaded coil, each one addressed at the top of the page, call sign, MGY, three little letters, not to be confused with CQD, they didn't know it but they would follow soon enough.

Chapter Thirteen

'This is the second time tonight, they must have hollow legs' she said, pouring piping hot water into a stainless steel pot flipping the lid closed to keep in the heat, she twisted it to sit properly on the tray, a mixed plate of sandwiches, two cups and saucers and garnish never to be eaten. Wiping down the surface with her cloth, she pushed the tray forward and signalled it was ready to leave, a single nod at the waiter stood propped against the wall, balancing on one leg as he polished his shoe on the back of his trousers. He was in no rush, flirting and teasing her as she folded the napkins.

'Thanks Essie, I'll drop by when I've finished perhaps we could have a night cap?' he said, winking at her as he lifted the tray balanced above his shoulder, waving goodbye. Before she had time to answer he was out the door, a smirky grin, more in hope than anything else belied his chances, gauged by the hair clip in her mouth, chewed with more vim and vigour than was necessary. His charm, like a lead balloon, fell on deaf ears but he was nothing if not persistent, undeterred he would try again as he made his way up the corridor to the canteen on C deck reserved for the Marconi and postal workers. It was small but less of a hike to the boat deck where he was heading, practicing the *gift of the gab,* it needed work, a little rough around the edges but Essie smiled when she heard him talking to himself, perhaps he had broken the *ice* after all. You wouldn't have known it from his summing up, the précis a cruel account indeed had her laugh out loud, his voice echoing up the stairwell, 'Francis, you couldn't pull a tooth!'

There would be more than pride at stake if that bloody radio couldn't be fixed. Both men back on duty would work through the evening and into the early hours, the *backlog* only partially cleared, made worse now, trial and error, the process of elimination, coffee and sandwiches.

They could always navigate by the stars, the skylight their only contact with the outside world, tucked aft behind the officers' quarters, the Marconi suite, centred at the rear of the superstructure forty feet from the bridge. The radio transmitter capable of communicating thousands of miles at night, relied on *shanks' pony* to engage with those at the helm, messages sent back and forth, up and down the passageway on the port side, a strange arrangement given their connection to the fifty line exchange, an obvious flaw perhaps but there was no telephone to the bridge, an oversight or design replicating life, and the difficulty we have talking to those closest to us, either way, it was just too close to call.

'I'm sure that wind's shifted, it's getting bitter outside.'

In from the dark, the young operator threw his top coat over the arm of a chair and slumped back down, the freezing air clinging to his clothes brought shivers from his colleague, like someone had walked over his grave, or was just about to. A sense of dread without explanation had settled in the nape of his neck, quiet apprehension that would materialise into goose flesh, made worse from the lack of sleep and nothing to show, well nothing but an edginess that would have him jump to the slamming of a door, and shouts of, 'You'll catch a death of cold!' The advice, suitably ignored, as the hatch to the boat deck swung closed, sealing their three roomed existence, the *silent room* with padded walls housed the main transmitter, as noisy as hell, its *shouts and hollers* muted by isolation, incarcerated in darkness, it spoke, *chatting away* with not a breath for silence, a conversation of one half, it would *hear* nothing, not a single reply. The Marconi Room, the *ears* of the ship captured the dots and dashes, translated into clipped messages, typed up and delivered, their content *handed on a plate*. Stewards in white cotton gloves and small silver trays slid telegrams beneath cabin doors, to be opened in private, the final journey, both men the bearer of news, two insignificant rooms, one crammed with machinery, the other a lone desk, wrapped in paraphernalia floor to ceiling, ordinarily oppressive, but at night with the daylight gone, the skylight covered darkness like the walls came in on them.

They had worked almost ten hours straight before it was fixed. Hopelessly behind, they'd have to prioritise, deal with the weather warnings, notices from Cape Race, ice warnings marked *Urgent Priority*, that's another three since the radio failed. They daren't look in the basket, the White Star communiqué unanswered; you could feel the pressure, the intensity of the situation. Working in silence they barely spoke beyond the task, exhausted there was nothing left to say, this was it, a solution bound by insulation tape, breaking the short, the cable encased, the final coil sticking to his fingers, one last glance between them, more in hope than expectation, the radio groaned slowly into life. Switched on, the lights warmed to a gentle glow, pulsating at first and then a constant burn, waking up, stretching, the radio ready for the day.

'That's it, we've done it! Thank Christ for that! Now let's get this mess cleared up!'

That was all they could muster, both men out on their feet, they hadn't noticed the daybreak, it was light outside, almost five thirty, their test message sent and received, a quiet satisfaction carried the moment, suitably subdued they enjoyed the silence, a *lull before the storm*, today was going to be absolute hell and they knew it, and as for the third room, well, neither men would see much of that, neither would be sleeping.

There's something about Sunday mornings, something that defies explanation and this day would be no exception, April 14th 1912 in the North Atlantic.

It was quiet in the crew canteen and Archie was grateful for it, happy to sit alone and drink his tea, yawning repeatedly he pressed the warm mug to his cheek, rolling the heat into the side of his face, barely awake, he rested his head in the palm of his hand, and thought of home. With eyes closed it brought him closer to them, the boys both fast asleep, the new mattresses like magnets would pull like Sunday mornings should. A day off for Charlie, he'd make the most of it and spend some time with Will, they'd help mother with the chores, *fetch and carry* and later, when they were *under her feet,* Charlie would take Will to Kingsland Market for bruised fruit, pestering the traders they'd often get an apple or pear just to move on.

'Take it, bugger off, and don't come back today!'

Happy to oblige, they'll do the rounds before heading back, a few ounces of currants that Charlie would haggle for, damaged fruit, milk and eggs brought from the *travellers* in town for the day, mother counting out the *coppers* would deliver the same message, 'Bring back as much as you can'. It didn't seem so bad from a distance, sat here on Titanic drinking tea, a plate of toast devoured, the taste of jam in the corners of his mouth, but the reality of home was never far away. He knew the money left in the jar wouldn't last long, Charlie would do his best selling papers, but it was the sense of helplessness that played on him, made worse now with time to reflect. It was the start of his fifth day, the longest he'd ever been away, more than a thousand miles apart, and an hour before his shift, he'd finish and take in the air, it would cheer him up and in a week or so he'd be home with a pay packet clutched in his hand. Excited they'd be down on the dockside waving frantically as he came ashore and in the evening they'd sit around the scullery table, the boys hanging on his every word, mother listening intently would pretend not to hear. The sound of plates scrapped clean, his favourite bread and butter pudding wouldn't *touch the sides* and later, with the fire no more than embers in the hearth, he'd take a second look, a secret peek at the *notes* poking up from the top of the jar, unfurled they'd look like all the money in the world and in that moment it would have all been worth it.

On deck the early morning sunshine barely up welcomed in the day, the stern bathed in amber glow warmed to the attention, steaming westbound Archie basked in the sun, his face held up like an offering to the gods. It was a beautiful day, fine weather, the temperature as mild as could be, a gentle breeze the only reminder of April, a picture post card, the wake trailed undisturbed in the distance. Flat calm and twenty two knots, it was a magical sight, and one saved to memory as he left to start his shift. Slow at first, the morning lumbered into life. The smell of coffee, bacon and sausages wafted through the passageways, cutlery and china chinking in the distance called them to breakfast. A *full English* taken at leisure and hymns in the *church* aptly staged in equivalent hallowed ground, a dining saloon, the perfect venue or ironic bad taste, would witness lyrics dismissed in verse from the hymnal, it was mid- morning, their wake up call, belted out in all its glory, the bitter illustration that *truth is stranger than fiction*, but lost on them all, they sang.

'Eternal father strong to save whose arm hath bound the restless wave, who bidd'st the mighty ocean deep, its own appointed limits keep, oh, hear us when we cry to thee, for those in peril on the sea....'

Sunday six bells wouldn't travel to the Tank Top, the sentiments confined to those in earshot and whose souls were not in question. Prim and proper, the *stiff*

194

back played the piano, not a single note prepared to leave or deviate the seven decks down and into the furnace, *hell in damnation*, the *divine punishment* was real enough for those working the shift. Archie and Lyle back in number five bunker, two hours on two remaining, their worship limited to the higher power of coal, driving her on, driving them all on, closer than they could have ever imagined, judgement day, just thirteen hours away. Whoever they were singing to could almost wait, their chance would come soon enough, *sheep on the right, goats on the left*, there'd be no account for pocket book or favour. Lyle ran the barrow down the tunnel feeding the furnace, a stoker slamming the door; its clatter lost in the mayhem, flames licked the casing as they turned a page in silence, hymn number 418, *O God our help in ages past*, the last of the service. It couldn't help them now, the congregation swollen they hadn't noticed his arrival, the *visitor* sat quietly at the back of the hall, content to be amongst them made no attempt to sing, watching as they filed out with clean conscience, their morning activities would prove the perfect preparation, library books returned and swimming in the salt water pool. The *church,* empty now, with song sheets left behind on chairs, the key to the piano lid, its silk ribbon gently swaying, the makeshift altar, temporary in every sense, adorned in candles their tiny flames flickered violently as *he* stood to leave, a last chance for life had walked amongst them. A young woman, her scarf fallen to the floor, had returned to retrieve it, a wedding gift, her relief apparent she tied the cashmere knot and tucked the ends into her topcoat, frightened as the door slammed closed behind her, a double take she watched the shadow pass the window without the sound of a single footstep. A sense of foreboding accompanied her as she left to join some friends, unaware of what she had seen, her momentary distraction overcome, she would give it no further thought, preferring her share of gossip with morning tea, but she had *seen* it, the future, clear as the leaves in the bottom of a cup, a *sign* waiting to be read, its message lost in translation.

****

'Archie! We need you and Lyle up here a while, let's get the last of it out!'

The two of them exhausted from the previous shift had witnessed the coal bunker fire come to an end, the last of the *smoulder* dampened down with fire hoses and a huge effort to clear what remained of the stack. Lyle had volunteered them to *oil* the damaged bulkhead, warped with intense heat they did what they could to cover the buckled steel, its paint charred and blistered doused in black oil, covering the distortion still visible at a glance. Stood in the empty bunker the enormity of what they had achieved was clear to see. The height of the shaft from deck to deck, like an empty cave, its contents burnt or shifted, tons of coal moved with bare hand, they had earned their passage and more, enjoying a moment, the unspoken moment of a Sunday when somehow it was alright to catch your breath to lean on the shovel, a resting head, cradled into tattooed forearms, Kath barely visible his youthful attempt with ink and a needle exclaiming his love, smeared in coal and sweat, no greater love than toil. He wiped his brow into the sleeve of his shirt, and smiled at the sight of her name, in a few days' time, with luck, he'd be on his way home, he and his new mate Archie Mullins. Kath would take to him right enough, his manners, the way he'd put others first, his *place* understood, he had done his best and more. Lyle watched him as he warmed his back on the burnt steel, waiting for the shift to end, the clatter of the bell, like rats up a drainpipe they'd go, washed, fed and watered, Sunday, the seventh day, the day of *rest*, they'd do like any other, heads down and sleep, catching up as if sleep would be in short supply, not every battery would need recharging.

197

Chapter Fourteen

Lunch was almost upon them when she realised he was gone, her head count short, she should have noticed the peace and quiet, the bundle of energy, the constant, 'Did you knows?', as curious as a kitten tugging on a ball of wool. Mary put down her knitting and pulled her daughters front and centre, moistening a cloth with her mouth she *flannelled* their faces, a *wash and brush-up* they'd pass her inspection, a Sunday ritual like any other, determined to keep their routine. Mary had read from an old pocket bible, the three children lined up on her bed, cross legged they'd sat and listened to passages from Psalms, Proverbs and Jeremiah, messages of love, hope and faith, something to cling to in times ahead. Their Sunday morning wasted they'd fidget through it, their confinement over she'd send them off to play, her holy book its worn pages loose leaf to the spine, a prayer for old man O'Shea, his Sunday waistcoat out twice in one week had brought her close to tears. Snuffling back, she told herself off and checked the lid to her emotions, there was no time for weakness not now, her faith tested soon enough, read and re read, the chapter stained in salt, a private place that no one else could find, just her and Joshua 1:9, her mantra, the comfort in its repetition, wherever they were going they were not alone, skipping a beat, she was saved by cruelty, her imagination full of happy scenes, children playing in the park, a home small but clean, food on the table and work, as much as her bones could endure, cruel thoughts indeed. She swapped the bible for her knitting and spent what was left of the morning lost in day dreams, planning the future and what might be, living every scene, their lives enriched by opportunity, more than she could ever hope and far beyond her expectations, each thought as brutal as the next, framed like a picture, remorselessly they settled behind her eyes, the prospect waiting to be realised, each one set beneath an April New York sky.

He hadn't gone far, just enough to *shake off* his sisters, down one flight to the Orlop deck, stopping momentarily at the mail room packed to the gunnels, huge cages filled to bursting, the gunny bags tagged and labelled waiting to be sorted. Thousands of jute sacks, their smell as comforting as chestnuts, piled one upon the other, those at the bottom slumped beneath the weight compressed to half their size, millions of letters with stories waiting to be told, much of the mail carried would never be touched, distributed shore side it wouldn't see the light of day but upstairs in the post room the sorting had begun. Five men, one task to prepare Titanic's mail for dispatch offloaded at Quarantine Station New York Bay, three thousand three hundred and sixty four bags, another two hundred registered, distributed into sacks marked up with *facing slips,* the final destination, the clerks name stamped upon the label, a simple trace for repercussion not warranted on this occasion. The men of The Seapost, the mail entrusted to them, carrying the pride of the postal service, their bravery yet to be recorded, but unaware that every piece of mail aboard touched or otherwise had something in common, a prerequisite for those who'd bought the stamp, the fundamental flaw, they would all be delivered to the wrong address.

****

Thurle Duggan ran his fingers across the iron cage and pushed on the locked door, more in mischief than anything else, he didn't expect it to be open.

The detour complete and content he wasn't followed, Thurle made his way back, skipping two steps at a time up to G deck, his mother not one to be messed with would be waiting, a thousand questions where he had been and more Irish guilt imaginable for such a heinous crime, desertion at the very least, his lunch, peppered with every conceivable disaster, as if *life* had it in for them, the burden of responsibility heavy, but for them not heavy enough. She'd berate him, the shame of it and

God giving him roasted pork with sage and pearl onions, plum pudding with sweet sauce, three courses and what did he do, abandoned his own. Thurle loved his mother for it, the very way she thought through every little detail, his responsibility driven home like a hammer to a nail, he was just nine years old, and going on a hundred. He'd tried to fight it and would again, telling himself 'I might as well be hung for stealing a sheep as a lamb', he was late back anyway, whatever happened he was in trouble but somehow he could never get past the barrier, the sense of unease, the sadness when he watched his mother grind her teeth with worry, the anxiety gathered in the lines around the corner of her eyes, a constant fear, like impending doom was waiting in the wings, fretting over everything, she worried about them constantly. God knows what she was going through now, their lives thrown in the air, she'd do her best to catch them, to put them down gently, somewhere that gave them all a chance, working night and day, she'd take anything, the filthiest of jobs and more than one and later, when time allowed, she'd read them stories before bed, their stomachs full, they'd kiss her one by one and climb beneath clean sheets, the smell of soap and effort scrubbed across the washboard and for tomorrow, its arrival soon enough, they'd wear clean clothes and hold their heads up high. A new beginning, she'd not let it slip through her fingers, unlike the handfuls of hair pulled from the bristles

201

of her brush, a lifetime of trouble, her worries would end soon enough.

He almost made it, sliding on the polished floor he skidded past the squash court, the faint smell of sweat hung in the air.

They were up near the bow, the third class births, open dormitories full of bunks and a scattering of chairs, it seemed an odd place to have a squash court but there it was, next to the post office on the starboard side, tucked away behind the first class luggage and boiler casing. It was a comical sight, his little feet slipping on the floor, adding to his cadence as he spun around the corner, legs one way, him the other, his ears pricked like a *jack rabbit slim*, doing what he did best, explore, as nosey as a neighbour, he nearly made it, sailing past the post office, the door pushed back against the wall was an open invitation.

He had used the ploy on more than one occasion, hunkered down taking the opportunity to tie his boot, unravelling a knot making more of it than was necessary. Staring down the length of the post room, the five men, chatting like today would be their last, catching the gist of the conversation, they had got their own way, moving to separate accommodation, far enough from the singing and late night chatter, fingers pointing at the *continentals* as if it mattered now. But it wasn't what they were saying that had him spellbound, it was how they were saying it, the first American accent he had ever heard, the strangest twang from the back of the throat, all the way from Brooklyn and in a day or two the *voice* would be home.

Thurle watched the men sort the post, letters thrown into huge racks, floor to ceiling covering the entire back wall, the pigeon holes almost full, they'd know at a glance where each of the letters should go. Back and forth they'd twist and turn, lobbing parcels into canvas sacks, each sack its mouth prized open by a steel rimmed frame, swallowed the packages and five thousand letters each and every day, enough to distract anyone and Thurle was no exception. He hadn't noticed the clerk back from the canteen watching him snoop as inquisitive as a cat with nine lives, one for each of his years, standing up to get out of his way the tray of teas manoeuvred above his head as the man stepped passed, 'Have you come down to help us son?' he said, his colleagues stopping momentarily to see who he'd spoken with, Thurle docked his cap, aware it was back on his bunk, he'd been caught *red handed* eavesdropping on the men of The Seapost, his punishment nothing more than friendly banter and a few rubber bands.

He'd not forget what they'd told him, the post carried to the USA, some eighty million pieces through Quarantine Station. Royal Mail Ships reliant upon the revenue, it truly was a precious cargo, handled with care, the ex-railway workers knew what was expected of them, protect the mail at all costs, whatever the consequence, even with your lives. Thurle pondered on the conversation, sharing nothing but his sheepish grin over lunch, it was never a price worth paying to lay down your life for a few sacks of mail. What chance of it anyway, the notion dismissed as fanciful, but real enough to those on the Elbe taken by the North Sea, the widow's grief, the letter landed on her mat, she didn't need to read the lines of ink smudged into a blur of salt stained rain, his absence at the table, his place still set, she stared at the knife and fork, collapsing into a heap of pain and heartache that would never heal. A *letter*, it had found her door, unopened and unread, the final line soon to be repeated, this time on a scale unimaginable, loved ones, their lives *waiting* to be shattered, waiting for the postman and that final line, *With Deepest Sympathy.*

You could hear them talking down the empty corridor, the sound filling the space, more often deserted, the clerks shift but part way through would have them work till early evening. A supper of ragout of beef, served with potatoes and onions, and the small matter of Woody's forty fourth birthday, another year older, they'd help him celebrate whether he liked it or not, a drink or two amongst friends and back to work in the morning for more of the same. He would never see the clerks again, the corridor *filled* but not with laughter, his lunch finished he'd play quietly on his bunk and weave a rubber band around his finger, it was almost two thirty, a beautiful spring day, the post sorted, checked and signed for, it would make one last appearance, *return to sender* no longer possible, the young boy, waist deep in death, watched as it floated past.

****

Six hours into his shift and Sammy was looking forward to a rest, he'd finish at four and take the weight off his feet, the plan to meet Archie at seven down on F deck, the third class dining rooms adjacent to the galley where he'd spent most of the day. With lunch prepared by the time he'd arrived, the afternoon would be spent on clear away ready for dinner; it might have been Sunday but nobody had told his boss. Running errands for the next hour or so, up and down the Orlop deck, the bulk stores, refrigerated cargo, fruit and vegetables, all manner of supplies, stocking the pantries, dry goods mainly, the policy of rotation strictly monitored, his own shelf life limited if he did those stairs again. '*Dogsbody*', he

205

said, his breath heavy from the exercise, in truth it was probably good for him, a few pounds over and flushed to the cheek Sammy wasn't built for speed, but grateful for small mercies he was working down with his own, the dining rooms and kitchens much less intimidating than those upstairs. It was something he'd remember for this evening, something to tell Archie in between arrangements for when they docked. God, New York will be manic, maiden voyage and all, they'd need some sort of plan, at the very least a time and place, he was fretting already, resisting the temptation to make a note in his book, 'Must remember to tell Archie this is my one and only trip', the decision made that it wasn't for him, his dad's pub more appealing by the day. He'd not sign on again and that man the other day who told him to pick up the cloth, it was only yesterday the penny had dropped, the conversation overheard in the kitchen describing him to a tee, no one knew what he had come down for but he made more of a *stir* than the soupe du jour, if only to give them something to talk about. The manager of the *Ritz* and everything else on B deck, the À la Carte restaurant like nothing seen before, pure sumptuous luxury, a members club like no other, elegant and refined, the lavish menus beautifully conceived, it was a privilege to dine there, and tonight would be no exception. 'Thirteen courses! You'll have to wheel 'em out!' he heard the pot washer say, others adding comments less flattering, *effing and blinding,* they laughed and joked, taking the piss out of everyone, stopping short when they mentioned his name. It was the shift in tone that had caught his attention, a reputation worthy of respect, gossip and tittle tattle passed from one shift to the next offered nothing on the subject, Mr Gatti was held in high esteem, a man of good repute and fair in his dealings, responsible for every minute detail, his staff from far and wide, not a single one of them worked for The White Star Line. Handpicked from London's finest, he himself poached from Oddenino's to head up the team, most of them foreigners by all account, a kitchen scullion chipped in listing the countries flags, blended together the colours fused to create the perfect recipe, French and Italian, Spanish with a pinch of Belgium, English, Swiss and a few besides, an intricate balance all working beneath his watchful eye. The graceful *dance* from kitchen to front of house, catering for every whim and whisper, the rich and famous would be out again this evening, and waited on hand and foot; sixty eight men and women, trained in the art of discretion, the service would be nothing less than exquisite, much like what was to come, it could take your breath away.

He'd caught them just in time, glancing across the kitchen to see if he'd been seen, stirring the eggs he saved them with a splash of milk and showed no interest in the *chinwag* that had caused the initial commotion. He could *natter* with the best of them, but on this subject nothing would be gained by talking. Sammy kept his head down ignoring the advice aimed in his direction 'You see young man, work hard and you could be up there with *'em'*, the fountain of this counsel, up to his armpits in grease, it hadn't worked for him, scraping plates his life seen through a mountain of filthy dishes, he was only trying to help and besides, he was reading Sammy's mind. Many a true word said in jest and of times not said at all, a simple glance, a knowing stare, a smile of encouragement through sad eyes, urging you on, the subliminal message 'Don't end up like me'. Friendly advice it carried no stigma, they were lucky to have work, his decision perhaps a little hasty after all, he'd ponder on it, it wasn't like he had to make it now, maybe one more trip, he'd speak to Archie, perhaps next time Drippin would come. Sammy laughed out loud, the thought of Drippin leading Spike up the gang plank, 'Where I go mate, he goes!', the absurd idea they could ever be parted, back home the pair of them would be stuck like glue, Drippin counting the days, if not the hours, until they returned, he'd be missing them terribly.

They were a long way from home, none more so than Luigi Gatti, the man with the keys to upstairs, perhaps the keys to a new life, another risk worth taking, one of eleven children his family left behind in the northern town of Montalto, Pavese, Italy.

Heartfelt his letters would send money home, a life in London unfolded like a serviette, the white Egyptian cotton embellished with the restaurant name embroidered in silk, taken from the package, they'd be proud of their boy, he had arrived and was carving a life for his own family. Married with a son, the desire to give them a future had brought him here, the North Atlantic, a big fish in a small pond, soon to be reversed, a role model, he was unaware they both had something in common, something that wouldn't see the light of day. It wasn't spoken of yesterday, the grapevine pressed of all its facts but one, trivia perhaps but vintage to Sammy, had he known he would have seen him differently, the pedestal a little less intimidating, one of his own by association, the chance lost but nothing that couldn't wait. The insignificance held to order in the small canvas bag, *Effects of 313* stamped in black dye, a gold watch, a pair of cufflinks, two lead pencils, five shillings with a sixpenny piece, a pocket knife and his wedding ring. The drawstring tightly pulled scrunched the top of the bag, his restaurant keys bulging against the sides, bulk and weight not appreciated by those who'd deliver it, and that was the thing, the insignificance that Sammy would have loved to have known. The string threaded through the label, marked his address *Montalto*, his birthplace, carried in his heart all the way from Italy, the house name carved in a plaque by his door, *Montalto*, Harborough Road, Southampton, his personal effects had finally made it *home*, one bag amongst fifteen hundred and twenty nine, disproportionate to a few square miles, something in common, a town they called their home.

Sammy's thoughts drifted to this evening and a chance to catch up, he'd eat first and rest a while, his notebook never far away, a recipe for the perfect chocolate cake, sworn to secrecy by Freddie the Baker. Each ingredient and measure reluctantly divulged, a guarded family secret dating back to who knows when, Sammy was sure he regretted the disclosure, his family from Winchester marching over St Catherine's Hill, something else to worry about. Sammy scribbled notes in the margin writing over the entries, thickening the lines like flour to milk, the decision made, he altered the sugar from four to five ounces, protecting the innocent, unaware there was a greater power at work, the *recipe of disaster* already baking in the oven, he needn't have bothered, the family secret was secure.

His work done, Sammy nipped downstairs to clean up before returning to Scotland Road. He'd pick up his book from Clemmy Booth, a scullion working on C deck, *mad as a march hare* with a permanent smile, he was never short of a story and impossible not to like, turns out he knew Drippin and would often see him down Deanery Way along the Chapel Road, it was like walking Below Bar, familiar faces scurrying from one shift to the next, something in common and much more than they could have possibly known. It wasn't the only thing either, the goose pimples on his arm witness to the falling temperature, it was cold down here, outside the weather looked as it did this morning but it was on the change, the winds had shifted, straight across Canada Newfoundland, the cold front pushed on by a bitter north westerly breeze, a bearable 6 degrees Celsius would fall to zero before the day was done. Sammy returned to his cabin, the heavy green *jumper*, army surplus, would fend off the worst of it, packed by his mother just in case, a spare one he'd check with Archie, it'll *drown* him but at least he'd be warm, the weather gauge, to no one's advantage but those with time enough to plan. The first of the ice warnings this morning, setting the tone for the day, another received from the Baltic eastbound to Liverpool, passing on Athinai reports of bergs and field ice ahead, it wouldn't be the last of them, the next just three minutes later, direct to Washington DC, Amerika reports two large icebergs, her coordinates uncomfortable reading, well would have been had it reached the bridge, 41.27N 50 8W April 14th 1912. The cold front announced its arrival and out on the bow just hours away, icebergs, growlers and heavy pack ice waiting in the darkness, the clear skies beneath a new moon, just two days before an eclipse, as black as the smirk of death, the night was young and things were hotting up.

It wasn't like a bump in the road, or *Spike's* cart clattering across the tram lines, the turn had gone unnoticed. A gentle steer to starboard they'd follow the rhumb line true to New York, the decision to delay half hour beyond *The Corner*, marked on every chart that passed this way, a turning point for traffic making final alterations, longitude from the chronometer, latitude from dead reckoning brought forward from the noon fix and one last check of the pocket watch, its lid flipped open and closed just long enough to share a secret, the silver casing slid back to the cover of darkness and *his* waistcoat pocket. It was almost six o'clock, 266^0 True and heading back towards the ice field, further south of the intended position. They'd follow *the great circle*, its invisible line lifted from the charts strewn across the desk, a visual of the *dog's leg* firmly implanted in *his* mind's eye, the final changes had been made and calculations checked, the deviation card consulted as if magnetism would play its part, east is least west is best, variation true to magnetic, speed, wind and tide, it was all accounted for, New York was out there on the bow. Ever closer *she* carved her path through the freezing waters of the North Atlantic, twenty four of the twenty nine boilers fired up, they pushed on, early thoughts of their arrival on Wednesday coming to the fore. The welcoming party was just around the corner, you could feel a sense of excitement with little more than a thousand miles to run and as for Sunday, of all days, it would show no effort as the daylight bid farewell and slipped effortlessly into the darkness.

He'd leave the chartroom now, the guest of honour in the À la Carte restaurant, *his* party already underway, the pre-dinner drinks flowing as the champagne flutes chinked to the captain. Time was pressing, it wouldn't do to be late, a final glance at the chosen course, *he* switched off the desk lamp and felt his way to the door, pausing long enough to throw a pencil back onto the open chart, the sharpened graphite caught in the floodlight from the boat deck window, glistening as it came to rest casting a shadow across the Eastern Seaboard, its nib pointing the way to safety like a beacon of light doused out with the door closing behind him. The chartroom, silent but for the clock never to be wound again, counted down the moment when all the planning in the world wouldn't save them. But hindsight is a wonderful thing, guaranteed never to be there until after the event, the *perfect flaw*, it would carry no criticism, unlike the toast of the soirée. Down from the Boat deck he made his way to the restaurant, flush with *society* calling him to the fold, from the biting winds of an open deck to the warmth of insincerity he'd notice little change, the muffled sound of piano and laughter, sharpened with each footstep, a faithful smile well-rehearsed, another evening to endure rubbing shoulders with the *clique*, as comfortable as a new pair of shoes. He would grin and bear it and suffer the inconvenience, paled in comparison to what was to come. Due west the arms of the clock were veering and in five hours' time *their* good opinion would be lost forever, his fall from grace soon to be complete, this was his swan song and they were all in the choir together.

Chapter Fifteen

'Third time lucky' he said, scrunching the paper into a ball, his previous attempts lying *dead* on the floor beside the waste basket.

Bernard Hendrick was sat on an old wooden chair, his feet on the desk, balancing on the back legs in search of equilibrium, teetering back and forth throwing missiles at the bin, two down one to go, he'd bounce it off the wall, celebrating his efforts with an Irish jig, the *lead around* as good as any, his metal toe caps clunking on the floorboards *keeping time*. Light on his feet he gave it his best, toes out, straight carriage and arms by his side, *fasten the leggin* he did a double turn, his reflection in the window unkind around the waist as he pulled up his britches and gave a bow, with a mischievous grin he stared back at himself and watched as he raised a smile. Life hadn't beaten him yet and that was enough for today.

Four on four off, his shift pattern would see *her* arrive on Wednesday, a maiden voyage but not like any other, he'd watch the throng in front of Chelsea Pier, down to catch a glimpse or collect relatives whose lives would change forever. He was almost done for the day, in truth the evenings furnished very little, the dockside stores locked from six o'clock, he'd ferried the crates down to pier fifty nine and stacked them on the wharf for the porters. Boxes of bunting and ticker tape, balloons and spools of ribbon still to be hung, the band stand assembled but yet to be *dressed*, he'd sort it in the morning and collect the hundreds of chairs stacked in a warehouse up on West 14th Street, his afternoon spent setting them out in rows of fifty at the end of the quay, close enough to hear the band, far enough to drown the speeches, his work appreciated but never acknowledged by those that would sit there. He liked his new office but what wasn't to like, the old docks a collection of wooden sheds and ramshackle buildings condemned to hardcore and fire wood, the future, a mile of stone facade stretching back from 12th street running the West Side of Manhattan all the way to West 23rd. This was New York and the Chelsea Piers had something to say. A gateway to the rest of the world you could see it in the architecture, the same designers for Grand Central Station their hallmark, like a signature to a drawing, it carried a simple message, *Pass through here but once and you will never forget it, embark upon a new life, or arrive to make another.*

In two days' time they'd be here, through the archways, echoed footsteps on stone floors, the smell of leather, wet cases and trunks piled high onto trolleys, cigarette smoke, conversation and laughter rising up to the ceiling furled around ornate columns of polished marble. The gargoyles watching from their vantage point, grotesque faces smirking and scowling, shouting to each other across the halls as you pass beneath them, their shrieks so loud the pitch beyond our register, pointing you out, an evil undertone, like death, playing with you, waving you on your way. Out into the morning sunshine, blissfully unaware, like lambs to the slaughter, their warnings unheeded, the streets of New York unforgiving. Life replicating art but on this occasion, for more than fifteen hundred souls, there'd be nothing to fear and for those *returned* to Chelsea Pier, they would *see it* with their eyes wide shut.

If it wasn't for the hallway light he would have been in complete darkness, the end of his day he'd rundown the clock and watch the island ferries back and forth across the river.

Alone with his thoughts he closed his eyes and pictured his youngest snuggled down, his wife in the kitchen, the smell of *scrag end* stew simmering on the hearth, a bottle of stout, like mud it would *cling to the sides* and steal what little energy he had left. The embers in the grate holding on, their fading amber pulse barely breathing he'd watch their final moments and pick at the armchair cloth, threadbare and torn, the gaping hole developed over time, he'd tug on the cotton strand wound around his finger and drift off to sleep, open mouthed, twitching like a stray dog basking in the midday sun. *Once bitten twice shy*, she'd leave him alone to rest. Like love, some things are best left undisturbed.

With his back to the window, the shadows from the blinds dissected him in equal measure. An orange glow washed across the empty room smudging the reflections captured through his spectacles, a false sense of warmth and comfort competed with the image outside. The early evening darkness concealed the Piers in the distance beneath a blackened veil, their structures picked out from the dearth by upturned lights of galvanised steel swinging gently on a northerly breeze. Biting cold etched on the faces of those down below him, dockside workers shuffling along the quayside, their s*ideways* glances and private banter directed at those whose offices watched over them. Shapeless figures they'd congregate against the warehouse wall huddled in circles below the overhang still dripping from an earlier shower. Faceless objects lost to the dark side betrayed by the burn of their cigarettes and muffled laughter, *taking the piss*, his own insecurity reliable to the end soaked it up and staked a claim to all that was undirected, sarcastic tones *egging him on*.

His thoughts re-arranged for this evening, dinner at the table, the chance to talk and broach the subject, he'd do his best with hint and innuendo, his feelings, or something close to them, called upon to surface.

The slings and arrows of fortune, twelve hour shifts and hungry mouths to feed, a tenement block due for demolition, her days spent in search of somewhere else to live, dragging the youngest from door to door, out on her feet with exhaustion, they'd settled for something neither could recognise as the life they had hoped for, from Ballymore to Greenwich Village, a marriage unravelling in his absence. Bernard Hendrick had work to do, a pang of guilt flooded over him, he'd let things slip, it was up to him, Christ he was the man of the house, their own lives like those who'll arrive on Wednesday, a handful of dollars and hope as if that would save them even from *their own*. The *runners* will be waiting, speaking the Gaelic and working the street, the Irish enclave, from *promise* to rat infested slums without water or sanitation. Shovelled ten to a room at four times the going rate, they'd arrived, from immigrant to *boarder* and grateful for it, *frying pan into the fire*, they'd travelled the same path and in a week or two many would be out on the streets, homeless, penniless, their new life all but over. A harrowing end before it started, possessions confiscated for back rent, squalid shanties they'd share a floor with filth and despair, broken sleep, huddled beneath a single blanket, the mayhem stepping over them, while petticoats were lifted for a dollar a time.

He wasn't sure what he was feeling, his own thoughts muddled like a drunk on a corner, lurching back and forth he tussled with the picture etched on the back of his eyes.

That's all he seemed to do, head down work hard, the only response he could muster and look at him now, caught in the middle, his efforts to get on alienated from everyone; *no man's land* was proving a difficult place to be but he'd chosen it, to supervise, moving up, taking the chance when it went begging, he didn't get a say, not really, the constant threat to lose his job made worse by the daily queue of men that would gather outside the gates, looking for work, looking for anything. He was one of the lucky ones, the *right side* of the railings, cast iron segregation that would see those unlucky scatter and disperse into a backdrop of misery, they'd try again tomorrow, as would the rest, a sense of hopelessness. He'd make up the list at the start of each day to take on the labour, *casuals*, as if any a word could be more misplaced, twelve hours straight with barely a break, humping goods the stevedores whose job it was, exercised their bloodline while others took the strain. A dockside run by each generation, the *family*, like any other, a melting pot of pressure that would show itself in stabbing pains, his temples, the resting place for conflict that would plague him, neither worker nor boss, the shift in attitude from outright aggression to hushed tones and looks down the end of the nose, a friend to no one. Bernard Hendrick was on a hiding to nothing, he knew it, of course, but this was his chance, a chance to shine amidst a palate of grey murk that hung above their grim existence, stripped of the colours *they* once took for granted. His youngest was born here amongst the Dumbbell Tenements and putrid air trapped like them, her lungs slowly filling with mucus, a constant reminder as if the squalor wasn't enough. His decision made, made for them all, he'd brought them here like those before him, his *mind's eye* nothing more than green haze of the life they'd left behind, its harsh reality diluted with each day, scolding him for what he'd done, unbearable sadness only known to regret, the type that would have him wince at the sight of *her* this morning.

There was nothing more he could do, not today, and in a strange way he took comfort from that. The air horns in the yards, already long sounded, had seen the usual stampede for the gates, a thousand leather boots and britches kicked up the dust as they funnelled through the exits spilling out onto West Street. Milling about the open expanse of wasteland soaked up the overflow of men as they poured through the pillars set between pink granite stone; blistered hands rubbed aching backs as they made their way, absorbed beneath a canopy of chatter that would thin as the crowd drifted off. For them Sunday was over, but for others it had only just begun.

Two more days, it wasn't long but enough to finish what was needed. The blackboard, witness to progress hung precariously above a scattering of chairs, chalked up in straight-line capitals with underscored jobs yet to be done and a flourish of crosses administered with gusto beneath a message thickened for effect, **RMS Titanic (59) Wed 17th/AM**. Like nothing before, the Pier scrubbed to an inch of its life roped off waited *her* arrival. Inside the halls polished and buffed fell silent but for the huge stone clock, its marble face tickled by the movement counted down the hours while an old negro pushed his broom as gentle as a *brush* on a snare drum. Bernard stepped away from the window and slurped the last of his tea, the dregs cold and bitter offered nothing but a mouthful of leaves unseen in the shadows. His mood troubled by the image still haunting him of his wife Lillian, sat upon their bed, a rusty nail in one hand she used it like a braddle adding one more notch, a leather belt loose around her waist, searching for the *puncture,* closing the buckle like a chapter on their lives. His judgement portrayed in a single act played homage to blind faith and the innocence of love incapable of blame and deep like the ocean that had brought them here.

With one arm in his sleeve he stabbed at the other in frenzied bursts, probing the lining behind his back, straining and contorted pulling the jacket across crooked shoulders, the twisted collar straightened with all the grace of a man deranged cursing its unwillingness to co-operate.

He'd walk the eight blocks to Grafton Street, into the evening chill and follow the shoreline to the Church of St Luke, his pace quickening past Cherry Lane crossing the street to avoid the dogs that would gather beneath the gas lights, running the gauntlet of teeth and attitude. Content to fight amongst themselves he would slip past unnoticed and make his way back home, a single street of blackened brick merged into the bleakness, redeemed in part by the smell of burnt timber or somebody's furniture, broken up, another chair sacrificed in private, the family eyeing what was left, they'd do what they had to, holding on, waiting for the spring to come. *Out front* as far as some would ever get, mothers and children would gather on the steps, *her* pride in scrubbed stone something to cling to, idle gossip and the wait for a pay packet already spent, they'll watch their neighbours watching them from across the street while eldest daughters practice a life without expectation, disinterested hands resting on the push bars soothe crying babies in beaten old prams, spring loaded heaven they'd drift back to sleep oblivious to the filth they were lying in, while sisters rocked them gently to a place beyond the reach of reality.

This was Bernard Hendrick's chance, the here and now and he'd not get another, if all went well on Wednesday the promise of a full time job, a member of the permanent staff working the Piers from West 12th to 23rd Street. He'd heard loose talk, an opening working dockside for Cunard, another covering shifts at the White Star Line, general dogsbody but either way it was a huge step forward and he'd take what was offered and be grateful for it. A regular wage not usually rendered to the likes of him, *the brotherhood* broken, an *outsider* hired in favour of men known to others with a decade or more beneath their belts, men whose accents, if not their efforts, would see work shy friends' noses out of joint, the consequence of hard work, if nothing else seen by some as the tip of an iceberg and something to avoid at all costs.

Whatever the repercussions, sooner or later he would have to deal with them, however uncomfortable or difficult his life was made, it would be nothing to the pain delivered from a single glance this morning, his doubts quelled at the sight of her, any second thoughts he may have had vanished as quickly as they came. No, Bernard Hendrick was ready, but for the churning stomach yet to be convinced and the keeping of a promise made to himself in the solitude of darkness, the type never to be shared or cross the threshold door. His resolution sure to be tested would do little now to change his state of mind, a blend of apprehension tinged with the fear and excitement of better things to come. His efforts had finally been noticed and in just a few days' time all his hopes and dreams would be carried on the morning tide, up the Hudson River, the bearer of a better life, or absolution for bringing them here.

With a spurt on he could make it back by eight, stuffing the muslin cloth in his pocket, some torn bread and a wedge of cheese long since gone, his cap lost and found by a process of elimination hiding on the desk in front of him, gathered up. The silence broken by a cleaner as she passed the frosted glass, her silhouette impaired by the signage painted on the door did nothing to conceal an identity betrayed by mop and bucket as the clatter faded down the hall. A wet floor her sworn affidavit, the acrid tarry smell of disinfectant and carbolic soap strangely comforting as he made his way down the wooden stairs and out across the yard checking padlocks and storerooms along the way. The open concourse brightly lit burnt energy with scant regard for those whose evening would be spent in darkness, his neighbours' plight best gauged at night amidst the flicker of candles, the shameless glow incapable of lies throwing truth up the walls of dimly lit rooms. The spotlight of poverty as brutal as you like illuminates in open glare, as if humiliation lodged in Grafton Street.

He didn't know what had made him stop. It was as if he'd walked the length of a rope, like something was pulling him back, a chilled hand across his shoulder. Stood frozen to the marble floor, the last piece on a chess board his next move unknown as he tried in vain to leave. A solitary figure alone in the terminus building he'd made it not a half way across the huge expanse before the weight of silence nailed him. The vast hallway as opulent as any encased him in a tomb of stone that sparkled like a new penny, while shards of light refracted back from cut glass fashioned into pearl drops above his head. The huge chandelier chinked in the draft that rushed beneath a line of oak framed doors adding to the chill that ran the length of his spine and had settled between his shoulders still cold from the touch.

It was coming from the antechamber. A gentle weeping sound as haunting as any he'd heard, its tone pure and innocent captured the acoustics of the room while muffled echoes of stifled tears carried *her* grief exhumed in wailing lament. Its raw edge was sharp enough to tear him open as the sobbing trailed to a mournful groan, her breath snatched with all the skill of a *tooler's hand*, gasping for the promise of life while breathless whimpers called him to her side. *They* were watching him, the sense of *their* presence crawled across his flesh like death itself had tried him on. Gulping back whatever courage still intent to leave, wiping his moistened brow, his *gallies* rooted no more he shuffled slowly toward the door. Squinting eyes caught in the glare of advertisements hung down the wall from timber poles, huge banners twenty feet or more competing for attention. There, above the door, a picture of a young boy *drenched* in yellow oilskins, drowning beneath an oversized hat, a box of Uneeda biscuits at five cents a time tucked beneath his arm, smiling down at him, no, laughing at him like *he* was the last to know, the child's mouth pursed tight to keep a secret, beyond reproach. He was nothing if not true to his word, in confidence but for a day or more, drawing him closer, goading him towards the door, wide open and as hungry as the mouth of a cave. The room was in darkness but for the light flooding in from the hall. Peering inside his whole body shook uncontrollably, her snivels, subdued now, had taken on a calmness as if her fate already decided, catching up, his eyes adjusted to the shadows tracing the sound to the far end of the room. Privacy booths set in timber frames and buttoned leather obscured in the murk and the bleakness of misery. A shape in the corner, perhaps nothing, distorted, his mind playing tricks, could he see *her*, withered like an unloved plant, rocking back and forth, her mind lost to grief, *washed up*. The figure huddled like an orphan yet to be chosen fell silent to his calls.

'Hello?! Who's there?! Hello Miss? Don't be afraid, please come from the darkness. Let me help you?!'

It was as if they had been lost along the way, bouncing off the walls, words returned like a creditor when least expected, the element of surprise, his voice suddenly behind him brushed the nape of his neck and with it every hair on his body.

'Who's there?'

'Miss? I heard your tears, please don't be afraid, step forward into the light!'

He tried again, not least because it reinforced what the hell he was doing there. This building was *deadlurk* along with Pier 59, empty and had been for days, the next forty eight hours would see nothing but caterers prepare the welcoming parties. This very room, one of many already set up for what would be a truly splendid reception, locked down until Wednesday with keys shared between shifts, the main gates manned by *uniforms* with an officious interest in authority, guarding the perimeter walls like a well-kept secret, the ebb and flow of those that worked here mirrored by the ships tied to the quays. No, everything about this was wrong and he knew it, a sense of dread impossible to shed coursed through his veins swelled by the blood that had drained from his face, pallid and sullen the hush tinged with a helplessness from which there'd be no return. But that wasn't it, there was something else, an edge difficult to define, an inevitability had consumed the moment and all those in it as he walked toward the future, like impending doom, it waited patiently for his arrival.

'Miss? Come from the shadows, I can help you!'

There was no reply, just a gentle sobbing diminished to all but a whimper. His take on the room never conceived when the trestle tables were assembled earlier in the day. Row upon row they lined the room, *undressed* the tablecloths folded away would soon adorn their *bony frames*. Cold and skeletal the iron legs barely sufficient held aloft the rough wooden planks worthy of any morgue, the mid-morning buffet yet to be arranged around a centrepiece of white lilies, each bench dressed in exacting fashion creating an avenue from where he stood to the back of the room. His path laid out before him consigned whatever choice he may have had, waved away like they all were, their fate already decided. Staring into the abyss he moved into the darkness and gingerly shuffled toward *her* calling as he went, a nervous glance across his shoulder checking on the open door. He took what comfort he could and gulped back the little spit he had left, his mouth as dry as a house of sobriety soon to relapse.

It was as if she waited for him. Watching as he felt his way down the room, arms outstretched his silhouette, a fumbling crucifixion, moved beyond half way and the point of no return. His footsteps competed with a heartbeat pounding violently beneath his jacket, a button loosened with clammy hand as if a signal to begin, the moment his life would change forever, her screams standing witness to revelation and the pain released through tortuous wailing as heart wrenching as any a man should endure. Sobbing uncontrollably she cried out, her voice breaking off into a weeping sorrow so disturbing he flinched at the sound of it, fighting his instincts to run. The door slammed shut behind him closing off the exit and with it the only light in the room engulfing him in darkness and the touch of her voice.

Blind panic and nothing else had taken hold, its grip like a vice, orchestrating what followed when the first of the trestles went crashing over. The metal frame bouncing off the stone floor like a crack of thunder had him struggle to stay on his feet. Clambering over the obstacles like a bull in a china shop, cutting through the undergrowth to the side of the room, his palm slapped the marble, *walking* down the wall to the light switch recessed beneath an alcove positioned to avoid detection, failing to quell the sense of relief manifested through fingers numbed by fear. Willing them on, it was as if time stood still, waiting for the row of lamps above his head to fire up, a surge of power kicked them into life, each element crackling one after another, the register called, marked present and correct, he stood amongst the chaos that surrounded him. Frozen beneath the glare, his vulnerability was difficult to deny, as was the throbbing pain in the side of his hand; a shard of timber buried deep into his flesh. Pulling on the splinter he grimaced and yelped its release in contrast to a moment of madness before the room had fallen silent.

'Miss? Come out from behind the booth?!' he shouted again, there was not a murmur.

With only one door to the room he knew *she* was there, perhaps fearful of the consequence and delaying the inevitable, hiding in the corner curled up in a ball, the very sight he expected to meet him as he took the last few steps to her side. His face ashen as he peered around the timber frame, the smell of damp leather, fousty like a tannery, so strong the image of drying hides stretched on wooden frames flashed through his mind's eye, his attention diverted momentarily, it would steal the opportunity to soften the blow. Peering into the closet, wavering for a moment, he gathered whatever will he could muster, his whole body like a wound up spring waiting for recoil, but nothing could prepare him, nothing could warm the *hand* cold as death itself now resting on his shoulder.

It was the shortest of gasps, as if a single breath had been stolen from his lungs. A step back, then nothing, frozen at the sight of it, his eyes wide open like they'd never blink again, his mind racing with every connotation, fighting the fear that would have him run for the door. There was no one there, the empty stall soaked in water, salt stains like *tears* ran off the leather seats, sopping wet, the press button holes filled to the brim, an hypnotic sound syncopated as drips formed puddles on the floor. Seeping from the *pew* a pool of water, the *future* catching up with him, a vision like any other open to interpretation, its strongest clue the pungent smell of seawater hung in the air. Clinging to *her* top coat, the saturated cloth heavy as a lead weight *pulling her under*, a crunch of ice stuck to the soles of his boots and the image of a woman, fully clothed, her lifeless body lapped against a blackened hull, its vertical wall of frozen steel and despair had her wash back and forth like a rag doll. Her powder white skin and purple lips captured beneath a starburst of blinding light, a final act void of all resistance to fate and as pitiful as the splash that would signal her fight was over. Waiting to be taken, she kissed the beads wrapped around her hand, a garbled prayer for mercy lost beneath the freezing waters of the North Atlantic, alone, surrounded by others, Mary closed her eyes and was gone.

It was a second, maybe two, before making for the door, slipping on the floor his footsteps followed him out toward the hallway, chasing him step by step like a bailiff with a writ, waving proof as to what he had seen. The significance *sinking in* he pieced it together, his sanity questioned but for the trail of water strewn in his wake. Running down the aisle the tables lined up and waiting, their adaptability soon to be utilised as would the ton of ice and crates of embalming fluid stacked against the wall, a deathly hush of respect offered to those whose needs were long since gone and the sweet smell of rose water that hung in the air. Whatever *this* was he wanted *out* and in every sense of the word. His traction lost on the marble floor spilling him into the hall, a parting glance across his shoulder leaving *it* behind, an apparition like no other, yet to be verified, his solace taken from his own counsel bellowed at the top of his voice.

'Pull yourself together!'

'You're tired that's all! It's just an illusion, your imagination playing tricks!'

Belting it out he crossed the terminus heading for the exit like a man possessed, any justification undermined by his britches long enough to soak up the *evidence*, sopping wet they slapped together stealing all but the faintest attempt at denial, the sum of the parts screaming at him merged with every conceivable thought that dared to enter his head. He could *see* the chalked up blackboard outside the Pier roped off for those first down the gangplank, the bandstand, its silhouette like a carousel of galloping horses waiting to turn, Titanic's thrilling climax played out on the dockside. New York was ready and so was Bernard Hendrick, ready for a better life, kicked off on Wednesday by an ocean of ticker tape, the culmination of effort and reward, a small part played in making what would be a day to remember, a day written into the history books and captured in sepia tones. Families piling down the timber bridges stopping momentarily to wave at loved ones in the distance, the crowd five deep bustling to catch a glimpse amidst shouts and hollers lost on the breeze, their relatives held behind barriers as temporary as the moment itself. Now look at it, all thrown into question, a melting pot of turmoil like no other, a premonition so real he could have saved her, should have saved her, his anger directed inwards re-living the moment when she slipped away. As terrifying as it was, it left nothing but a sickening ache gnawing at the lining of his stomach, an emptiness not driven by his failure to act but the cruel possibility now stabbing at his conscience, a struggle so intense he'd try in vain to block it out, his only response, the crutch of stubborn ritual searching for order amongst the chaos that had set up camp. Straightening his jacket he brushed the woollen cloth and took what little comfort offered, his stride gradually slowing as he reached the outer wall, the sign read, West Street, his escape to denial, the other side, shedding the weight of responsibility, that nagging doubt hell bent on snatching everything away, perverting the course of *injustice*, leaving him with nothing but conflict and the overwhelming possibility that it wasn't too late.

It was like watching in slow motion, grappling with the handle his shoulder pressed against the door forcing it to open, his second charge enough to see him fall through the gap and into the darkness.

A memory re-ignited, stirring his consciousness he tumbled into the gloom, lunging for the railings at the top of the steps, Bernard steadied himself and gathered what composure could be found in a momentary pause, his ungainly exit worthy of *closing time* in Clonakilty. Turfed out by the clock, he'd stand outside the pub wrestling with his coat, tugging on his collar, the first line of defence already breached, a bitter night as cruel as winter bones made worse by the wind howling through the alleys, raw as a bereavement it swept up from Galley Head, wiping smiles off strong constitutions as if inebriation was a match for the Celtic Sea. He was back there for a moment, his thoughts broken only by the sound of a dog barking in the distance and the sense of unease stood alone on the dockside.

Striking a match his silhouette and shattered nerves betrayed by shaking hands cupping his cigarette from a northerly breeze, the Pier black against the night sky offered little comfort to his mood as he closed the door, checking it twice he tugged on the padlock before walking away. It was nothing but relief at first to be out of there, grateful for the chance to make sense of what he'd *seen*, his breath deep and measured witnessed by the rise and fall of his chest, pensive agitation appeased in part if not for the conflict still raging in his head, bedlam or something close to it, pouring over the detail, unaware the answers were but a few days away. The New York Times, his resolution bellowed from the sidewalks to a waiting crowd, held aloft the newspaper headlines, sombre but factual would change his life forever:

Titanic sinks four hours after hitting iceberg, 866 rescued by Carpathia, probably 1250 perish, Ismay safe, Mrs Astor maybe, noted names missing.

It was quiet when he left the yard, West 18th Street deserted but for the waifs and strays, rundown buildings improved by the darkness followed the path of the river to a kink in the bend and disappeared behind Pier 54. Strangely eerie the evening silence made worse by the night sky exaggerated his awkward shuffle as he passed beneath the street lamp, a brief distraction as a moth danced around the lantern, unaware of the danger beyond the glass.

'How fragile this life?' he said, blissfully unaware how close he had come to something better. The aftermath come Tuesday, when the world would be told what he'd *seen*, Bernard Hendrick, stolen by remorse, as if anyone would have believed him.

Chapter Sixteen

One final check and the Maître d' was ready, the evenings reservations completely full, he made his way to the first class lounge and that all important announcement.

'Ladies and gentlemen, dinner is served!'

It was going to be such a lovely evening, champagne, the perfect aperitif, captured the atmosphere as they made their way through the Ritz and the Palm Court already busy filling with those lucky enough to have booked. A gathering bursting with excitement fused with a sense of anticipation, beautiful gowns filed one after the other taking their places to the sound of music and laughter, appetites defenceless to the wonderful aroma, their senses teased with what was to come. The hum of chatter, a *lifetime* away from Wednesday and their arrival in New York City and, for many, that's exactly what it would be.

Spick and Span the Chelsea Piers were waiting, the party that would never come just two days away, a neighbourhood like no other, running down the west side of Manhattan, the Hudson River within spitting distance depending on the wind, little West and 12th up to Gansevoort and beyond, *the meatpacking district*, home of the *Knackers Yard* and the end of the line, the irony as cruel as it was, would not go unnoticed.

'Archie! Over here Archie!'

Sammy called him from across the dining room, standing briefly to ensure he was seen, waving him over he pointed the shortest route through a sea of heads lost beneath a haze of cigarette smoke and conversation.

'Archie! This way! I've saved you a seat!'

He called again, discharging his responsibility of the chair, watching his friend weave a path, their smiles connecting them together like a piece of string, handshakes and ruffled hair the obligatory welcome.

'Sorry Sammy, I overslept. God, I could have gone right through till the morning.'

They would only have twenty minutes or so but long enough for a natter before Archie's shift at eight, two mugs of tea, strong and sweet, enough for now, Sammy would eat when he'd gone, this evening's fayre of Lamb and mint sauce, green beans and new potatoes, a tempting prospect but one that could wait. *Chomping at the bit*, Sammy, ten to the dozen with barely a chance to catch his breath, running through his list, slowing momentarily to emphasise a point, 'No, I didn't realise who he was?! It was only later when they were talking in the kitchen. Gatti, yes Mr Gatti, Luigi that was his name, the Manager of the Ritz. Can you imagine Archie running such a place?' Archie never said a word, in truth he never had a chance, he was on a roll from kitchen stories to the drudgery of stocking the pantries, his mood noticeably subdued before blurting out what he wanted to say.

'It's not for me though Archie. I've thought long and hard about it, as soon as we're back I'll be working for me dad. Even cellar work is better than this.'

He didn't mean it quite like that; if he could have said it differently he'd start again. It wasn't like Archie had a choice, his best friend shovelling coal, grateful to be here, in truth grateful to be anywhere, the opportunity to earn a few *bob*. Archie would never judge him, but he was pleased all the same when he replied.

Slurping his tea, Archie gave a knowing smile, the type only friends would understand, acknowledging Sammy's awkwardness as if in some way he had let him down.

'I'm glad you've said that Sammy, I've been worrying since we came away; if you hadn't mentioned it I was gonna bring it up myself. I think I'll do a couple more trips, just long enough to put a few quid in the jar and you saying that has made it possible.'

Archie didn't stop; he could see it required explanation, Sammy's blank expression a mixture of *help me out* and anticipation stared back across the table.

'You see, I've been worried after Drippin? In all honesty I couldn't do another trip, he'd never survive without the both of us, but with you at home that's one less thing on my mind, if you're sure Sammy you'd be doing me a big favour, besides even *Spike* must be fed up with him now.'

The two boys broke into laughter, conjuring thoughts of *Spike* and Drippin, the old cart off up the high street, their sympathies firmly with the horse, *bending his ear*, the poor thing's had five days of bickering, 'Cruelty to animals' Archie said and with that they fell about again. 'That's settled it then, now let's sort out Wednesday as we might not get a chance to speak again. I've brought you the name and address of the pub just in case either one of us is held up. Tully said he'd be glad of your company, besides I wouldn't go without you. Now here it is, I've written it down, all I know is you take a left out of the docks and its a few streets up on the right, West 21st Street, The Liffy Tavern, number 408.'

Sammy smiled and took the scrap of card, a pack of Player's cigarettes he'd written on the box, his final instructions delivered between a slurp of hot tea.

'I'm not entirely sure what time we'll all be finished but I've heard it said that we'll be done by mid-morning. Now that gives us plenty of time to get washed up and meet at the pub by 12:45; either way if I'm not there ask after Tully or Lyle and they'll see you right.'

With the arrangements made the two boys finished up, Archie using what time was left talking about the Tank Top and how lucky he was to be sharing a cabin with the others, slapping Harry's gloves on the side of the table the unspoken confirmation that it was time to go.

'It's been really great to catch up Sammy. I doubt we'll see each other again until Wednesday; so, you know the plan and I'll meet you in New York as arranged. Can you imagine it, a couple of urchins from Southampton walking the streets of Manhattan, I can hardly believe it's going to happen and it's not long now.'

It was almost five to eight when Archie left, dragging it out as long as possible before saying his goodbyes, they had made a plan, or something like it, and enough to bind them together. The smile on

Sammy's face confirmation, as if any was needed, in the value of a friend. There was nothing to rush off for, throwing his jacket across the back of his chair, staking a claim to the table he joined the queue. Piling his plate with *comfort* and a fresh mug of tea, four meals a day with supper back on his bunk; he was missing it already, his plate balanced with thoughts of home and a future working for his dad. It was like a weight had been lifted, Archie dismissing the *news* to a favour; he had turned it on its head concealing any disappointment at the prospect of another trip out here on his own, his *choice* stolen by Wickham Court. Sammy's pang of guilt eased by the sight of his dinner and the mystery of life's circumstance and, for now at least, that was something not even he should worry about.

He was oblivious to those nearby, his rituals almost complete, the condiments lined up before him, salt and pepper like soldiers on parade. Gathering his knife and fork, pausing for a moment while he bathed his face held over steaming gravy, you didn't need to know him, it was clear from a hundred paces that Sammy loved his food. It would be almost an hour before he'd look again, hunger pangs the priority all but diminished, rummaging in his pocket, as awkward as you like with one leg out stretched beneath the table, searching for the card hidden in the fold of his trouser pocket, Archie's note pulled out like a rabbit from a hat, its value beyond explanation. He could have been sitting there alone, unaware of the racket going on around him, filtering the noise to the back of his mind, its dull drone broken by the scraping of a plate as a young stewardess cleared dirty dishes from across the way, smiling as she passed, her hair pinned beneath a white cotton cap trimmed with a black velvet ribbon, as pretty as a picture, her *movement* appreciated as she made her way to the galley. The swing door pushed open with her hip, disappearing out of sight, leaving nothing but the rhythm of motion swinging back and forth to a gentle close.

He hadn't read the note when Archie passed it to him, content to listen while the arrangements were explained, weaving the torn card through his fingers, the image of a sailor circled inside a life ring. The packet ripped and stained dissected him across the shoulder, while *Navy Cut*, cropped but visible, encased the *hero*, leaving Archie's writing scrawled down one side. Sammy grinned like a Cheshire cat tickled by the message, 'Cheeky little git' he said under his breath, as he read it for a second time.

Sammy be there at quarter to one,
don't be late,
and don't bring your note book!

Archie

Sammy sat for a while pondering on all and nothing, putting the world to right, his continual state of agitation cleverly disguised, worrying about what money he should take come Wednesday and the likelihood of getting robbed, convincing himself it required more thought. He'd head back to the cabin and make a list, the do's and don'ts of Lower Manhattan, Sammy was never one for spontaneity and there was little point in changing now.

She wasn't coming out again, the swing door firmly shut, showing no sign of activity he would take that as a *no* and be on his way. His stomach full to bursting, working it off he'd rest on his bunk and save himself for supper, cabin biscuits and a coffee top, the end of a perfect day witnessed by the glow of his cigarette stubbed out on the metal frame of his bed. It was almost ten o'clock before he drifted off to sleep, the Monday morning red eye shift, he'd be up before he knew it, woken by a thud on the door; his wake up call was coming, but unbeknown to him, this time it was for everyone and a lot earlier than expected.

'Talk about ships in the night!' Tully said, the cabin in darkness when he returned from the washrooms, the smell of carbolic soap hanging in the air from Harry's long johns drying on the end of his bunk. They'd be eating their supper now, he and Albert, 'A couple of right old-timers' he said with affection, like everyone over forty were all but done. 'Mind you, I'll give 'em their due, the pair of 'em are as fit as a butcher's dog, if not a little hard to train', he said, his cheeky smile breaking through as he added the extra line. They'd probably be back within the hour, long enough for Tully to catch a nap and get downstairs for dinner. Scotland Road, quieter now as the eight o'clock supper was all but cleared away, following the whistles he passed the *Glory Hole* steward, door ajar with his galvanised bucket, moping out the cubicles, his song cut short as Tully passed.

'Alright mate?!' he said, the obligatory acknowledgement shared between them. There are worse things in life than shovelling coal he thought, disappearing down the stairwell to F deck, his dinner of grilled sausage and mash, buckwheat cakes covered in maple syrup waiting to be polished off, his six hour break, barely two hours in, fed and watered and back on his bunk for a sleep. He'd be down there again at four and be done in time for breakfast; their daily routines well established proved more of a chore for Tully and Archie than it did for the oldies. Harry and Albert, up and at 'em, Christ they didn't even need a shout, the pair of them, like a couple of old soldiers, wind 'em up and point them in the right direction, work, eat, sleep and more work, they'd been doing it for years and in truth it was impossible not to admire. 'A couple of good eggs' my old man would have said and pleased enough to know them. Both back on again at midnight, unaware their shift would never come. *It* was little more than an hour and forty minutes away but time enough to finish up, a cigarette, perhaps a game of cards, their dinners going down, Albert's indigestion the curse of growing old but he didn't need to worry, very soon he'd have all the time in the world.

****

He should have drunk it sooner, in truth he'd forgotten it was there; lukewarm the coffee had left a ring around the cup, tepid and miserable, a little like him right now, not helped by the splitting headache that had settled in the back of his eyes. Working alone, Phillips maintained a listening watch, deciphering the incoming and working the messages that had built up during the day. The wretched breakdown hadn't helped and neither had the ADVISELUM almost 250 since leaving Southampton, the backlog of telegrams yet to be sent adding to the pressure he was feeling, subdued, the bitter cold draft straight off the boat deck did nothing to improve his mood. Outside the temperature had dropped to near freezing, he was tired, no exhausted and it was probably fair to say the Marconi Room was a place best avoided.

He had been sat on his desk for almost forty minutes and was yet to make it to the bridge. An ice warning from SS Mesaba clipped in tone, its business like message clear enough to those who would read it, those on duty just yards away from where he sat. Across the *airwaves* it had travelled the darkness, its journey only to falter at the final fence, the Bridge and Marconi Room either end of the corridor, a distance to be counted in yards, Phillips drowning in passenger traffic working Cape Race, acknowledged its receipt but it would never be read:

In latitude 42N to 41.25N to longitude 49W to 52.30W. Saw much heavy pack ice and great number of large icebergs, also field ice, weather good, clear.

It could wait; they'd received several during the day, checking the form Phillips filed it for routine delivery, the standard procedure for any message not warrant of prioritisation. The prefix MSG or Master Service Gram replaced with *Ice Report* enough to have it set aside, the Masters acknowledgement not required he would deal with it later perhaps on change over when his shift was done or sooner if time allowed. They were out on their feet, Bride, fast asleep next door was completely done in and catching up with some well-earned rest, both of them still struggling from time lost repairing the radio, time that would never be recovered. Phillips propped up his head, a moment's breather taking stock of what was to be done. This evening's shift, dragging despite the workload spilling over from the previous day, a stifled yawn and the obligatory glance at the clock suggesting 0200 still seemed a lifetime away. *Shut eye*, yes that's exactly what was needed; he never thought he'd say it but Monday morning couldn't come soon enough.

Chapter Seventeen

'Time waits for no one!' Lyle shouted catching Archie as he ran down the tunnel, a friendly grin; he had already made two trips on the barrow before he'd arrived.

'I'll do this one! Go and get yourself sorted, you can take over when I get back. Pulling was she?' he said, referring to his bunk. Archie cutting it fine had nothing to offer in reply but his apology for being late and a look of disappointment like it was the end of the world.

'Sorry Lyle, I met Sammy to make the arrangements for Wednesday, I should have allowed much more time. Sammy doesn't do quick.' Lyle dismissed it with a wave of the hand, well almost a hand, more of an elbow pushing the barrow down the tunnel, a flick of his arm, as if to say 'don't give it another thought'. His grubby vest disappearing into a haze of red mist, the backwash from the furnaces waiting to be fed all one hundred and fifty nine of them shouting for more, their deafening sound Archie took as confirmation they'd not be quite so understanding. He'd let him do the ferrying for a while, if only so he felt he was pulling his weight, Lyle content to work the stack while Archie ran the barrow, bellowing to each other every time he returned, their conversation broken into turnaround segments, waiting for the next instalment or a punch line to a joke, both hard pressed to find anything funny about a life shovelling coal. It was almost twenty minutes before they'd swap; taking a breather Lyle wiped the sweat from his eyes and kicked some stray coal back to the pile. The sound of boots down the tunnel signal enough to get back to work; both looking busy, never to find out first nor last who it was. Their evening shift would finish at midnight and so far it was proving to be like any other.

It was the guilt doing it, Archie working flat out still chastising himself for being late, his mind drifting back to Sammy and thoughts of home.

They'd all be asleep now, the house in darkness, silent but for the clock in the parlour, the light from the streetlamp flooding through the downstairs window picking out the armchair, his mother's sewing, a work in progress on the seat waiting for daybreak, while the last of the embers were all but done in the grate. It was alone with time to think he found most difficult. He could see Will's face in the morning, his hair skew whiff, half asleep he'd slump at the scullery table, swaying back and forth nodding off, his mother scalding milk in a cast iron pot, mixing it with oats and heaps of granulated sugar, packed off to school, Will's belly full for now, making his way across the square stopping briefly to

251

wave goodbye. He could see every detail, smell the milk browning on the stove, his brother dozing while he chewed the cud, a mouthful of textured glue porridge and be grateful. He'd not go hungry, not today, Archie's daydream as real as it gets, cut short by the shouts and hollers bouncing off the bunker walls, like him it had nowhere else to go.

'You men! Yes, you two! Over here sharpish!' he said.

Lyle straightening his back and wiping the sweat from his brow, tugging on his neckerchief allowing his stare to break the silence.

'We need a trimmer *fore* in Six, leave that for him and come with me!' he yelled at Archie flicking his wrist at the barrow like it was being dismissed; a glance back at Lyle, his bark as mean as a dog on a corner, if not his bite Lyle thought, a step closer to Archie pure instinct.

'Don't worry Archie, I'll finish off here. I'll not even notice you've gone.'

Lyle made light of it, a nod toward the tunnel as much as to say 'don't worry' as anything else. Archie's face, somehow unconvinced stared back making no attempt to hide his anxiety, worse now as the man leaned forward and bellowed in his ear,

'Come on! We ain't got all day! Set that barrow down and follow me!'

With that they were gone, Archie trailing behind, his apprehension recording every step, a little grimace and thumbs up, his trademark response to everything be it good or bad. There'd be no say in the matter, not even for Lyle, like the rest of them, both as expendable as the ash they eject, nothing more than cannon fodder and it showed. Another link in the chain, the lowly engineer as brutish as you like, his voice deep and confident wasted no time on convoluted explanations. The order of the day, taking one man forward to bunker six, shifting coal and trimming the portside list; the first time since the off they'd not be working together. Lyle was convinced he should have gone instead, a sixth sense, intuition, call it what you will, something was playing heavy on his mind. The ringing of the midnight bell, less than two hours till the end of their shift, now superfluous to the situation, Lyle had no choice but to do what he'd always done in times like this, put his head down and take it out on the coal.

****

It was all going *swimmingly* well.

The International Brigade, a credit to Signor Gatti, were moving between the tables *invisible* to all but his watchful eye, the last course cleared with military precision, made to look effortless as the dirty dishes were whisked away. Sirloin beef and chateau potatoes followed by roast squab, garlic and a sprig of thyme, seven courses, the next ready and waiting lined up on hot plates, each row hanging on the call to service while Punch Romaine stole the show. The delicate blend of champagne and white wine served over crushed ice and rum fused with the juice of orange and lemon, the perfect balance cleansing the palate while adding to the drama of the evening. It really was just getting started with four more courses yet to be served, an army of crisp white starch rallied around the chosen few, white cotton gloves refreshed glasses of chilled wine, while others scraped crumbs off the tablecloths into silver trays, an act of theatre performed in the interlude working its way to the Pâté de Foie Gras, celery and Waldorf Pudding, the finalé, French Ice cream topped with polite conversation. There was something special about this evening, it was difficult to define, perhaps nothing more than the week drawing to a close. The mood noticeably lifted from sombre Sunday prayers yet to be tested to thoughts of New York, helped along with a splattering of anecdotes that would see the occasional table of eight burst into laughter, drowning out the hum of the room with a little more enthusiasm than some might have approved. But it wasn't the quality of the stories, amusing as they might have been, no, it was the contrast that was different, more than any other night it was impossible not to notice. Outside the sea state was as calm as a mill pond and merged seamlessly into a blackened night sky, already the temperature had fallen below freezing unnoticed by those whose black velvet shawls hung off the backs of their chairs. The room warm by any standard embraced the palm trees nestled at the foot of the stage, while the orchestra played the White Star repertoire and their own interpretation of the renaissance dance quickly followed with a blend of modern day parlour songs; light-hearted and touched with something only Irvin Berlin could have found hidden in the Bowery. There was something in the air, a sense of fun and gaiety, the room filled with conversation broken by the occasional cork popping gush of expectation, dampened momentarily as the waiters champagne etiquette wasted nothing to frivolity or a *head of mousse*. This was World Class dining, the Ritz Restaurant, RMS Titanic, somewhere in the North Atlantic, the finest experience one could have hoped for, the only place to be the big ticket everybody wanted and tonight the realisation that *they*, the privileged, were custodians of a night to remember, blissfully unaware; for those that would survive, it would prove nothing but one they would choose to forget.

The odds weren't great, in fact based on the previous night's performance it was only a matter of time, those having heard it before counting down the moment when his one and only contribution to the evening's debate would make an appearance. Pushing back his chair in anticipation, convinced the table had been squashed against his stomach, Algeron Ollard-Smythe dampened down his temples with the corner of his silk handkerchief, sweating profusely he gulped another glass of Burgundy and waited patiently for his cue slicing what remained of a chocolate éclair with the edge of his spoon used to summon the wine waiter with a civilised tap on the glass. A stocky man, rotund by nature, his chubby red face flush beneath a flop of grey hair, delivering his life's observations without a moment's pause, something about a pocket watch and a woman's place, the latter theme revisited, its slant somewhat different to what might have been imagined.

It was almost upon them, the first of the gentlemen taking their leave, quickly joined by others who'd prefer the company of brandy and cigars to that of their wives. The first class smoking room waiting at the rear of the Promenade deck, walled in Georgian panels inlaid with mother of pearl, a sanctuary for those who would choose it, nothing less than a

Gentleman's Club. The room, a little dark in appearance carried an air of gravitas not unlike a courtroom as seen from the *dock* the last place they'd have wanted to be, but in less than an hour this room would be as vulnerable as the next. The deep leather armchairs, empty from the evening debate, abandoned in front of an open fire, the centrepiece painting *The Approach of The New World* somehow inappropriate as the ship made its way into the harbour, while a fading blue haze settled to no more than a lingering memory.

They'd stay and while away the evening, long enough to discuss what pressing affairs demanded of attention, lost behind Havana cigars swirling cognac in crystal glass balloons, Courvoisier l'esprit or Hennessy Louis XIII, espresso thick and bitter, the perfect balance and sure to repeat. It would end as it began, the topic reverting to something closer to home, the markets past and present with new opportunities out there on the bow. Friendly advice yet to be heeded, facts and figures bandied between statements of mark my words. A recurring theme, percentages mulled over as they analysed the yield, odds yet to be considered, with forty per cent of *their kind* never to see the sunrise or to run a hand through dew covered grass, pick a flower for a loved one left alone in their stateroom; oh if only they had known. The band was in full swing, the tempo slowed to songbook twenty seven, *Mon Coeur S'Ouvre*

À Ta Voix, they could have taken that chance, smelt the perfume in her hair, witnessed the beauty of a smile as she danced across the floor, the pain of love binding them together, entwined in a sea of emotions and none more so than the ocean that would bring sorrow to their door.

****

'Never swim within an hour of eating a meal.'

For some it was time to call it a day. The adage it's tiring doing nothing seemingly holding water, but for most the night was still young. The passageways from the first class restaurant a hive of activity as guests ambled back and forth to the lounge in search of the perfect spot, somewhere to relax away from the thoroughfare, rearranging furniture borrowed to suit, a nod of gratitude here and there they settled back wrapped in sofas and comfortable chairs while waiters in crisp white tunics served night caps of brandy snifters and chocolate mints. Creatures of habit gathered in localised parties spread throughout the room, the lucky ones able to watch the band through the open doors, waiting for the decamp into the lounge. A lone piano already waiting for the ensemble to arrive, the rest of the orchestra playing elsewhere, they'd bring Scot Joplin's ragtime sound to life, the melody augmented with flush instrumentals each player waiting their cue, clarinet and trombone, piccolo and violin, defying each other to bring *it* to life, their reward measured in part by dancing feet hidden beneath the tables, their owners unaware of the *faux pas*, enjoying it for what it was and a chance to set aside the starch, shed the social etiquette and for the briefest of moments be themselves.

She wasn't always *a la mode*, her posture developed over time gave little if anything away, sat alone Emilie Broussard encapsulated everything known to be the French way. Beyond approach, her charm as graceful and refined as the pinot noir in her glass, warm and rich in tone, the perfect contrast to her pale complexion, the wine untouched, it would remain so, much like her dinner cleared away with an elegant acknowledgement so as not to offend. It was impossible to know whether she was enjoying the evening, her beauty as obvious as it was, carried with it an air of confidence of times misconstrued to other adjectives more easily understood. You could see her from the lounge, the first table of the À la Carte restaurant in full view, unwittingly enticing those already infatuated to stare longer than was necessary as they passed the open door. Her gown of white taffeta with the faintest purple wash pulled tight around the waist, a delicate corset tie finished with chiffon across her hips fastened with a tulip clasp, the bodice cut from the shoulder teasing those still blessed with imagination, if not the ability to look without being seen.

She would have joined the ship at Cherbourg, one of the two hundred and seventy four brought out to the roadstead by tender, the first and second class aboard Nomadic, her arrival as likely unnoticed but for the luggage and entourage in her wake. Parisian chic, reinforcing the stereotype of those that would grace the boulevards this spring and, for one night only as she made her way to the lounge, a chance to witness *that* smile, a smile that would ask much more than it would ever be prepared to give, leaving those that had seen it wanting more. A coffee before bed, Emilie watched as the sugar lump dissolved on her spoon, part submerged waiting till it was almost gone before stirring her drink, the evening's *activities* unnoticed by most, now quietly observed with a ruthlessness only charm could ever understand.

'Cherchez la femme' she said beneath her breath, a woman looking everywhere.

It was the honeymoon couple and what they represented playing on her mind, a sense of foreboding unexplained, Emilie Broussard knew better than most that things were not always what they seem. The back streets of Marseille, her instincts borne of a lifetime destined for compromise. She could *feel* something was wrong, something that had dragged the past kicking and screaming to the forefront of her mind, something so horrific it was beyond human comprehension, so gruesome it would bury her secret along with all the rest and unbeknown, in its own way, it would save her from herself forever.

Two strikes in and the only thing moving fast was the ship. The telegraphs set to *full ahead* or thereabouts, cutting through the flat calm at twenty two knots perhaps more. Seventy five and a tad revolutions as if that was going to bring the *feeling* back to frozen *plates of meat*, the new lookouts stamping their feet in a losing battle against the cold. They'd been up there since 22:00 hours, ninety feet in the air, the crow's nest, barely enough room to *swing a cat* and open to a bitter wind now full in the face, the temperature below freezing felt raw as a Sunday with a *head* and by all accounts it was getting worse, the salts saving grace as the sea fell to -3^0 degrees, both men knew they were in for an evening of misery but neither could have known just how right that would prove to be. Their watch was almost an hour gone; relieving Jewell and Hogg they had clambered through the hatch at the base of the foremast, a tight squeeze at the best of times not least in a heavy topcoat. Climbing the ladder up onto the platform, the last words from those they'd relieved a warning to watch out for *bergs* and something about 'Mind they don't drop off' a reference to the *nether regions* which was exactly where they were.

It was almost time, another five minutes to the next strike of the bell at 23:00 hours, six tolls with an 'All's Well!' they'd call from above, neither keen on moving frozen hands buried beneath their armpits; shivering uncontrollably they did their best to shake the worst of it off. It would take more than half an hour to adapt to the night, their eyes streaming in the wind chill blurring everything and anything, the distortion, much like what happened to the binoculars, probably best avoided. A moonless night, clear and crisp, they had both commented on the sea state, a flat calm the like neither had ever seen before, not even a swell to rely upon should anything be out there on the bow and that was it, the clues, every one of them systematically removed with not even the *Ice Blink* to rely upon. The horizon lost to a blackened sky hid the signs already in part drifting on the ocean current down below, thin at first, super cooled the Frazil Ice was starting to form, the early signs of crystallised needles forming platelets as they knitted together, an oily appearance, their initial introduction as to what was to come. Their wait would not be long now and when *it* finally came all the rehearsal in the world would not have made a difference.

262

Porous in construction, the iceberg offered little if any light reflection, reducing the distance from which they would see what death itself looked like waiting in the darkness. The *black* shape coming slowly into focus, still as a rock with an eerie silence that could have drowned out thunder, they'd squint and wipe away the tears from their eyes and peer through faces frozen solid in the wind, beyond the bow of the ship out into the blackened abyss.

Let's call it intuition, the ability to look inside, a general unexplained belief without foundation nagging in the back of the mind, call it what you will Emilie Broussard was not alone in her thoughts.

Out on the open wing bridge, first officer Murdock stood looking out like those above him in the crow's nest. A sense of unease a fair assumption given their situation, his final watch relieving Lightoller at 22:00 who in turn had been advised to rouse the captain 'If it became at all doubtful', as if there was any doubt ploughing into the unknown at full speed in the dead of night with a handful of ice warnings was in any way ambiguous. There was a lot riding on it, a knowing nod passed from one another, some vague attempt to pacify any obvious requirement to slow down to at least have a fighting chance, a pause, perhaps a moment's contemplation. *Top Down* pressure to push on, driving them headlong into the unknown, soon to be replaced with pressure of an altogether different kind; starting at the bottom up, the Tank Top and Orlop deck first to make its acquaintance and by evening's end everyone would have been introduced, but this time it would show scant regard for grace and favour.

It was relentless and with it bore all the hallmarks invisible to those who couldn't see it, no, couldn't feel it, those not dealing with the stress, unlike Phillips still working the Marconi Room alone. He was getting through them, the private messages and commercial traffic, a pile still to be dealt with on his desk, each one in turn tapped out across the air waves while their authors retired to bed, his own prospect of getting some sleep diminishing with every click of the *straight key* leaving the pressure of the last few days to surface momentarily delivering its own unique sign even the untrained could have deciphered. It was almost 23:00 hours, three hours done, three more still to go, the end of his shift felt a lifetime away and on this one occasion unbeknown to him, it would prove to be exactly that. It wasn't the first message received from Cyril Evans aboard the Californian, the radio operator's earlier report of three large icebergs north of Titanic received by Bride and delivered to the bridge and now with their own circumstances conspiring against them Evans would communicate once more. He hadn't planned on the encounter but had he done so he could have hardly expected the response he'd receive. A close shave south of the Grand Banks of Newfoundland, the Californian was stopped and surrounded by ice, her reactions quick enough to avoid a collision but not so as to keep clear of the loose edge to the drift. The decision made to wait it out till morning Captain Lord was about to leave the bridge when spotting a light to the east of their position making enquiries of Evans as to what if any ships were in the vicinity. Evans confirmed 'Only Titanic' and was instructed to make contact and explain what they had intended to do given the circumstance together with a warning regarding the conditions, and that was it. That was all Evans was trying to do, nothing more than was expected given the imminent danger, *where others fear to tread* or at least should, having been given ample warning.

In truth it was just something else to add to what was already a catalogue of disasters, mostly small in nature but when added together would take on a significance all of its own. The message, when it came would carry no MSG, the prefix requiring a response from Titanic prioritising its importance beyond ice warnings received throughout the day; this, compounded by the informality to the transmit, would leave what happened next as nothing more than a *simple twist of fate,* rooted in human frailty and manifest in a moment of pressure, a genuine misunderstanding, the consequence of which would live on forever.

'Shut up! Shut up! Keep out! I'm working Cape Race!'

It wasn't any more than that, it was just the heat of the moment, letting off steam and as uncharacteristic as could have ever been imagined, but for that split second, Phillips had snapped.

He didn't mean it, well in the moment, yes, but not literally, not so as to offend, Phillips was nothing if not professional, it was just a symptom of everything up to that point, the lack of sleep, the constant pressure, the endless stream of messages yet to be sent landing in the basket, none of it was helping the situation and that coupled with something that has plagued us *all* since time immemorial, something that should never be relied upon, *timing*.

Evans couldn't have got it more wrong if he'd tried, his message bursting through Phillips' own transmission with all the force of a freight train. The very fact that both ships were less than nineteen miles apart, their close proximity cranking up the volume in his headset, an unbearable squawk piercing his eardrums as the whole signal bled across the spectrum, impossible to filter out he did what he could as he listened to the broken reply. His own transmission bouncing back from Cape Race, picking out what could be salvaged in the hope of piecing some of it together, cursing the intrusion that had caused his outburst and cursing himself in the process. He hadn't meant to be so abrupt, his response as terse as it was did nothing to ease the frustration, a brief pause to scratch his head and reseat the headphones all in a single move, as if to say 'he'd had enough' and in that moment he probably had. It didn't matter now; it was out there, floating through the airways his rebuke clipped and to the point, leaving no room for interpretation.

It had stopped him dead, Phillips, returning his attention to the wireless and the shore station MCE on Newfoundland, he continued where he'd left off.

'Sorry, please repeat, jammed.'

That was the whole business, Phillips continuing with Cape Race while Evans, unaware if his message had been delivered to the bridge, monitored the situation, well for a while at least, listening out for any further communiqué that would shed some light on the matter, perhaps not directly, perhaps a reference to the situation as he listened in, his own desire to speak with Phillips somewhat tainted if the truth be told, after all, he was only trying to help. He would give it a little longer before turning in. Evans, the only radio operator aboard the Californian, sat in isolation much like Phillips and waited on developments, a wait that would take him to the sound of *Seven Bells* before he'd gather up his things.

Glancing back he caught the flicker of light from the pilot bulb and the sound of a *voice* fading to a gentle hiss, switching off the equipment at 23:00, he closed the door on the radio room and with it, any possible hope they'd have to survive.

Chapter Eighteen

On any other night it would have gone unnoticed, her emotions held on a tight lead, Emilie Broussard had never allowed herself the luxury of self-pity.

She needed no explanation, it was already amongst them, she could smell *its* presence as if *it* were stood by her side, a shiver as cold as the North Atlantic crawled across her flesh, its final touch like death itself inviting her to stay. They couldn't see it, couldn't feel anything as it walked amidst them through the room, a gentle kiss, the elderly woman pulled up her shawl that had slipped from her shoulder, its significance lost to conversation and laughter. She could see the injustice, not only for herself but for everyone, like lambs to the slaughter, unaware their evening was about to take a very different path and while they didn't know it, they were already *walking through the valley of the shadow of death.*

It was like shouting but without a single sound having left her mouth, waiting on something to happen, she watched as the young couple meandered back to their cabin, arms linked like a wishbone soon to be broken. She could visualise their final moments, her anger welling up inside as they said their last goodbye. The absurdity of suppression despite the gravity affecting how they'd part, his sense of duty borne of a marriage but eight days old, overpowering everything but the fear that was surging through his body, as real as his love for her and as equally terrifying. She could hear the creak of the davits as the lifeboat hung precariously over the side, his wife's tears disguised by the bitter cold fell silent as the order came to lower away, their lives, over before they had started, stolen by circumstance, only to end in a stifled and awkward denial of public affection, *stiff upper lip* had a lot to answer for.

'Tell him you love him! Tell him now before it's too late! Can't you see this is your only chance?! Tell him! Tell him or you will regret it for the rest of your life!'

Regret was something she had learnt to despise along with those who'd taken her newly born daughter in the early hours of the morning; taken forever and with it, the shame.

There wasn't a day went by when she didn't think of her, where she was, what she was doing, was she still in France. *Le Scandale*, covered up and wrapped like her child as they bundled her away. Late Sunday evening, much like now, the door latch closing, voices beneath her window, a strangers footsteps echoing down the narrow alleyways, leaving nothing but ten years lost to the darkness, a life filled with empty distractions, memories that for the most part lay buried and undisturbed. But not now, whatever *this* was, whatever was about to happen, she knew it would touch her, no *them*, in such a way as was unimaginable and for some, like her, they'd be set free from the shackles of remorse, while for others their sentence would have only just begun.

Emilie Broussard finished what was left of her coffee placing the cup and saucer down on the table; a glance around the lounge before gathering up her bag, twisting the kiss clasp she rummaged in search of the key to her room and returned a silver match box in the process. It was quieter now, a scattering of tables still intent on having fun, while others, like those before her, were in the process of leaving. Out through the double doors next to the À la Carte restaurant, past the grand staircase she would make her way down the passageway on the starboard side, her stateroom the fifth suite on the right, a distance counted in yards but long enough for her to make the comparison. The finality of it, the image of the table deserted after dinner, dead chairs pushed askew beneath a white cotton cloth hanging dishevelled part way to the floor. A silver candelabra, its base splattered in hot wax that had dripped persistently throughout the night, the centrepiece to what was probably a wonderful evening enjoyed by those who'd graced its table, those now safely tucked up in bed. Emilie stood outside her door, pausing for a moment while she opened the lock, the corridor abandoned but for the distant sound of laughter echoing from the stairwell mingled with the contrast of silence. It should have been a pleasant thought, replaced instead by something the origin of which was understood only by that written in a *book*, from just outside the old walled city, *The Room of the Last Supper* and tonight, as she closed the door behind her, she was quite sure that for many who had dined at that table it would prove to be exactly that.

****

There was something of a false truthfulness about it, the sky blackened by an absent moon still truant from the night before, cold and still it would reveal not a single gasp or fidget.

There was no given method, scanning left to right in quarter breaks each section scrutinised before moving on, out across the bow nothing but darkness and the smell of isolation to ponder. The banality interrupted momentarily with what appeared to be a distant light low on the portside, it disappeared into the black expanse and hid behind the curtain waiting for the final act, proving nothing more than a walk on part in what was about to unfold. They'd squint once more, both men's faces scrunched against the weather, each hunkered down in the nest out of the wind and in contrast to the water down below, eerily still it sat beneath an icy haze reluctant at first to give up its secret, adrift in open water and floating on the ocean current, death but comes on an ebbing tide.

With not so much as breaking foam, *its* outline slipped slowly into view, silently edging closer in peaceful stillness. A rock carved of ice and with it the strangest aura and sense of serenity reserved for those envied from afar. *Her* beauty impossible to deny, she came without malice or intent, stealing the sound of eight bells. She'd leave nothing but the euphemism for those whose loved ones would refer, the reading delivered from high in the altar, written up their obituaries recording them done, time and date, their demise scrawled with flourish of hand in blackened ink, each column inch a capsule biography to be read, *her* description best left to the living, after all, almost none would have made her acquaintance.

It was short and sweet, the third toll still ringing as he made the call to the bridge, straight and to the point the question came, 'What do you see?' said Moody.

'Iceberg right ahead!' came the reply from Fleet.

'Thank you!'

That was it, nine words would complete the whole exchange and unbeknown to them, the entire event would be written into the pages of history and, quite literally, frozen in time.

****

'No, she thought it was a map of the Sahara desert not the sandpaper, she bought the sandpaper thinking, oh forget it!' he said, shaking his head in disbelief, another wasted story, Harry disappointed it required further explanation but then with Albert, well, he was used to that.

'Butt me!' he said taking the open pack of cigarettes from off the table not waiting on a reply, some things are expected and that was one of them; their friendship, as solid as *her* double bottom hull forged in steel, had stood the test of time, the pair of them like an old married couple.

'One more brew before we go', Albert offering to 'Get them in', he was already standing by the time he'd finished the question, neither bothered either way, it would pass the twenty minutes or so before their shift. If he'd yawned once it must have been a dozen times, rubbing his eyes he sat beneath a haze of blue smoke staring vacant across the dining room floor, smudging the spilt milk off the edge of the table and into his hand, the plan ill-conceived, there was nothing else for it but to wipe it in his britches, an indiscretion safe enough with the graveyard shift, it wouldn't matter anyway, seen or not, he was about to be saved by the bell. He had almost made it back to the table, mugs of steaming tea one in each hand, Albert's face a picture of concentration before he'd set the first of them down. Harry poised for damage limitation, watched with amusement as his cack-handed friend spun the mug back to front, oblivious to clumsy invitation sharing his awkwardness seen through left handed eyes, dexterity aside, not even Albert could be blamed for what happened next.

It wasn't much more than a nudge in the back, Albert's balance broken by a single step widened his stance like an old sea dog, his *good* leg anchored to the floor while the rest of him lunged for the table. Cursing the *lag*, his instincts quick but not enough to stop his tea from slopping over the lip and dripping on his boots, both feet shaking as the steel deck quivered beneath him, the sensation drowned out by the strangest of noise. Like grinding metal dragged down *her* side, screeches of contorted pain, its high pitch cry silenced for a second, returning with a vengeance, bouncing down the hull with each glancing blow like nothing either had ever heard or felt before.

They waited for the rebound, staring at each other mouths agog, each void filled with the peculiar impression something had passed beneath them, scraping the underside and jarring as it went, a shudder releasing them on their way, *she* heeled to port while they watched the whole room twist gently out of shape*, springing back,* it was over before it begun, ten seconds maybe less, every strike down the starboard side, each impact landing further aft, knocking them up, *it* had found a path to their door and, for the most part, the introduction would pass barely noticed.

'What the bloody hell was that?!' Albert said, shaking hot tea from his hand.

'That, Albert, was the sound of bad news!'

'What do you mean? Have we lost a prop or something? Perhaps an anchor?!' repeating the comments and murmurs of those around him.

'No, I don't think so, but if it's what I think it is, we may well have lost our way home!'

****

If he was tired before, he was showing no sign of it now, Harry literally threw himself across the room and pressed his face hard against the porthole glass, shielding his one good eye, the other scrunched tight as he peered into the darkness.

'What's out there? What do you see?'

Harry narrowed his eyes straining downstream aft of where they stood, cursing the freezing glass for sticking to his face, wiping it clear it made no difference to the outcome; whatever it was, it had gone.

'Nothing Albert, I can't see a thing, if we'd hit another ship I'd have seen her lights, it's just pitch black out there, it can only be ice.'

Harry tugged on Albert's sleeve and nodded simultaneously pointing with his head, steering him out of ear shot where they could talk, the noise and vibration of engines running full astern had fallen silent, replaced in part by passengers spilling into the corridors on E deck. It would all come clear soon enough, those still in the dining room milling about, each talking over the other in a bid to be heard, their own version of events much the same as the last and none showing any regard for danger.

Five hundred yards or thereabouts, that was all the warning they had, both men on the bridge thrown in the deep end when the call had come, they'd barely had more than thirty seconds to coax her around, their terrifying sequence well-rehearsed, took no account for a rudder incapable of such deflection, woefully inefficient, her lumbering tonnage showed little interest if any in getting out of the way. It wasn't as if they didn't try, the engine telegraphs set to stop before pulling full astern, Murdoch's calls 'Hard a Starboard' saw the Quartermaster frantically turning the wheel, his own acknowledgment to the task shouted loudly above the alarm now ringing in his ears. Murdoch pulling the lever to release the hydraulic system holding up the watertight doors, sliding down the tracks, the cast iron promise sealed by gravity and settled by arrestors on the floor and as for those close enough to hear the thud, the offer of nothing but false hope. Watch and wait that was all that was left to do. Up in the crow's nest their job was done, both men completely helpless as they watched it unfold, played out in slow motion, the bow shifting a point maybe two, teasing every fibre in their bodies, willing it on they had shouted and screamed at *her* lazy response, braced for impact, in itself as misleading as any a sideswipe, leaving the steel plates staved below the waterline with nothing but puncture holes of truth.

It was a hopeless task and they knew it, the decision made soon enough to port the helm and swing the stern away from danger, and in so much as that was the intention they had achieved it. Unaware at that very moment water was pouring in through open seams, the flesh wound of steel plate ripped apart as rivets sheared like buttons sliced from a coat, each impact buckling the hull crushed against a solid wall of ice, hundreds of thousands of tons rising up from the surface, sixty feet or more and washed in a warm amber glow, the ships lights thrown across *her* face found little beauty as she drifted off the stern and slipped into the shadows.

They were starting to stir, it had taken a while to sink in, most having retired for the evening but as the minutes passed, more and more would make an appearance.

'What's happening?'

'What's all the fuss? Why have the engines stopped?'

'Excuse me? Could you tell me what's going on? Why the commotion?'

Up and down the corridors bleary eyes peered out from behind closed doors, like rabbits from their warrens one after the other, heads on stalks twisted in both directions as others scurried back and forth in search of answers. It wasn't the noise that had woken them, it wasn't the impact that had thrown them from their beds or the passive violence that lurked beneath the North Atlantic as they shuffled up and down the passageways in slippered feet, no, it wasn't that, what had brought them here was nothing but the sound of silence. No not now, there was noise enough now and colourful too, all manner of dressing gowns, pyjamas and other apparel, faces blotched with night cream stripped of makeup, stripped of everything, faces reserved only for those close enough to share their darkness, their reality and here they were, out for all to see, stood beneath the spotlight, a naked vulnerability etched into the moment, its poignancy unnoticed much like the lines concealed beneath tired eyes. The engine's song as reassuring as it was unconsciously heard, its gentle hum sung in low tones vibrating up through the decks and felt by every soul whose head lay upon a pillow, a lullaby of comfort shut down, they had awoken to the aftermath and unbeknown slept through the most fateful few seconds of their lives.

It would prove the perfect alibi, the usual suspects still drinking in the Palm Court, unaware of the kerfuffle down below. They'd heard the fuss, well more like *felt* it, the brandy glasses quivered on the table as she recoiled off *her* side, twisting under it and springing back, whip like she shuddered beneath an avalanche of ice, dislodged on inpact, two tons maybe more strewn across the forward decks and back towards the bridge, another shift landing on the promenade. For the inquisitive it was enough to leave their drinks, as good a diversion as any, tomorrow's conversation and a chance to make her acquaintance, a handful at first joined by others from the bar, their evening attire little defence against the bitter cold as it swept across the weatherboard, the open deck desolate but for her *calling card* and the crunch beneath their feet.

It was as if they had to do something with it, a compulsory response when they saw it scattered across the floor, chunks of ice, grubby white against the wooden deck broken into a thousand pieces like confetti left on the chapel steps, the *service* over and the only visible sign of what had taken place, those venturing out left in the lurch with their awkwardness as to what to do next. Some picked it up brushing it off, connecting with the absurdity held in their hands, out of place and like them out of character, slipping back to a childhood moment when inhibition knew nothing of self-inflicted boundaries, a lesson learned from those down below, their impromptu snowball fight as natural as the laughter echoing across the open deck, a painful reminder driven home by the slamming of a door, leaving nothing but insecurity and the cut of a good suit. They had missed *her,* the caller dressed in white and with it the opportunity just for a moment to let go, most throwing the ice back to the floor suppressing the urge to lob it clean over the side. One last chance to find themselves, one last chance before they'd face the truth, regret was waiting in the darkness, the real and unspoken tragedy most would take with them to the grave.

Back inside the majority had forgone the excitement, unaware of the upshot to the evening's activity, they'd finish off and make their way back, each stateroom rendered a different version of events as the story unfolded, embellished to suit the circumstance and *mood,* most still unaware something greater than a late night excuse was developing beneath them. *Menace* had come with a quickening step, her visit paid, she had left without so much as a by-your-leave, satisfied the contrast to *silence* would soon increase by a single word, deathly, and all that that entailed. Slowly but surely the chit chat would increase, a hum of excitement its tone changing when the penny dropped, drifting up the stairwells as groups gathered in conflab exchanging what little, if anything, they'd been told. Sleeping babies awoken by the kerfuffle cried beneath the glaring lights while mothers tried in vain to comfort them, a world left for gentle slumber now shocked back to *life* and intuitive of their surroundings, no longer crying wolf, their sense of danger as sharp as the ice that sliced *her* side and as yet both unnoticed. They would plead with them to quieten down, mothers not wishing to irritate those nearby, ushered the rest of their brood along, while Scotland Road slowly filled, families joined those loitering in the corridors waiting for news, pacifying their tired bundles, a chore soon to be stolen forever, along with something as equally mundane, their lives.

It was twenty minutes short of twelve when the log book entry was made. *Her* little visit barely more than a glance and already she had caused a stir, the price to be paid for a *midnight kiss* soon to be counted as the ship's carpenter confirmed flooding at the bow. They'd verify it soon enough, Smith and Thomas Andrews their post inspection chinwag enough to settle it, but for now, the tally was all but over, her starboard list slowly evident and witnessed by ungainly compensation as the last ten minutes collected payment on account, it was 11:50 and the damage done, leaving nothing but an awkward tilt and 14 feet of seawater above the keel.

'Shut the dampers! Shut the dampers!'

That was it, that was all the time they had, both engineers talking by the passage aft of the boiler room as confused as the rest of them when the telegraphs rang to stop. It wasn't like they could question it, bellowing across the filthy floor at the stokers to get them shut; their conversation over, they would barely have time to return to their stations, each checking the illuminations on the wall, the order down from the bridge to the starting platform, like faith it would have to be placed somewhere. A lifetime at sea and never before had either seen the call to stop, both men running back in disbelief as much as anything, the ship in mid ocean passage, close to midnight and closer still to something beyond her steel plate.

You could see it in their eyes, the uncertainty, it was only for a second before something kicked in, overcoming every instinct to wait and see, hoping upon hope that others would step up while the comfort of procrastination blurred the moment, their validation, arriving quick to order amidst alarm bells competing with the roar of the furnace. Blackened faces blinked beneath soiled cloth caps, the *Black Gang*, the first to feel the fear settle in the nape of the neck, waiting on the impact and waiting on their fate as the watertight door hung menacingly above the frame, their escape in full view beyond the thickened steel, tugging on every sinew to make a dash nullified only by the shouts and screams, part direction most part warning the second engineer finding something from within, call it instinct, call it what you will, either way when he barked his instruction it had kept them rooted to the floor, each man looked about the room, their cold sweat the only clue as to how they were feeling and all they could ask that it wouldn't give them away.

'All hands stand by your stations! All hands stand....'

There wasn't enough time to repeat it, not before the warning light flashed above the door. Another bell ringing out the danger pierced every fibre left in tack, each stoker's dread adding to the tension before the first twitch of gravity pulled on the mechanism. Slipping from the friction clutch, tons of cast iron grinding on the teeth that had held *it* back, the way out pleading with them not to wait, its gaping mouth the door slowly falling closed, their hopes pinned on something if not what they'd waited for, a higher grace, entrusted to others, those that had flicked the switch in the wheelhouse or on the bridge, those unlike the men stood helpless on the footplate, those on the Tank Top at the bow of the ship, those like Archie Mullins in boiler room six.

Nothing could prepare them for what came next. Their wait over, the doors of hell bursting open as *she* hit the side, the impact, brutal like a hammer blow to the head, flooding the boiler room with the sound of thunder. An almighty crash the like of which was beyond comprehension, throwing everything into chaos and most to the floor, the noise as horrendous as Satan's laugh, its high pitched screech like a million chains being dragged across the twisting metal plate, grinding each seam into submission, the steel buckling, it crumpled like the faces of the men, etched in fear and blackened coal they were as helpless as the ship itself.

Archie wrapped both arms around his head, burying himself beneath his safety blanket as he cowered in the corner, the coal stack shifting above, he tried in vain to fend it off as it tumbled down, the foot of the pile his only refuge he lay petrified as the amber glow from the tunnel flickered on and off. Terror stricken he watched through scrunched up eyes the whole floor flexing in violent bursts, each second a lifetime as she rode her luck, riveted plate ripped apart like paper mache, bucking up, raking against the twisted bulkhead, below the waterline her beauty deformed, exposing an open gash as she ran the ice ledge, her body punctured with each stabbing blow, peeled back like a tin can, her under belly as vulnerable as the next. Every hair on his body stood on end, every nerve consumed with fear he clung spread eagled to the floor, pressing his face in coal dust and the sweat dripping from his nose. It was like he was dreaming, a nightmare, he was watching the wheel of his upturned barrow spinning like the roll of a dice, his fate hanging in the balance, willing it on, willing it to land on a *six*, his every fibre desperate to escape the deafening roar engulfing everything and everyone. *Her* cries of pain as wretched as any as the blows moved aft, each strike inflicting damage unseen by all but those who would *bear the brunt,* those whose lives were yet to be taken when *Holds* one and two caved in. A flesh wound open and defenceless to the freezing waters pouring through the mangled steel, engulfing the space, submerged it spread like a cancer as it climbed the walls, her bow heavier now in every sense, while those aft of boiler room six still unaware of the flooding already taking place. Their own knock soon to come and nothing more than where they stood when the *visitor* came, and for many they were just too close to the *door*.

He could barely lift his head, the whole event witnessed from beneath a sleeve, blurred in a mist of vapour, coal dust and emergency lights, the pitch black bunker a sanctuary to what was beyond the open door. Shouts and screams, drowning in their own panic from across the tunnel floor, a desperate voice overlaid with pleading anguish distorted to a slow motion drawl, deep in tone and mingled in blood shot red, each burning lantern washing the walls down to the footplate and, for the briefest of moments, nothing less than a river of blood. The whole floor was moving, those still standing cut off at the knees by a salty foam, a foot maybe two, wading between the fireboxes, spitting venom from open mouths as the boiler room filled with steam, his gaze fixed on burning coals piercing the mist, adding to the pandemonium only those condemned could testify, those like him, those that had missed the closing of the watertight doors.

It was clearer now, like a film removed from his eyes, what he'd seen and the voices inside his head, back in sync the words making sense or something like it, the man was calling to his friend, calling him out to leave before it's too late, the boiler room abandoned, he could see the icy water flooding the passageway, swilling through the entrance to the bunker where he lay, the man's cries fading to nothing as Archie's fragile consciousness played its final trick.

'Run man! Get out of there! Leave it Francis, leave it now!'

Archie could hear the words hanging in the air, as the claw of the water reached out to smother him, beyond the tunnel his escape blocked by a cast iron door, The North Atlantic gushing in through every crevice. He clambered further up the stack, dazed and confused he watched what appeared to be a black linen sack sloping back and forth against the wall, its resistance futile as the water rose, lifting it off the footplate and carried toward him on the midnight tide, the corridor deserted but for the lifeless body of Francis Rickman, the ultimate confirmation that *he* didn't heed the advice.

He would have sat there forever, clutching his knees to his chest and gulping at the fear that had settled in the back of his throat. His hands shaking uncontrollably he wedged his boots deeper into the coal for resistance, pushing against it in an effort to get away, the water slopping around the stack, swirling into circles as the current from below forced the ocean into the bunker, under pressure and rising faster now climbing the walls and engulfing everything in its way, not least every rational thought that he had. It was as if it was happening to someone else, the realisation brought home as *it* passed the open doorway, adrift, his body rolling over in the swell, not the whole way but just enough to catch the side of his face, Francis Rickman, *Ricky*, shy of twenty and someone Archie had made as a friend, his acquaintance, much like him, short lived. It was difficult to tell, perhaps the shock of seeing him, his dead eyes staring up as they broke the surface, or perhaps the banging on the watertight doors, it didn't matter, not now, either way, it had brought him back to his senses.

'Archie?! Archie Mullins?! Can you hear me Archie?!'

It was like his head was exploding, the noise unbearable, crushing every attempt he made at thinking straight, *his* name called out mingled with the sound of rushing water forced through open seams, the mangled hull and impromptu waterfalls, a deluge flooding back from boiler room six and into the bunkers further aft. He had to move and move fast, back up the passageway toward the torrent, a bolt from the blue, and the realisation this was his only way out. Sinking at the bow, there was nowhere else to go, not for him, not for any of them still capable of climbing the emergency ladder. Archie would never know what took a hold, the strength he found from within, the will to live, the images of Charlie selling his papers, his mother and Will sat at the kitchen table squabbling over something of nothing; images flashing across his mind of *Ricky*, barely four hours past, smiling and waving as he crossed the dining room floor, a parting joke he left Archie to finish his tea and disappeared at the far end of the room. That was the last he saw of him, heading for the metal stairways that zigzagged all the way from B deck to the bottom, the vertical shaft housed like a test tube and the perfect vessel to settle the odds. Flooding now, but not when he skipped them, two at a time, his footsteps the last he would take, three down from F deck to his four hour shift, never late, always respectful, Archie's final thoughts of him stealing what breath he had left. He could hear him singing as he shovelled the coal, making up the words long since forgotten, *holding a tune*, if not his head, as his body floated down the passageway. Archie waded past, unable to look at him again, unable to comprehend that the obstacle, washed up in filth and slurry by the ash ejector door, was his friend; his earlier anecdote hanging above him like a cartoon bubble, 'knock

knock, who's there?...', Archie broke down before he got to the punch line.

He could hear him screaming through the watertight door, his fist slamming side on against the cast iron wall, each dull thud lost in the mayhem as he bellowed out his name. Panic stricken, his voice unable to hide the terror overwhelming every fibre of his body, each strike pleading to be heard, Lyle Benson pressed his head against the cold metal bulkhead, knuckles split and bleeding, he wiped them into his vest, battered and bruised the stains of blood and grease unnoticed as he awaited a reply.

He tried again.

'Archie?! Archie Mullins?! Can you hear me? Archie, get yourself out of there, get to the ladder Archie, do it now, quickly, do it now!'

It was all he could do to stand, Lyle slapped the flat of his palm against the solid door, slamming it helplessly to the metal, unyielding the *slap* like a pistol shot, he clutched at his head, 'Think, think!' shouting out, the *pitch* of the floor falling slowly at the bow.

'Make your way to the ladder Archie! Get out now! I'll climb it from this side. Do it! If you can hear me, do it now!'

Archie tried to reply, opening his mouth the words refusing to leave, gasping for breath he pulled himself along the passageway, the water waist high, his britches and boots heavy as lead weighing him down, clinging to both walls for leverage, cursing the lack of handrails as he went, each step calling out a name, talking to himself, answering his demands, 'That's it Archie! One step at a time, keep going now you're almost there.'

At first he thought it was something that he'd done. The final look across his shoulder, the one he'd promised not to make, he had made it to the boiler room door, his silhouette a crucifix, clinging on, his tiny frame as feeble as his chances, holding him up, knees buckling he could feel the water start to lift him off the floor, pulling himself through with barely a chance to look around or take in what or who was left behind before the banging stopped. Stood alone, petrified, he could see the ladder across the way, the lower rungs already lost to the freezing water, his *choice* as stark as it was vivid and as brutal as his life had always been, Archie was staring at his future, at least he was until the lights went out.

It was scarcely a second, thrown into darkness, the whole boiler room still visible in the back of his eyes, fading slowly the amber shapes a last ditch attempt to grapple with the obstacles between him and the prize. Archie's realisation, just when you think it can't get worse, his reminder, like the lid placed on an open box, trapped inside the blackened room as terrifying a moment as any he could share, jelly legged, one foot before another, watching as the overhead lighting flickered on and off, each illumination a clue to the maze, each hazard threatening to end *it* there, some like the *visitor* lurking beneath the surface, waiting for the moment, the stumble from which he'd never recover. It wasn't the distance, in truth he could have made it had the lights stayed off, the layout of the room familiar enough, four double ended boilers set abreast, six furnaces apiece, mostly closed, some abandoned with doors hung open, glowing cherry red the burning coals throwing light across the water, each fire box waiting for their time to come, doused out forever, Archie swearing at their insistence on being heard to the end as he passed each one, pulling himself along by the poke rods, tip toes now, it was almost ready to take him. Pulling off his jacket he set it adrift, gulping back a lungful of air and steam, the force of the water pushing up through the open seams, the footplate lost forever beneath the icy water. He could feel it climbing up his body inch at a time, colder now, his breath, short and sharp as if it was his last, consuming him with every passing second, holding his neck above the parapet, the greenish fate, broken by a salty foam, its quiet insistence filling the room from below. Archie launched himself into it, arms flailing, something like a front crawl, something like his memory falling from the pier at Mayflower Park, his friend, Drippin, yelling instructions from the Quay. 'That's it Archie, left arm over, now the right, keep kicking, keep kicking!', he could see Drippin running to the water's edge, see his panic stricken face, pulling off his shoes and clambering down the boulders to fish him out. Archie could barely hold his thoughts together, a mouthful of water bringing him back from the past, coughing and spluttering his way to the ladder, panting uncontrollably his chest heaving with it, clinging on to the metal rung he wiped the sopping hair from off his face and tightened his grip on the iron bar, a momentary pause, while copper cables hanging from a wall *shorted out* in spectacular fashion leaving him cowering terrified beneath a shower of sparks and luminous flashes exaggerated when the lighting failed once more. With his arm through the loop, he caught his breath, his boot already searching for that leg up, stabbing out beneath the freezing water, he could feel the relief as the iron rung nestled in the arch of his foot, but none more so as when Lyle Benson shone a lamp down into boiler room six.

He didn't see him at first, holding the lamp into the darkness, the light, weak at best, skimmed the surface as he waved the lantern from side to side, one arm clinging onto the bulkhead the other hanging free, his body balanced across the iron girder, Lyle Benson almost slipped and joined him catching sight of Archie's head.

Down below, fifteen feet maybe more, Archie clung to the ladder like a drowned rat on the river bank, his chin resting on his knuckles, peering up from the gloom of the boiler room floor. Pallid faced, vacant but for the fear of god he craned toward the glow as best he could, petrified of moving, his whole body paralysed rigid with the thought of *it*. The shaft of light passing overhead, washing the walls with something close to hope as the shadows danced around his head and shoulders; bracing his back against the ridge and baulk, he looked for all the world as helpless as to wait for the water to take him. Exhausted and all but done, the swirls on the surface, rounding on him, were visible more by the sounds pushing up from the plate as Lyle strained beyond the hopeless burn of gaslight to see his friend. Leaning into the blackness, his arm pulling on its socket he held the light firm and true above the rising water and watched as Archie did something only he could have possibly done, his response, summoned despite all that had happened, something that would stay with Lyle Benson forever, the moment his friend broke into a smile.

'Archie! Archie up here! It's Lyle Archie! You're safe! You're safe!'

Lyle choked on the words and shouted into the darkness. Clattering the ladder as he struggled with the lantern, the noise enough to wake the dead. Shuffling on his belly, he hauled the first of his legs over the side, scrabbling in the gloom as he slid off the edge, feeling his way and taking his weight with a *testing* stamp void of all trust. Pausing for a moment he placed the lantern close to the hatchway door and dangled from the ledge, the flame close to his face, he scrunched the effects from his eyes and lowered himself away, the ladder flexing back and forth beneath each step, stopping to wipe the sweat from his brow, hollering aloud as much to comfort himself, stifling back the pungent smell of sea water, if not the urgency and the realisation that whatever happened next, they were down there on their own.

Chapter Nineteen

Harry and Albert had watched like the rest of them as the chaos unfolded into something close to farcical, their own shift just minutes away they'd never made it down to the boiler room floor, stopped on the stairwell with others heading for the midnight run, all sent packing out of harm's way back up to F deck to wait for news. The canteen all but full, they could barely hear themselves speak, the atmosphere changing quickly when the truth drifted up from below. Both men squeezed through the huddle in the doorway and out onto the corridor, pushing past the throng now blocking the narrow passageway that ran abeam the aft engine casing and a wall of steel lockers jutting out into what little space was left, shouting above the din they weaved their way toward the bakery, past the Engineers' Quarters heading for the third class dining, Harry ushering Albert along, the severity of the situation as yet to reach his feet.

'Come on Albert, get a move on! Let's get back up front and see what's going on for ourselves!'

Tugging on Albert's jacket, Harry pulled him down the passageway against the tide of dishevelled passengers, complete families shuffling noisily as they went, children crying, some carried, some barely awake, the older ones in charge while parents did their best to hide worried expressions as they passed, bickering couples arguing amongst other things as to what they'd left behind. Harry watched as one man sent back by his wife to check their cabin door, a face like thunder, she stood aside to let them through, Albert muttered beneath his breath, 'Rather you than me' as the man came past, one arm in his top coat the other clinging to his life jacket, a life worth saving as if anything but time would tell.

It had all but gone unnoticed. The first twenty minutes or so without so much as an explanation as to why they had stopped, each account conflicting with the next, every steward doing his best to improvise as they made their way down the corridors, each cabin, *knocked up,* the urgency now impossible to hide, undermining the message to 'Stay calm' and 'Don't be alarmed', the parting comment to 'Wrap up warm, its bitter cold tonight' left hanging in the air, that, together with their life jackets pulled from closets and thrown across the bed, the final instructions 'Get them on' doing nothing to help the cause.

He'd never noticed them before, the huge fans whirling in their casing wedged between the Stewards' Mess and the Bakery, right across from the third class galley where Archie introduced his mate, Sammy or Samuel, he couldn't much remember other than he seemed a good'un, but now with the engines stopped the sound of the blades made eerie listening. It wasn't like it was quiet, there was enough going on all right, no, it was just that the drone from down below had gone and for the first time tonight Harry realised that it wasn't coming back. It must have shown on his face, the pair of them stood by the pantry doors, Albert propped himself in the corner and fell on his haunches his knees creaking badly as he sprung to a stop. Cadging a butt from Harry he took a long deep drag and pulled some tobacco from the tip of his tongue, pausing just long enough to catch his eye, his face pulled into something close to a knowing smile in need of practice, more of a grimace, the type used only with a tilt of the head, the type that asks for nothing but the truth.

'How long have we known each other Albert? No, don't answer that. I know, it feels like a lifetime.'

That was Harry's opening line, and in truth had he stopped right there it would have been enough for Albert.

Sliding down the opposite wall, both men crouched at the end of the walkway, close to the third class dining room but far enough back so as others could pass, back and forth they watched the endless stream of people aimlessly going nowhere as much in response to doing nothing as anything else, the same faces returning having made their way to the exits only to be redirected back down the stairs. Their turn would come, as it would for some of those asleep in open steerage when the *visitor* came, one floor down on G deck, those whose bodies would soon be washed up in the foot well outside the Post Office door, the *queue,* as orderly as any they'd have stood in, waiting to be *delivered*, but much like the millions of letters already lost to the North Atlantic, they too would never see the light of day.

It felt as if he was the only one to know, watching the restraint of those around him as they made their way, the third class dining rooms filling quickly, they'd become the only source of information, such that it was. Harry watched the toing and froing while Albert finished his fag, the passageways on F deck already teeming much like upstairs on Scotland Road, the main thoroughfare full of families all in search of the same thing, an explanation, some kind of answer, something other than 'stay calm, keep warm', anything in truth that would shed some light as to why they were all trussed up with a chest full of *cork*. The life jackets, cumbersome if not downright bulky, worn like a tunic and strapped around the waist, six squares stuffed into a canvass sack, tied off twice, they were for all the world as useless as the benefit of hindsight, much like the regret to steam ahead at twenty two knots. Harry chose his moment, the pair of them watching as a couple argued as to how it should be tied, 'That's it! Now wrap it around you again and tie the front!'... he didn't bother, instead he gave her a sideways glance and sighed, as much to say do you have to humiliate me, tugging on the hem of the jacket, straightening it up, as if any of it would matter.

'Look at the poor bastard! It's not enough he'll be dead within twenty minutes of hitting the water, she wants him to look good!'

'Do you know the sad thing Albert, most of '*em* will break their necks in the fall, that cork ain't going under for anyone, if the water don't kill him, then as sure as night follows day that jacket will.'

And that was the moment the penny dropped, Albert stubbed his cigarette into the floor, twisting it to make a point, blowing a haze of blue smoke into the air, he took off his cap, never once offering a single glance, picking at the label sewn inside as if not looking up would somehow change the outcome.

'Do you think we're all but done for?'

'It can't be that serious Harry; they'd be moving this lot off wouldn't they?'

'It wasn't like we've hit anything full in the face, Christ they said she's unsinkable!'

'Listen to me Albert, I don't rightly know what's going on, all I know is something ain't right, look at '*em* in their jackets, forty minutes ago most of '*em* were in bed and there's no good reason to knock '*em* up for the hell of it. No, whatever this is Albert, it won't end pretty so you and me would do as well to get used to it. Christ it's minus four in that water, it's only the salt keeping it from freezing and you know as well as anyone....' he didn't get a chance to finish his sentence and even if he had it could have never had the same effect as to what happened next. No one could have prepared them for the scream that echoed up the corridor, a single cry as harrowing and as raw as to stop them in their tracks, the sense of anguish amongst those that had heard it rooting them to the floor, the wail fading to an eerie silence, they stood outside the dining room, colour draining from faces etched in fear, the realisation despite what they'd been told, lives were now in danger and like it or not they too were a long way from home. It was without dissension, the silence broken en masse by the overwhelming sound of panic, those in earshot reacting to what they'd heard, staring down the passageway back toward the cry, the sound of footsteps followed by a dullish thud, another hatch door closing, sealing her up and one last attempt to cut off at the pass, the warning clear enough but

302

disguised from all who would hear it, unlike Harry who was already back on his feet.

'Ok Albert, whatever happens now let's stick together! We'll have a better chance, such as it maybe, if we do, besides, I'm not telling your missus I left you, Christ I'd rather take *me* chances here! Now let's get forward and see for ourselves.'

For everyone on board, their turning point would come, the gravity of what was happening slowly dawning, Harry could sense it, no, feel it physically changing those around him, for some the tension spilling over into anger, while others seemed oblivious to the significance of what they'd been told. Families gathered in small groups around dining room tables strewn with top coats and paraphernalia as mothers wrapped life jackets in spare clothing for makeshift pillows, their children, some fast asleep despite the noise, huddled together on benches while parents kept one eye on the growing crowd gathered by the door. In truth it was difficult to tell what people were thinking, some calm others not, their final meeting place the dining room amidships spanning more than a hundred feet across the beam, a mushroom cloud of W*oodbine* smoke as thick as a blank expression filled the air, gathering up all those beneath it, once strangers, no longer so, speaking freely, they helped each other cope as babies cried in sympathy and hapless fathers went in search of news.

It wouldn't stay like this for long, the din growing with every passenger that had made their way aft, several hundred maybe more, their mood darker now as the fear settled like nausea in the back of the throat, ever present, its persistence overpowering any positive thought as to how the night would unfold. Exposed to the bitter cold and packed off into open life rafts, hours maybe days waiting to be rescued, the very detail too unbearable to contemplate, those with children beside themselves with worry, but they needn't have, their anguish nothing more than a match struck upon a box, quick to burn and soon to fade away.

Harry wasn't one to hang around, it was as much to find out for himself, offering a helping hand to Albert he pulled him to his feet and gave a nod as if to say follow me. The pair of them headed down the passageway around past the bakery and the third class galley, Sammy, only yesterday stocking the pantry adjacent to the dining rooms, the same pantry, the decision made this trip would be his last; Albert instinctively tried the door, a gift horse in the mouth, 'Worth a try' he muttered, and followed Harry as he cut through the rank and file. 'All dressed up and nowhere to go' Albert called ahead, zigzagging the four hundred and seventy *covers,* half as many empty seats taken up with bags and *what not* destined to be left behind, their owners oblivious to the fact that, on this one occasion, they were never to be parted.

'Move your ass Albert! I'm telling you this deck is definitely falling away, I can feel it under foot, it's like running down Latimer Street!'

Out through the double doors and down toward the Turkish Bath, the corridor narrower than before, exaggerating the *list* to port from the bunker fire recently doused, the weight of her bow pulling them forward with each clumsy step, Albert sticking close behind he could feel the unease magnified by the sense of confinement. The walls and ceiling closing in like depression on a rainy day, an atmosphere strangely disturbing having been abandoned by those who were down here, the shortest of passageways but its smell was for all the world as good as Archie described it. *He* almost walked into the back of him, Harry stopping abruptly, *shushing* Albert quiet as he raised a hand, both men motionless for a second before moving on, Albert's explanation, deferred but soon to be satisfied, if not wholly understood when it happened again.

'Pipe Down!'

'Can you hear that Albert? Can you hear that banging, that dull clunk, from outside?'

In truth it was impossible to miss, a ringing lifeless thud, metal on metal, the call of the blacksmith vibrating through the airwaves and down the stairwell behind them, as ominous as was the direction from which it came. 'The boat deck sure enough' Harry said, listening to each blow, he could almost visualise the movement, struck with purpose, every delivery bringing those in the dining room closer to their fate. The racket oblivious to most, lost in the pandemonium that had taken hold, *the sound of menace* as the wishbone pegs fell upon an open deck, each davit swinging free from its stay, the first of the life rafts ready and waiting to be launched, waiting on the order that may never come, but if it did, Harry knew, they too were at the beginning of the end.

He could have walked around, Albert stopping to pick something up off the floor, placing it gently on the handrail, bluish green, a child's glove from peasant wool, rough to the touch with the smell of sour milk, a memory of a life long gone, Harry watched as Albert left it balancing so as not to fall and wondered what was going through his mind. Down toward the swimming pool, left at the dead end and sharp right, the *kink* nothing more than a *dog leg,* Albert's face pitiful if not down-hearted with the prospect it might never be recovered, a simple act, but one that spoke a thousand words. Old beyond his years, his skin course, leathery and deeply grained, he was without denial a rugged man, stood alone, the empty corridor stretching out behind him bearing witness to something not even time could attest to now. Pausing for a second, he gave a solitary glance back, checking it was still there just in case and in that moment, however brief it was, Albert Hemmings belied every possible clue as to the person beneath the filthy clothes, gravelly voiced with *pluck* borrowed from a taller man, at five foot three he was nothing short of a *gentle giant*, but given the circumstance, one whose attributes few would ever likely come to know.

It never seemed right first nor last, neither man much able to *fathom* its appeal, talked about by those on board unable or unwilling to waste a dollar for the privilege, the swimming pool abandoned beyond the double doors, stripped of all exclusivity by the very thing that had made it so, salt water. The pool house like any other, finished plainly by comparison beneath a ceiling of girders and pipes, modesty booths hiding nothing but a coat hook and bench and secrets shared only by those that had used them. Harry couldn't resist a look, wedging the door with his boot, holding it open while he and Albert took their chance for *a butchers* inside, their voices, *Chapel like*, echoing off the water, that hollow empty sound, its origin disguised with muffled distortion, as spontaneous calls of 'Hello?' fell upon deaf ears. The water too shallow to touch and beyond the reach of stretching fingers, Albert tried in vain to skim the surface with his hand, a childhood memory, or still in denial that it too would be full soon enough.

Harry noticed it first, that strong pungent smell, *briny like*, lingering in the air, the door to the Lido closing behind them.

It was as strong if not stronger than before, head long into it they walked, down the passageway, the icy chill full in the face clawed at the temperature plummeting with every step. Down to the *seafront,* the smell of Kelp and Iodine clinging to their clothes, each breath a little more intense, the reek of the ocean overpowering every rational thought, wrestling with the notion it could have made its way to here. F deck, three above the Tank Top, the very idea dismissed completely out of *court,* closer to the bow, the corridor narrowing as they squeezed past each berth, single cabins built to house, if not to *isolate,* third class males that were travelling alone. Feeling their way in the darkness neither of them spoke a word, the shadows replaced by electric lights that flickered like a stammer yet to be beaten. The generators still working or at least for now, they took what little comfort from the power surge lighting the hallway, single file, they could sense they were close to *it*, the end of the corridor and sharp left, Harry's whole body tensing when the carpets squelched beneath his feet. The moment of truth, the pair of them stopping dead in their tracks, listening intently for direction, the token gesture, they knew as well as anyone, they'd arrived on the *front line*; the warning, as overpowering as any could have possibly been, the disturbing sound of silence.

It didn't much matter now where it was coming from, it was clear enough it wasn't going to stop, everywhere beyond the bunker hatch impassable, the view that had met them as they rounded the corner, as horrific as could have ever been imagined.

If Albert didn't get it before he did now, the main corridor running down to Hatch No 2, disappearing somewhere just beyond the midpoint, freezing sea water rising rapidly up from below taking with it everything fore of where they stood. The corridor filling quickly beneath the sound of a million salty bubbles bursting as the tide flooded toward them. Pumped under pressure and forced up through the open stairwells and hatches cutting off everything and everyone closer to the bow, wall lights exploding on contact, while those encased remained burning beneath the surface, aqua blue, the backlit water as beautiful as it was surreal, a quality completely lost on Harry as he bellowed his instruction.

'Quickly, check the main stairwell on the port side!'

Albert did as he was told while Harry tried the aft stairwell starboard of the squash court, the water, already up to the mezzanine turning him back as quickly as he came, the bottoms of his britches sopping wet with the force of it catching him unawares, climbing the last few steps, slipping on the tread bar as he clambered out from the shaft, racing back to Albert, the sense of being followed ever present, both men square on with fire point and muster station, as if anyone would contemplate waiting there. It wasn't for long, peering down from the viewing gallery, Harry perched above the back wall, he could see the door below left open, the squash court, its whitewashed walls cast in shadows but for the light spilling over from above, the sight, as grotesque as it was tragic, summing up the lunacy of what was happening. He couldn't get his head around it, for all the world he was staring into a swimming pool, seawater climbing rapidly up the front wall, the *court* floor, down on G deck fifteen feet or thereabouts, the *Tin Line* already gone and the strangest sight as harrowing as it was bizarre, a single wooden racquet floating on the surface, spinning gently with the swirls of current from below, those last on court, their recreation cruelly interrupted, neither player waiting for the score but much like Harry and Albert, despite their obvious differences, tonight, they would all be part of a losing game.

'Let's get out of here Albert! Let's get back to see what's happening!'

It was on the tip of his tongue, Harry choosing to keep *it* to himself, the reality of what they'd seen still *sinking* in, pushing Albert ahead of him, a friendly pat on the shoulder and a shove, both men headed back the way they'd came. Ten to the dozen now, Albert's questions scrutinizing every possible option, the noise louder than before, drowning out the one probability neither wanted to discuss, the commotion upstairs on the boat deck a timely distraction, reinforcing the issue both had been trying to avoid, the very real prospect that unless another ship came to their aid and quickly, neither of them would be going home. They were all but running, covering their tracks back to the dining room, the uproar in the distance as good a steer as any, the hallways full with passengers milling about, a congregation waiting for divine intervention, or a *tip off* at the very least, the noise and uproar measured by agitation, every passing minute, another lost.

How could he resist, Albert stuffing the *glove* in his pocket, 'I couldn't just leave it there' he said, running to keep up, the sight of it, as cack-handed as you like, Harry's smile short lived as they made their way back to the dining room. It was like the middle ground, no-man's-land right in front of the stairwell, an impromptu centre stage for anyone with news, both men mingling with the crowd gathered at the foot of the steps. It was all they could do not to shout. The lowly officer doing his best, baited by some, heckled by others, flush and flustered, Christ he looked as fresh faced as a walk on the beach, sent to calm it down, the senior crew placating passengers from the upper deck, not least those queuing at the Purser's Office, the return of their valuables was all that mattered now, it hadn't as yet been explained, *you can't take it with you when you go*, but then that would all depend on *who* you were and where you were going.

'Please stay calm; there is nothing to worry about. We have the situation under control, we'll be transferred to another ship should that prove necessary, now please stay in your seats.'

'Look at the poor bastard', Harry said 'He hasn't got a clue, wait till the water comes gushing up those stairs, we'll see how calm he is then.'

He was trying his best, his efforts to fend them off spirited if nothing else, some of the passengers old enough to be his dad, doing what they could to *oik out* the truth, Albert gave the young lad credit for holding his own satisfied he was unaware of the danger. Harry peeled off the back and moved away keeping a closer eye on the stairs and corridor behind him, those gathered stood beneath the flood lights bathed in the full glare of darkness. Moistening her finger tips to turn the page had caught his eye, her hands shaking she clung to the bible and did her best to hide the fear. Three innocent souls, her children sat and listened intently while their mother finished the prayer, Harry's 'Amen', whispered softly, the sight of her alone with nothing but her faith in printed word. All hopes and dreams, she gently closed the *book*, their fate given over to a *higher power*, an image so strong he could feel the raw emotion of it welling up inside him. Her strength, as humbling and as comforting as could be for a man late to God's acquaintance, his own mortality, as fragile as those around, and for the first time the beam of light had found *him* amongst the crowd, carried on the morning tide, the *Truth* laid out bare before him, it was 12.37 am Monday, 15th April 1912.

All life was in that room, all death was in that room, and all they had to do now was sit tight and wait.

****

Forty three feet above the keel, and enough water for anyone, whatever the reluctance to launch the life rafts, it had been removed along with the covers.

From down below it was difficult to understand exactly what was happening, most of the lower decks from E to G awash with blank expression, the information patchy at best, it was clear early on a sense of disarray had taken hold. Upstairs the sound of running feet across the boards, the only clue as to gauge the urgency, the tone of their voices becoming ever frantic, as much in disbelief it could be happening, but it was, what made it worse, it was happening to them. How to describe it, like a lag, a general malaise, the reluctance to accept it was real, the crew woken, with those not on duty assigned a task, thrown in the deep end, the focus now on keeping everybody calm, on the bridge, all the musing in the world couldn't help them now, the ship was sinking and fast. Down the hallway, the Marconi Room, Phillips and Bride already working the *wire*, the first CQD, the first of many, *tapping out* history when they switched to *SOS, This is MGY Titanic position 41.44 N 50.24 W. Require immediate assistance, come at once we've struck an iceberg. Sinking.*

They were just ten minutes or thereabouts away from those infamous words 'Women and children first', life boat number 7 on the starboard side already waiting to be loaded, the clamber to survive

314

reserved, if not completely misunderstood; partially loaded with but 28 of her 65 capacity with no one else ready to go, well, no one waiting on the boat deck, assuming you could have ever got there. Some things are better left unsaid and for a while at least, while a vague sense of order prevailed, there was always hope to cling to. Mary's prayers as yet unanswered, she would have held not a grudge for the newly-weds as bride and groom were given priority, the rest of their lives laid out before them, her own children sat beside her, orphans, or perhaps part of something much more profound, *it would be better to have loved and lost, than never to have loved at all*, she knew whatever happened now, it was all or nothing, their fate already determined by those whom she would never meet. Mary Duggan, waited for something that would never come, sat quietly, she mulled over the passage that she had read, Psalm 23:6 'Surely goodness and love shall follow me all the days of my life: and I will dwell in the house of the Lord forever'. God's mercy, when it came, was that she wouldn't have to wait for long.

They could hardly hear themselves speak, a piercing shrill so loud it would have them cover their ears.

Down below the boilers had been closed and dampers shut, the excess steam vented up through the funnel relief valves, lifting the lid on what was going on, those in the know already aware what had taken place while others guessed as to the benefits of such an infernal din. Standing on the boat deck the screech was nothing less than unbearable if not impossible to communicate. Shouting across the open deck, Murdoch and Pitman struggled to be heard above the deafening noise, hand signals and gestures aside, they did their best to lower *her* away. The first of the life boats to leave, together with lookouts Jewell and Hogg and seaman William Weller as crew, brought about to the rear gangway before disappearing into the darkness, their instructions, 'Wait for further orders', much like those in steerage many of whom could barely speak a word of English, waiting for orders they too were all at sea. Harry lit another cigarette, his second in as many minutes, both hands shaking with something other than withdrawal, his stab in the dark close enough, 'We've lost two, maybe more boiler rooms', aware that others further aft must still be working, a head of steam powering the ships generators, the whole place as yet still ablaze with light. 'Do you think they made it?' he said, not even looking across to gauge Albert's reaction. 'Archie and Lyle, do you think they both got out?' Albert didn't reply, his only response was to bite his bottom lip and stare at the floor, picking at his thumb with the nail of the other, seconds that would last a lifetime while he weighed up the odds. Neither man was aware Archie had been moved only hours earlier from bunker five to six, his silence enough to warrant acknowledgement at least to the question, while the sadness that had settled in his eyes would be all the answer that Harry would ever need to see.

'Don't worry Albert; Archie will be alright, besides he's got my lucky gloves'.

'I've been saving it' he said, 'but you know what Albert, I think this is as good a time as any.'

Harry pulled himself out of the chair and got to his feet, leaning on the edge of the table for support, his expression somewhere between a smile and a look of resignation to what was about to take place, a look that said, he was ready.

'It's the best you'll get Albert, I stashed it away in my overcoat pocket, I only have a quart bottle but enough to get a taste for it, Paddy's Irish Whisky, all the way from Cork and right now I couldn't think of anyone better to share it with.' With that Harry was gone, shouting back across his shoulder, squeezing through the huddle congregated by the door, 'I shan't be long Albert, while I'm up there I'll pick up both our overcoats, just in case. Don't let anyone nick me seat!' It wasn't like he had far to go, he'd take the aft stairs to E deck then back along Scotland Road past the Scullion and Plate with visions of their cabin already under water. Well that was the plan and in isolation it was as good as any,

317

past the bakery toward the linen cupboards by the hatch, down the starboard side, the corridor as narrow as the minds of those that had brought them *here*, but the best laid plans of mice and men and, tonight of all nights, nothing could be relied upon. He'd barely cleared the swing of the door, his name, 'Harry Price!' bellowed up the hallway, the second engineer calling out with all the charm of a Sergeant Major, Harry stopping dead in his tracks, any confusion soon evaporating at the sight now walking toward him, ten men, maybe more, each and every one of them covered head to toe in filth and grime, *The Black Gang*, his own kind, several of them soaked to the skin their faces fraught with the anguish of loss and a sense of relief he was back in the *fold*. 'No time for a catch up, we've lost *six* it's completely under, *five* is filling if not already gone, it can't be held, all we can do is draw the fires further aft. You'll have to come with us Harry, we've got thirty furnaces, we'll pull as many as we can, we need power for the lights and radio, without it we're all finished as sure as you're stood before me.' There was no time for anything else, spoken like a request, in reality an order, the blank expressions disguised beneath a layer of coal and sweat. Percy Holloway clung to Harry's sleeve, tugging it once as if to say *he was glad to see him*, the cut above his eye weeping into a lump of congealed blood on his forehead, grimacing with pain, the shard of metal still buried in his flesh letting him know it was there, the *sharpest* of

318

reminders as to what they'd been through. It was the first thing Harry did, explaining Albert was sat in the third class diner, another stoker already sent to *round them up,* his relief at the thought of it clear to see, they'd all meet down on the Tank Top. Every one of them ready to shovel coal, their ending when it came, side by side, doing what they wanted to do, selfless and as brave as could ever be imagined, keeping the lights burning, right until the bitter end.

He never would have gone had he known, those supposed to do the *round up* sent instead to the engine room toward the stern, gone for lanterns to be used in the boiler room, the main lighting having failed once more. A farewell drink that would have to wait forever, a price too high for either to have paid, as unbeknown to them, Harry Price and Albert Hemmings would never see each other again.

Chapter Twenty

It was nothing but a flash in the pan, the first of the rockets detonated from the bridge, the starter's gun, setting the scene for what would follow.

Until that point those down below had clung to hope and the comfort of ignorance, unable or unwilling to accept what was happening, the first signs of *those* leaving, the dull thud upon the side of her hull, lifeboat number 7 close enough to clatter the oars down the side before moving off. It would be wrong to say it didn't cause a scene; it did, as did the moment the steam vented from the funnels, the sound so great as to be sure to wake the dead, but the sight of a rocket released into a clear night sky that was the moment most would *see* their time was all but over.

Officer Boxhall worked alone on the starboard side of the bridge, removing the first pyrotechnic from its box, the launching point, a socket recessed into the railing. Clearing away those that stood beneath him, he made the final adjustments to his aim and let the first of them go; it was 12:55am. Down below, lifeboat number 5 was being launched, Murdoch ordering Third Officer Pitman aboard, a shake of hands with 'Goodbye. Good luck' overheard by those close by, their exchange, captured beneath an illuminated sky. A single pull on the lanyard, the noise, deafeningly loud with a blinding flash the like of which would stun those unprepared, six hundred feet maybe more, cascading into a shower of white, the burning embers watched by those below through porthole windows, half to a dozen rockets or thereabouts and yet not a single one of them would signify the ship was in distress. It wasn't that they wouldn't be seen, they were, every discharge monitored on the bridge of the Californian, but the random sequence in which each would be fired *would only serve to confuse,* and as time would stand witness, it did.

'Be sure and see the plug is in that boat!' Murdoch called to Pitman as he climbed aboard, not the best of starts considering, the water flooding in the drain hole as she settled on the surface Quartermaster Olliver plugging the hole, another incident to add to the dislocated ribs of Annie Stengel's, the Frauenthal brothers jumping aboard landing on her as they lowered away. They were allowed to stay despite the hundreds of women and children still isolated below, the second boat to launch and the first of five to leave within as many minutes, oddly numbered on the starboard side, evens on the port, each boat equipped with blankets, provisions and flares, a level compass to navigate and a beaker of water, enough to sustain the 40 passengers and crew, launched adrift into the early morning darkness; the life boat 30ft of Elm, Oak and Yellow Pine, 30ft of England.

With over two thousand souls on board it was difficult to see how anyone could have felt alone, but that was exactly what they were.

Down on F deck those gathered in the dining room had all but given up the ghost, some having made it to the boat deck while others struggled with the signage, bringing them back to where they'd started, back to those rooted to the floor. They were the same as when they'd left, frightened rigid, too petrified to move despite the opportunity to *take their chance*, every stairwell manned by crew, themselves unsure as to what to do, did the *rules* apply, were they still to exercise *selection,* were they ever instructed to do that at all. The crowds gathered at the exits, held up more because they didn't want to part from loved ones as anything else. 'Women and children first', the steward said, a scuffle in the doorway, one of many as those at the back tried to pass, fraying tempers lost amongst the pushing and shoving but all in vain. When their moment came who would vouch for their character, each of them clinging to a life, each of them dealing with a death, they could hear the lifeboats being launched, shouts and screams from up above, rockets bursting overhead, the struggle to survive in conflict with the dignity of death. Stood in the foot well with the early morning sky clearly visible beyond the brow, all huddled against a bitter chill tumbling down the cold metal steps, *dragon's breath* hanging from their lips betraying those who muttered to themselves, and in the air the pungent sweet smell of Cordite mingled gently with the faintest whiff of despair.

He'd clear up as he went, gathering the brown grease paper strewn across the floor, *Ship shape and Bristol fashion,* some habits dying hard, the first box of detonators still being fired, with Quartermasters Rowe and Bright doing what they could to assist. Both men had brought another box apiece up from the aft stores, forty eight rockets in all, more than enough to communicate the ship was in danger and yet less than a quarter would ever be used, as for those that were, they would all be seen. On the bridge of the Californian, Officer of the watch, Herbert Stone, thought he saw what looked like shooting stars above a steamer that had stopped, alone at first, then joined by Gibson, together they would watch a further three released up into a clear night sky, eight rockets confirmed, their efforts on the Morse lamp futile before the ship they'd *seen* disappeared into the darkness.

'Listen to me! Please be quiet! Most of us will not be leaving by boat, stay calm and remember to stay out of the water as long as possible, good luck and God be with you'.

It was just an impromptu appeal, the man clambering up on his chair shouting out across a sea of heads, some, like him, facing the inevitable with the courage others could only have prayed for, lurching forward as he spoke, most feeling the shift beneath their feet. The bow pulling them down, suffocating and straining against the weight of *it*, dragging her under silently from within, each compartment flooding to the next, slowly but surely slipping away, the sea, washing over the Gunwale forward of the bridge, taking with it everything not tied down, much of the debris floating off into the shadows leaving those that had seen it in no doubt as to what to expect.

The Post Office was already under with three of the five clerks dead, the other two soon to follow, urged as they were to save themselves; they'd sacrificed every chance of survival. A lasting image, wading waist high in the freezing water hauling mail sacks on their backs, up the stairs to higher ground, one trip too many, the Registered cage door left swinging open as the force of the water took them by surprise, not the surprise Oscar Scott Woody had in mind, today of all days, his birthday, he was 44 years old.

****

It was nothing but relief when the knocking stopped.

Sat alone he stared at the back of the door and flinched with every thud that landed, watching the handle twist and turn, willing him to go, the Steward shouting as he made his way along the corridor.

'Is there anybody down here? Hello, is there anybody there?'

Quiet now, with those reluctant to leave their possessions long since gone, the passageway silent but for fading footsteps that would never return, Yusef Gans gave a heavy sigh and enjoyed the simple peace of it. He was losing track of time, twenty minutes maybe more since the last of them came, his *pledge* soon to be redeemed, he tidied up the bits and bobs left over from earlier in the day, out of sorts for most of it, having struggled to finish the garments now hanging on the rack. Yusef ran a hand across the cabin slips, one pinned on each piece, odds and sods for the most part, stopping at his last repair, a critical eye, he examined the quality in detail holding it beneath the lamp, his judgement confined to a hum before putting it back, the final stitch, not bad for an old man *under the weather*, or one *under* anything at all.

He didn't have long, straightening his jacket he stood before the mirror and struggled with the button on his collar, 'Always one', he said, running a comb through a wisp of silver hair, moistening the tips of his fingers he flattened it back in place, stopping only briefly when he heard the noise rushing up the corridor toward him. It was here, outside the door, the first sign as it seeped beneath the gap like blood from a head wound, the icy water reaching out across the workshop floor, circling his feet while he brushed his lapel, not long now, but time enough for one last glance, would he do, would she come today and sacrifice her life on him. Colder now, the temperature in the room falling sharply like a winter's day, Saturday 15th November 1862. He was back there, waiting inside, the freezing rain blown across the village green and into the vestibule, the tiny church damp and gloomy beneath a blackened sky. The start of their lives together, etched out of hardship and suffering binding them tight for almost fifty years, their wedding day and for the briefest of moments, there, beyond the reflection in the glass, he was staring at the groom.

Yusef dragged his chair across the floor and wedged an armrest beneath the lip of the bench, forcing it into place with a shove, twisted from side to side, far enough under to be secure leaving just enough room for his tiny frame to slide in. He was ready now, everything was done. Switching on his bench light, he walked toward the door hesitating slightly, unsure in truth as to what to expect when he turned the key in the lock. It was instant, the strength of the water completely overpowering as it pushed on past him, flooding in with a violent rush so strong as to take him by surprise, the room filling quickly he waded back to his seat, the freezing water swashing above the knee and rising fast. Yusef Gans would not have long to wait.

RMS Carpathia: *SOS Titanic sinking by the head. We are all about down. Sinking.*

It would be one of many frantic messages sent, the Marconi Room hard pressed to do more than was already being done, each message the same, SOS - *CQD 41.46N 50.14 W Sinking.* There'd be variation but in essence the substance was the same.

MGY *Titanic. Come Soon. Sinking. Require immediate assistance. Putting the women and children off in the boats.*

Some replied, others not, but all delivered by Phillips and Bride; the next half hour spent talking to those with any hope of coming to her aid. The Californian, her radio off, the closest by a mile, while Frankfurt, Baltic, Virginian and the rest either too far or too slow to make a difference, speed equals distance over time and none of them could change that.

They'd stay and see it through, both men, relieved from their duty at 02:05am. Captain Smith, his first attempt followed with a final plea, 'You look out for yourselves, I release you!', that was the last time they would see him alive, Phillips and Bride still working till the power failed, *every man for himself*, a sentiment that would prove lost on the both of them.

Up on the boat deck things had gone from bad to worse, scuffles and punches couldn't save them now, the last of the life boats swung and ready, increasing the unbearable. Too late to make amends, those in denial, no longer under any illusion as to where they stood, while for some, money would be changing hands. It would all take place, those last frantic moments that would draw the best and the worst from each and every one of them, *stiff upper lip,* or ripping a life jacket clean off of someone else's back. Gunshot, a warning to those preparing to launch themselves from A deck, Lifeboat 14, under siege, Seaman Scarrott holding back the *boarders* with the stub of a tiller, broken bones and soon, for those that would wait for news by the dockside, nothing but a broken heart.

How could he have known, alone in the darkness, Yusef Gans listened to the water as it climbed up the wall, the lighting failed, pitch black but for a shard still visible through an air duct above the closet. Shaking, his whole body shaking and numb, the icy water chest high or more stealing every breath, short and sharp, he gasped through an open mouth and pulled *her* toward the edge of the bench. His sewing machine, cast iron and as stubborn as a mule, the weight of it dragged off the side and into his lap, his ankles twisted around each chair leg, holding him down, clinging to a life, waiting for a death. He was all but done, his soft voice whispering, ramblings of incoherent thoughts, Hulda waiting by the river bank, 'from this day forward, for better or for worse, for richer for poorer, in sickness and in health, to love and to cherish, till death us do part' 'Yes I do', he said, 'Yes I do', louder and louder, shouting it out, calling her to come to him, tears streaming down his face as the water rose around his neck, 'Yes Hulda, yes, yes I do'.

****

The middle ground was a dangerous place to be, and so it would prove, not least for those of *The International Brigade.*

'For Christ sake man cut that rope!', he bellowed; Loading Officer Moody keeping them level, tempers fraying as was the *falls* as he sliced them clean away. It was one of the last to go, lifeboat number 13 washed beneath the path of those above, the engine outflow holding them directly underneath, sat helpless but to cling to the sides, petrified passengers mostly mothers and children could do nothing but look on in horror. It was just a moment but almost their last, Barrett and Hopkins screaming across the open boards, both men evening up the odds, grappling with the lines and tackle, every yank setting her straight as the davits flexed under the strain of it. Stern to bow releasing her slowly, their descent as harrowing as was the uncertainty to remain, unceremoniously dumped the last few feet, cut free, their belly flop like a slap in the face, panic over, but for others it had just begun. It was disbelief at first, in contrast to their status, handpicked to grace the *Ritz*, the À La Carte Restaurant staff, Luigi Gatti himself poached from Oddenino's in London. Sixty eight souls and not a single one employed by the White Star Line. Out on the Boat deck they were easy to spot, noisy and animated, their shouts and screams glued together in a barrage of broken English, huddled into small groups, united in the language of fear, their *standing* of little account to those charged with loading the last of the lifelines of hope. Lifeboat number 11 on the Starboard side, number 4 on the Port, the four Collapsibles, *C* having launched already, the final possibility to leave the ship, the two cashiers Miss Bowker and Miss Martin lucky to make it, both women rescued aboard number 6 with only one other to pull through, the Maître d', Paul Mauge, *The*

International Brigade, with just three mortals to survive, sixty five of them would remain behind and none would see the cold light of day.

He never knew them, how could he, making breakfasts for those on F deck, Third Class Dining as close as he'd come, Sammy was all but finished, the last few hours frantically searching for his *friend,* he couldn't have tried anymore, literally scowering every last corner in a desperate bid to find him, the stairwells to the lower decks flooded by the time he'd arrived, a last ditch attempt going further aft then forward on G deck, the whole area blocked. He was sick to the stomach, sweating profusely beneath his topcoat, cold chilled, his habit back, another sign of distraught emotion eating at him from inside. What will happen with Tully's birthday, Archie's invitation, their plans to meet, Archie's note, 'No!' he shouted, 'No!', his screams lost among the many, lost as he fell through an open door. He'd been up here earlier, forced now, the icy water all but ready to take them, the open Boat deck, an outpouring of raw emotion, heightened tenfold with every splash, prolonged agony no longer the choice of some, those stood nearby looking away, death, in fairness, never having claimed to be a pretty sight.

Right there, that was when life was chosen for him over death, a *simple twist of fate,* as they lowered her away. Collapsible *D* with only twenty two of her

331

forty seven spaces filled, in charge, Second Officer Lightoller, bellowing at him above the din, 'Grab the line! Get in man and don't let go until I say!' He just did as he was told, petrified he'd mess it up, the rope released through his palms as he copied the man on the bow, the excess *fall* pulled through the block leaving it swaying in the breeze and there it was, over before it had begun; pushed away from the blackened hull they drifted off her side and into the early morning darkness.

'Take the tiller and keep her straight', he said, clambering across the bench seat, the other oar already manned, both men rowing her slowly away, those rescued shocked into stunned silence but for a prayer delivered between the sound of stifled tears. 'What's your name son?' he asked quietly, Arthur Bright, the Quartermaster in charge, glancing up at him while he pulled on a blade full of freezing water, a single nod to acknowledge his reply.

'Samuel Sir....Sammy Fuller.'

There was nothing more he could do, looking back toward the ship the light reflecting off the surface, *holding her true,* its shimmer like a flame burnt into a memory that would haunt him for the rest of his life, the moment when he realised he was on his way home.

Chapter Twenty One

He could feel the pattern pressed into the cold steel floor, the darkened gantry, the last refuge before it was claimed; sat on his haunches, he leaned against the wall for balance and gasped for breath. It was all he could do not to end it, his wife and children fast asleep at home.

Head bowed, he steadied himself for a moment, drenched to the bone, his jacket torn at the shoulder, weighed down in saturated clothes clinging to him as he crouched on the narrow ledge. Alone in the darkness, shivering to the sound of water as it breached the bulkhead wall, its fall from grace down into Boiler Room five, a waterfall of blackened rain echoing as it hit the floor. He could hear himself breathing, no heaving as he gathered his thoughts, the shock of *it* reeling through his mind's eye, an image so brutal the like of which no man should ever be forced to see, the sickening replay captured by a tortured expression etched across his face. There wasn't much time left, not now, lapping at the underside of the shelf, the surface of the water eerily still but for the ripples of an appetite forced up from below, swallowed whole, boiler room six was all but gone. Lyle pulled himself up on his feet and edged slowly along the ledge his back pressed flat against the wall, the urge to look back forcing him to turn away. Hands shaking and hollow legged it was all he could do to stay upright, the emergency escape closer with every step, his only chance of life and one that, despite everything, he would take alone. Nothing could have prepared them for what had happened and nothing he did or didn't do would have ever made a difference, the truth is that when *it* came, it did so with all the full force of religion.

'Don't look back, come on keep going, there's nothing left!'

It would make no difference, the pull toward the water's edge like *time immemorial*, and when he did look back, he would fall apart.

Everything was captured in that glance, the emergency ladder bolted to the boiler room floor, one single rung still visible above the waterline, the rest lost beneath the North Atlantic. He had almost made it, five maybe six steps more, Lyle clinging to the scruff of his neck, a kitten rescued from a tree curling his leg around the back of the ladder for leverage, one hand holding on the other hauling him up by the collar, each pull a *dead man's weight*, like swinging from a crane, Lyle's hook working the pulley block, his arms bulging beneath the strain, reeling him in, Archie's foot sliding off the metal rung, slewing waist high in the freezing water as he gasped for breath. Panic stricken, both overpowered by the terror of a loosening grip, Archie's shirt slipping through his fingers as was the time they had left, flailing in the water desperate to hang on amidst the shouts and screams, the fear unbearable, calling out his name, helpless as his hold faded away, a life hung in the balance and nothing they could do would change it now. It came from nowhere, the surge engulfing *him* in a blanket of death, wrapping him up on a winter's day, smothered beneath its reach, Archie choking on his final breath slipping free and dragged beneath the surface, his body lost to an icy darkness, and that was it, taken from the clutches of hope right before his eyes. Archie Mullins, his little face, helpless as he disappeared beneath the water, reaching for the ladder, the fingertips of Harry's glove reaching for a life, but it was all in vain.

In time he too would learn his fate, but for now Lyle Benson needed to move and move fast, clambering down the ladder into boiler room five a deluge of water raining down upon him, the footplate already four maybe five feet under, now completely deserted. It was like a bad dream, wandering past the bunker door where *they'd* shared their stories, watching as he shovelled the coal, determined not to let him down, his first day, God, he could barely stand at the end of it, back breaking work but Archie Mullins never once complained. Stood by the open door, the barrow upturned like he'd have left it, Lyle

335

gazed into the darkened pit traumatized by what had taken place, the amber lights flickering up the tunnel wall in one last stand of defiance. This was where they'd met, amongst the filth and coal and for now, this was where they'd said goodbye.

There was nothing left for him, nothing but a memory yet to be shared, his future, bleak at best much like the early morning darkness. Alone on the Boat deck he watched the misery unfold, the initial malaise filling him with an overwhelming sense of anger curbed only by his need to survive, those in charge still in denial he would place his faith elsewhere. Whatever happened now he knew that he was on his own, the stark reality laid bare and a promise made to those back home, 'this trip would be his last', the very words he pledged on the day he left, a promise made without expectation and one they had both understood to be so, their mutual smiles silent confirmation as she fastened the button on his coat. How could he have possibly known what price he'd pay, her beautiful smile, one Lyle Benson would willingly die for, love's declaration, but tonight, even that might not be enough.

Chapter Twenty Two

It would start like any other day, cold and damp beneath an overcast sky, an early morning chill carried on a freshening breeze, felt by those whose day had already begun.

He would never forget the moment when he first heard the news, up until now nothing but an uneventful day, Drippin still haggling with Mrs O'Sullivan on Lime Street, the *old biddy* determined to hold out for a shilling or two, the iron grate, something he could shift if she could ever bare to be parted. It was nothing more than a throwaway line, something he could have easily missed as he loaded the spoils onto the wagon, her remark hanging in the air as he swallowed to take it in.

'Don't go banging on next door Drippin, her old man *was* on Titanic.'

He didn't get it at first and, in truth, even when she'd explained what they'd heard he didn't believe it and neither did the majority that would hear the news during the course of the day. Seeping out across the town, the story gaining credibility from sources sworn to silence, gradually what had first been nothing more than incredulity was now being treated with the reverence it deserved, RMS Titanic by all accounts, had been lost to the North Atlantic. He couldn't move at first, a blank expression vacant but for the cruellest signs of panic that had crept across his face, clambering up on the wooden bench, *Spike* whinnying at the imposition, another knap disturbed, but Drippin barely had time to say goodbye. Everywhere he went crowds gathered on street corners while people huddled in shop doorways, pubs spilling out through open doors, those outside shouting what they'd heard as he passed them by.

'Drippin! Does Charlie know? Have you seen Archie's mother? The bloody thing sank!'

His head was spinning, everything all at once, a thousand questions piling up and not a single answer to be found, did *they* survive, did anyone survive, how could that have happened? Sketchy at best, he would try to find out what he could and head down toward the docks, the place busy by the time he'd got there with others much like him, all camping out on the doorsteps of the White Star Line. It was nothing but a sea of black, Canute Road filled with relatives and loved ones desperate for news, the entrance to their offices buried behind a wall of desperation, some refusing to leave, while others drifted off into the early evening when they realised there'd be nothing more. It would prove to be an excruciating wait, two full days before the lives of those lost were known, Charlie in a state of shock, his mother refusing to leave her room, a house thrown into darkness and a morbid sense of dread.

Charlie couldn't bear to look, the office wall draped in sheets of paper rolled down the brickwork for all to see, hand scrawled lists of those aboard, passengers and crew alike, their fate, if known, written in bold ink, smudged and corrected beneath the glare of those that would share their grief in public, shouts and screams, heart wrenching cries, harrowing sounds that would cut through the air, the deepest sadness as loved ones buckled at the knee, held up by those around them, an image that would not be lost on Charlie as he and Drippin pushed their way toward the front of the crowd.

'I can't do it! I can't do it!', he said, his eyes filled with tears, clinging onto Drippin's arm as he scrolled on down the list, the names blurring into one, hundreds and hundreds of them in alphabetical order, all numbered, their fate recorded beside them. He could barely breathe, a hand held patting his chest, not stopping when he saw the names of those he'd known, a loud gasp of relief, he allowed every ounce of emotion to flood over him when the *first* of the names came into view;

Fuller, Samuel (Crew) – Rescued - Carpathia.

'Where is he Drippin? Can you see his name? Where is he?'

He never replied, he didn't need to, the reaction of his friend was enough to know he'd read it for himself, breaking down into a heap on the pavement, broken hearted he sobbed uncontrollably, shouting his brother's name while Drippin and those around tried to comfort him. It was over, a life, one of fifteen hundred and twenty nine lost in the early hours of Monday, 15th April 1912 and nothing they could do would ever bring them back.

Mullins, Archie (Crew) - RMS Titanic - Last Known Address.